SOLDIER ON: SURVIVING THE ZOMBIE APOCALYPSE

SHAWN CHESSER

CONTENTS

ACKNOWLEDGMENTS

For Mo, Raven, Caden and Penny, who is now flying up
in Cat Heaven. Thanks for putting up with me clacking
away at all hours. Mom, thanks for reading... although it
is not your genre. Dad, aka Mountain Man Dan, thanks
for your ear and influence. Thanks to all of the men and
women in the military, past and present, especially those
of you in harm's way. Thanks George Romero for
introducing me to zombies. All of my friends and
fellows, thanks as well. Lastly, thanks to Bill W. and Dr.
Bob... you helped make this possible. I am going to sign
up for another 24.
Once again, extra special thanks to Monique Happy for
taking Soldier On and polishing its rough edges.
Working with you Mo has been a seamless experience
and nothing but a pleasure.
Thanks Freddy Joe for allowing me to use your beautiful
apocalyptic cloud photo on the cover.

*****

Edited by Monique Happy Editorial Services
mohappy@att.net

Chapter 1
Outbreak - Day 4
Utah State Forest
Service Road 334
Wasatch Mountains, Utah

Cade Grayson, father, husband and former Delta Force operator watched the trees flash by as he maneuvered the Kawasaki dirt bike along the single lane gravel road in the Utah back country.

He was on a mission to reunite with his young daughter, Raven, and wife, Brook. Although he didn't know exactly where they were or if they were still alive, nothing was going to deter him from searching.

Cade rode east, away from Camp Williams. The Special Forces garrison was dangerously close to a large population center situated less than twenty miles from Salt Lake City, Utah and even closer to the smaller city of Draper.

Each break in the thick canopy of trees offered Cade a glimpse of the angry looking thunderheads above. The sooty gray clouds stretched up, bumping against the Wasatch mountain range directly in his path.

SOLDIER ON: SURVIVING THE ZOMBIE APOCALYPSE

Cade thought travelling through one of the many canyons dissecting the sharp granite peaks was the best way to avoid the walking dead. So far there had been few of them wandering the road, moaning and reaching for him as he sped by. Still, it was fresh in his mind that it made no difference how many of the monsters he came across, it would only take one bite to ruin his day.

Shadows flashing on the ground had a hypnotic effect on the already road weary traveler. Cade rounded a blind corner; he was riding too fast to avoid the crowd of zombies choking the road. Without hesitating he put his head over the bars and his upper body on the tank, trying to become as small a target as possible.

The first zombie met the motorcycle head on; there was no recognition of pain, fear or surprise as she was ejected out of her purple Crocs and sent airborne. The adolescent girl's blonde ponytail and blood spattered SeaWorld tee shirt was the only thing Cade perceived before she disappeared over the guardrail and down the embankment.

Adrenaline pumped through Cade's veins, heightening all of his senses and making the action around him appear to slow down. He could feel the bike going sideways under him and everything went quiet. Zombies flew by in his peripheral vision, their cold hands clutching and clawing for a piece of him. Cade momentarily sailed freely, separated from his bike, before gravity reunited him with earth. Pain exploded through his hip and shoulder as the unforgiving road took its toll, sending him into a flat spin on his chest. Cade got up on one knee with the Glock in a two handed grip searching for his first target. There was no need to chamber a round, locked and loaded had become the gold standard the day the dead started walking.

Cade picked Joe Dirt; the zombie sported a flowing brown mullet, NASCAR tee shirt, and khaki cargo shorts and was closing on him the fastest. He looked to be early twenties - the younger they were the faster they moved.

Joe let out a dry raspy moan and picked up speed, shredded bare feet slapping the gravel while his milky eyes focused intently on Cade.

The Glock held seventeen rounds in the magazine plus one riding in the chamber, more than enough for this group. The first bullet had Joe's name on it. The 9 mm slug punched through his Neanderthal forehead and exited the back of his head taking a sizable chunk of hair-covered skull with it. In between targets Cade checked on the bike; it lay on its side twenty feet uphill from his position.

The next zombie was a walking road map of lacerations oozing puss and blood; it looked like she had been wrestling with barbed wire and lost. The thing's short Peter Pan hairdo was home to twigs, bugs and the spider webs that caught them. Clothing was an afterthought. Save for panties and the remains of a short skirt, her pale tattooed body was bare for all to see.

Cade put the young lady in his sights and squeezed off three rapid-fire shots that walked up from her sternum. The first bullet shattered the breastbone and started the flying lesson; the second and third 9 mm slugs entered under her neck and chin, effectively popping off her skullcap and depositing the scrambled brains in a gory pile on the roadside.

The operator sidestepped while he backpedaled, keeping the remaining four zombies from flanking him. He had seen some instances of cunning behavior displayed, he had no answer for it, but he was glad it was the exception to the norm.

An undead Caucasian male worked Cade's right, while his African American counterpart, though much younger, tried to move in from the left. The last two were behind them, near the downed Kawasaki and were the slow movers of the posse.

The idea came to Cade from out of the blue; he rushed the clumsy corpses and sprinted between them, resulting in a near

face to face collision of the two zombies. Four more shots
from the Glock put the two ghouls down with vicious double
taps to the back of the head.

Four down, two to go.

Cade approached the final two threats from the low
ground. He shot the elderly zombie between the eyes and
watched her hit the ground and skid, leaving a black blood
trail behind.

The last zombie was having a hard time walking. His final
choice of footwear had been a pair of ostrich skin cowboy
boots that were no longer tan. A gash two inches deep near
its carotid artery painted everything from the neck down, the
black dried blood making his fancy western shirt crackle when
he walked. Tex had been having a bad week and it was about
to get worse. Cade circled around the Kawasaki and put a
mercy bullet behind his ear, being careful to keep the brain
shower off of the bike. The entire melee lasted less than a
minute; he had been given the nickname *Wyatt* for a reason.

Cade changed out the magazine and then he walked the
side of the road searching for the undead little girl; the body
was nowhere to be found.

After inspecting the bodies to ensure all were dead, Cade
picked up the bike and looked it over. There were a few
scratches and one of the saddle bags was cracked, but nothing
serious. The Kawasaki started on the first try.

With quite a few hours of daylight left, and a lot of ground
to cover, Cade had to get moving.

***

Cade used the time on the road to think through the
events of the last few days. He had made the decision to leave
Portland, Oregon when the outbreak first started. He needed
to go back east and find his wife and daughter.

From day one he had been thrust into the unwanted role
of protector, mentor and savior. Two neighbor boys had lost
their parents to the Omega virus, as the media had taken to

calling it, and since there was no one else to care for the two young brothers, Cade reluctantly took them in.

Soon, he and a band of survivors were travelling together in a mini convoy. After hundreds of miles and numerous brushes with death he remained unscathed.

It nearly brought the tired warrior to tears every time he thought about the smart aleck Ike whose personality was extremely large for a boy his size. Ike's teenaged brother Leo, always the protector, couldn't keep Ike safe in the end.

The twins, Sheila and Shelly, in their early twenties, each met their own horrible death.

Rawley, the rowdy neighbor, talented musician and crack shot with a rifle also met his maker violently.

Five vibrant souls lost and Cade felt like he was the common denominator. He had been beating himself up over the chain of events and cast himself as a pseudo grim reaper, in a way responsible for their deaths.

He made up his mind while en route to the Special Forces garrison outside of Draper, Utah. The second the Black Hawk landed Cade began to plot his solo journey. He firmly believed he would be better off distancing himself from anyone and anything that could divert him from his personal mission. Locating his wife Brook and young daughter Raven was his main reason for living.

Cade stopped reflecting on the past and focused on the present. It was time to find a place to stop for the night. After the near fatal brush with the group of walkers, driving on the narrow road with only the meager illumination cast by the bike's headlight was out of the question.

In the midst of a short straightaway, he stopped in the center of the road and let the Kawasaki idle. To get to the pocket where he put the topo map, first he had to brush off the armor of road grime that had worked its way onto every square inch of his body. Neatly folded, in the side cargo pocket of his ACUs, was the Bureau of Land Management map that Major Beeson had provided. According to the map

there was a junction five miles ahead and the River Bend
campground was only a mile further off to the right. If it was
free of undead, Cade decided, it would be a safe and secluded
place for him to get some much needed sleep.

He was busy refolding the map when he detected a
rhythmic scraping reverberating up the draw. The noise
seemed to be coming from downhill in the same direction he
was headed.

Spontaneously Cade turned the motorcycle perpendicular
to the road, gunned the engine, and roared uphill through the
underbrush and scrub oak, the bike's knobby rear tire
spewing dirt and rocks into the air. Cade had no idea what or
who approached, but on the road and exposed was the last
place he wanted to be. After charging twenty yards up the
incline he killed the engine and dumped the bike on its side.

With the engine noise silenced, the scrabbling, scratching
cadence grew louder. His gut feeling led him to believe that
many more zombies were marching on a collision course
towards him. Cade quickly retrieved his M4 carbine, attached
the suppressor, tromped uphill a few more yards and dove
behind the nearest cover. A semi-hollow fallen tree served to
conceal his prone body. Cade braced the carbine over the
rotting deadfall, removed the black protective end caps from
the optics and appraised his situation. The image framed by
the scope made him shudder involuntarily. A mob of undead
numbering somewhere in the hundreds noisily approached,
their shuffling gait propelling the fine talc-like dirt airborne.
The ochre cloud of dust rose to the treetops, obscuring the
rear of the long shambling column.

Cade harbored no reservations that the ongoing
commotion at the military base was pulling them in from the
city and he feared for his buddy Duncan and his mentor
Major Beeson. There wasn't enough ammunition in Camp
Williams to fend off the undead tsunami soon to be at their
doorstep. Knowing that fault lay solely on Beeson's shoulders

troubled Cade the most. In the days following the outbreak, Beeson's decision to illuminate the base at night had the adverse effect of drawing more walkers.

During his time deployed in Iraq and Afghanistan, Cade had spent countless hours observing targets and gathering intelligence. He was no stranger to laying low and staying quiet. He stopped estimating how many undead were marching past his position after the count exceeded more than five hundred. The monsters were shambling towards the base in silence; there wasn't any of the moaning, hissing or grunting Cade had gotten used to.

With nothing to do but wait, stay quiet and still, Cade thought of his wife Brook and eleven-year-old daughter Raven. The last time he hugged them outside of the airport in Portland was still fresh in his mind. The last words Raven said to him, with an air of confidence rarely exhibited, "*Nothing shall befall my mom when I am on the job,*" played over and over, a continuous loop in his mind. The last time he heard Brook's frantic voice on the other end of the phone, sounding alone and scared, also gnawed at him.

His thoughts turned to his neighbors back in Portland, and how he had been forced to kill Ted and Lisa after they were infected. The faces of Rawley, Leo and the twins Sheila and Shelly - all murdered by the redheaded outlaw biker - invaded his head as he pressed his face into the dirt, willing himself to blend into his surroundings. What an introduction to the new world.

A sudden commotion brought Cade back to the present. Three of the monsters were scrambling and clawing up the incline towards him. His finger tensed on the trigger as he watched the trio of flesh-eaters stumble over the motorcycle. One of the zombies began to frantically dig in the dirt while the other ghouls dumbly looked on. A flash of chestnut fur shot from the ground and raced between the kneeling creature's legs. Abruptly the zombies about-faced and tumbled down the hill after the speedy rodent. A humorous thought crossed Cade's mind, *chipmunk 1, zombies 0.* He smiled inwardly.

It took forty-five minutes for the walkers to trudge by his hide. When the road was finally clear of zombies, Cade assembled the satellite phone. He felt it his duty to warn Major Beeson of the approaching zombies and their approximate number.

The canopy of trees or some other atmospheric anomaly prevented the phone from working properly. Finding a better position to access an overhead satellite would require a long hump uphill, breaking through thick underbrush. Cade made the decision to use what little light he had left to distance himself from the dead. He slung the rifle over his shoulder and picked his way down the hill to the dirt bike.

Apprehension set in as Cade was about to start the motorcycle. It was hard for him not to imagine another army of dead waiting, out of sight, right around the corner. With his mind fully in check, he started the engine and pointed the front wheel towards his destination. Cade calculated that if he pushed the bike and rode hard, he might make it to the River Bend campground before sundown.

Chapter 2
Outbreak - Day 5
Shriever AFB
Colorado Springs, Colorado

"Bring more ammo!" Brook screamed without looking away from the stumbling ghoul bracketed in the scope's crosshairs. She smoothly pulled the trigger; the rifle bucked and the top third of the zombie's head evaporated in a luminous green cloud of bone and brain matter. The advancing corpse was cold; the superheated bullet warmed the detritus making it resemble a gory aurora borealis through the thermal scope.

A sidelong glance confirmed her worst fear. The gunfire from within the base was nothing but a siren song for the dead. Although it appeared the entire population of Colorado Springs was at the gate, the truth was the men and women of the United States military were presently taking the war to the enemy in and around the city.

***

Parker Bluff, Subdivision. Colorado Springs.

Lawson tested the door knob. Sure enough, it was locked. He looked at his superior. Captain Ronnie Gaines was in his mid forties and stood head and shoulders above most of the men he commanded. He was of African American descent and dark as night. His clean shaven pate and muscular build made him the center of attention wherever he went. Good attention or bad, he always took it in stride. One smile could charm the ladies or disarm the men; he was an equal opportunity killer.

Gaines was a member of the 10th Special Forces Group out of nearby Fort Carson and he was a decorated combat veteran of both wars in the Middle East and Operation Desert Storm.

The locked doors usually hid bad things behind them. The question was how many bad things?

Lawson rapped sharply. The other four men stayed abreast of the door, two per side, and waited the customary thirty seconds.

"No one home," Lawson said, a little too early as something heavy impacted the door from within. The moaning soon commenced; it was nearly always the same, a low pitched plaintive sound that caused grown men to get the chills. So much for hoping the house was empty.

They always followed the same protocol. The entry man would pop the door with the twelve pound Thundersledge and then stand back. Rarely did it take much more than the hammer. Occasionally one of the operators would be forced to blow the lock with a shotgun.

Lawson was six foot tall, although he was thin; his body was ripped with corded muscles. His pale complexion and wiry frame earned him the nickname Icky from his peers. It was short for Ichabod, as in Ichabod Crane, the timid character from the Legend of Sleepy Hollow. Ick was calm on the exterior; in battle he was anything but timid.

"Pop the door, Ick."

The sledge traced a well practiced tight arc, a perfect one timer. The door buckled as the hammer forced the trim on the inside to pop off, rendering the deadbolt useless. What followed was a little humorous, but deadly serious. A hefty female zombie who had been the source of the moaning became wedged between the ruined door and the jamb.

The trapped undead woman had been cooking in the one story ranch house for days. She was morbidly obese, pasty white and bloated like a beached whale carcass. The last shirt that she put on while still alive was stained with days old dried blood and other not so dry bodily fluids. She had probably been some soldier or airman's wife enjoying her weekend when the Omega virus stormed across the nation.

Gaines bellowed, "Clear!"

Icky stepped aside to allow the other two operators a clear field of fire. The three round burst from Gaines' silenced SCAR assault rifle pulped the walker's face. Her body performed a clumsy pirouette and crashed across the entryway to the house.

Sergeant Dale Williams stood back from the door, silenced SCAR at the ready, waiting for more zombies to appear. After a few seconds Captain Gaines stepped over the corpse and began clearing the interior of the house.

"Clear," was repeated after each room was checked for threats and deemed to be empty. With practiced precision the four man team swarmed the house from top to bottom.

"What does this remind you of, gentlemen?" Gaines said, subtly reminding his men to stay frosty.

"*Fallujah, sir.*"

"Ding. X gets a square. Good job Ick."

Williams dragged the corpse down the stairs and deposited it on the brown lawn.

Gaines pulled the door shut and marked it with a big chalk X and the numeral one. He had taken this right out of the hurricane Katrina playbook. The X meant the house was clear and the circled out one denoted the now deceased occupant.

Scenes like this played out all across the city as the Special Forces soldiers from Fort Carson prepared Colorado Springs to become the new capital of the United States.

Chapter 3
Outbreak - Day 4
River Bend Campground
Wasatch Mountains, Utah

The cutoff road was right where the map indicated it
would be. Cade followed it to the right and continued on
further until he saw the small sign that read *River Bend
Campground*.

The symbols on the map denoted that the place would be
unimproved - and it was. There were only eight sites and all
but one was empty.

A white Jeep CJ was backed in next to one of the sites.
The odor of carrion was evident; except for the flies he
detected no movement. A red, three-person North Face tent
was erected directly behind the Jeep.

The Special Ops motorcycle was very quiet, although the
exhaust was baffled; it still made enough noise to flush two
very large ravens from the tent. They cursed the intruder with
their caws and flew into the tallest tree where they continued
to let their displeasure be known.

Cade silenced the bike's engine, dismounted and drew his
Glock 17 from the holster strapped to his thigh.

Beer cans were scattered near the bumper of the old beat
up 4x4. He knelt and touched the back of his right hand to

the mound of ashes in the rock-ringed fire pit. *Cold.* Next he slowly traversed the front of the tent trying to ascertain if anything remained inside. All that he could see and hear between the open flaps was a cloud of small black flies. Using a long stick, he carefully parted the door to the fly hotel. A corpse - thankfully still dead - was splayed out on top of a pair of green sleeping bags. Maggots had made the remains of the dead camper their new home. The woman's head was only attached to her body with strands of dried skin and shiny corded muscle, the eye sockets had been picked clean. There was little left of her to explain how she ultimately met her violent end. Bite marks were visible on her exposed skin but Cade couldn't tell if they were human or animal. Some of the damage had obviously been incurred by the ravenous black birds, which were still in the trees making a ruckus.

Judging by the decomposition and the amount of flies and their larvae, she had been dead for a few days. Blood was splattered throughout the interior but had dried days ago. The smell in the hot tent was enough to make a normal person vomit. Cade had seen it all and had ceased being normal days ago. On the first day of the outbreak he had been forced to re-kill his favorite neighbors. They technically weren't alive, but he dispatched them all the same. That was the last time he had vomited. The former Delta Force operator was all business now. The sight and smell of the slaughtered woman didn't faze him.

Cade had only glanced in the tent momentarily. He removed his head from the opening and scanned his surroundings, seeing no threats in sight. Since darkness by his estimation was only an hour away he made the decision to stay the night at the River Bend campground. Seeing as how the tent was already occupied, he opted to sleep in the vehicle. It would provide minimal security but at least he would wake up dry. A low pitched rumble moved through the canyon; the thunder announcing that the mountain thunderstorm had arrived. Cade sniffed the air. The smell of

ozone was a portent that lightning might also make an
appearance.

Cade removed the silenced M4 from the hard plastic
holster on the side of the bike, and grabbed an MRE from the
saddle bag. As an afterthought he retrieved the night vision
goggles as well, and then wheeled the bike in front of the Jeep
and prepped it for a quick getaway.

The Jeep was unlocked and strangely devoid of the usual
cooler, stove, lantern, as well as any other normal camping
accoutrements. It appeared the owner only planned on a
quick overnighter. *The woman was probably trying to get away from
the infected on the first day of the outbreak and expected the government
to quickly get the situation under control.* Hundreds of millions of
Americans held the same false assumptions and it led to their
early deaths. The bad news was most of them reanimated and
now walked the earth in search of the lucky few that
somehow managed to survive. *Lucky few, what an oxymoron.*

It was impossible to get comfortable inside the cramped
Jeep but he made the most of it. He devoured the MRE
instantly and powered up his night vision goggles.

The sun disappeared behind a cloak of gloomy storm
clouds and darkness descended on the Wasatch. Thanks to
the clouds the night was moonless, and without the night
vision goggles he wouldn't be able to see a thing.

The goggles worked perfectly. He scanned the forest one
last time, and there was no detectable movement in the soft
green glow. After locking the doors and hooking the NVGs
onto the helmet mounting clip, he said a few words in his
head; they were directed at his wife and daughter, wherever
they might be. *I am alive and I will see you soon. I love you Brook
and Raven.* He closed his eyes. Sleep owned him seconds later.

Chapter 4
Outbreak - Day 5
Schriever Airforce Base
Colorado Springs, Colorado

Schriever AFB, home of the 50th Space Wing, Space
Warfare Center as well as the Ballistic Missile Defense
Organization. The sophisticated satellites monitored from
Schriever would provide a window with which to survey their
new reality.

The remnants of the United States government would be
trickling in during the coming days and it was rumored the
new President, former Speaker of the House Valerie Clay,
would also be arriving at the base sometime soon.

The installation was established in 1987 in the foothills of
the Rocky Mountains, twenty miles from the center of
Colorado Springs. The sprawling collection of squat buildings
rested on an elevated expanse of land blessed with heavy duty
fencing and excellent fields of fire. The base would soon be
fortified with troops and equipment returning from two
theatres of war and the many other bases the United States
maintained overseas.

Colorado Springs was home to a substantial military
presence before Omega, but now there were less than three
thousand soldiers remaining. Fort Carson, home of the
Second and Third divisions of the 10th Special Forces group,

was to the west of the city. Only a small fraction of the base
personnel returned to the base after the outbreaks. The
famous NORAD facility, buried deep inside of Cheyenne
Mountain, was southwest of Colorado Springs.

In addition to Schriever there were two other bases able to
accommodate flight operations. Peterson AFB housed a test
flight facility and Fort Kit Carson housed a large assortment
of rotor-wing and fixed-wing aircraft. It was no wonder why
Colorado Springs was chosen to replace Washington D.C.

***

Brook had begun the count to take her mind off of the
fact that before they became infected the walkers she was
putting down were like her. A number seemed less personal
and it seemed to work... so far.

The gun bucked again. "Seventy-th... damn." The shot was
low and right, the walker's right arm was blown from the
socket and backstroked away in a blurry green arc. Before the
outbreak the one-armed little boy had been someone's pride
and joy, and judging by the red and gold uniform he died
doing what he loved most. Before expending her last round
Brook rubbed her sore shoulder and readjusted the butt plate
where it met the muscle.

The long gun boomed again. The round entered the Little
Leaguer's head through the left eye, peeled back half of his
face and sent the contents of his cranium airborne. The
kinetic energy from the bullet's punch put the boy on his
back. Brook waited a second to make sure he wasn't getting
back up before adding him to her count.

"Seventy-three." She wiped her brow and popped the top
on the silver and blue can of god-awful tasting energy drink.
She guzzled it down in one drink, her face screwed up.
Monkeypiss. The petite woman had been awake for twenty plus
hours. Though the taurine- and caffeine-laced beverage made
her gag, it was necessary if she was going to do her part to
help protect the enclave and her daughter Raven.

"More ammo, *now!*" she screamed to anyone within earshot. Brook closed her bloodshot, red-rimmed eyes and cursed the impending sunrise.

Her introduction to the Remington M24 had been hasty. The bolt action rifle had a Leupold 10x40 mm optic attached behind the thermal scope and it magnified every grisly detail. Brook was presented with a target rich environment. Viewed through the scope, the zombies seemed like they were close enough to touch.

Each walker that she added to her kill count served to boost her confidence in the rifle as well as herself. The weapon was similar to the Model 700 that her husband Cade had taught her how to shoot. The M24 was a larger caliber, and it recoiled with more force, but she had to admit she was getting comfortable shooting her new long gun. Brook was also getting used to this new existence and her continuing baptism by fire.

***

The colonel had approached her the previous day. The softcover perched on his head was pulled so low Brook had a hard time meeting his eyes. By anyone's standards the colonel was tall, but to Brook he was a gigantic man with a booming baritone voice; the name tag on his chest read "Shrill" although he was anything but.

She had initially met him when the Chinooks, piloted by the men of the 160th SOAR, deposited her and Raven at the base. Colonel Shrill had been there to greet them even before the rotor blades stopped turning. Since then she had learned he was the highest ranking man left on base. Looking at the Airman's pressed camouflage utilities and clean-shaven face it was hard to fathom that there was a war with the undead being waged outside of Schriever Air Force Base.

"Young lady, do you have *any* experience with firearms?"

If only he knew, Brook thought before answering semi-honestly.

"A little bit sir."

"That's good enough, follow me." He pivoted and, without a backward glance, strode purposefully out the door.

His demeanor and bearing discouraged her from saying no; it was like she had been hypnotized by the man. Brook found herself following lockstep in his wake. The colonel recruited several more civilians before leading his ragtag group of conscripts to the armory.

Shrill silently looked at the survivors before addressing them. "Ladies and gentlemen, this shitstorm fell in my lap. If it would have been courteous and started on a Monday, then you probably wouldn't be standing here having to say yes to the question that I am going to ask."

One man in the back meekly raised his arm. Shrill ignored him and kept talking.

"The majority of the men and women that would be here on a normal day did not make it back. Most of the base personnel here at Schriever maintain and operate the space birds in our U.S. arsenal. Ninety-nine percent of our security force never came home." Shrill paused for effect and continued, his voice increasing in volume as he cut to the chase. "Ladies and gentlemen, I am humbly asking the..." he paused again and poked at the air counting the group standing before him, "...thirteen of you to help spell my men and women on perimeter security. They have been at it valiantly for days without any substantial rest. I need all of the help that I can get in fending off these abominations that used to be my neighbors, at least until the C-5s and C-130s full of combat veterans return from Iraq and Afghanistan. This isn't public knowledge, but before his passing President Odero ordered a complete withdrawal of all of our troops around the world. From Germany to the Korean peninsula, men and women from all the branches are coming home to help us pick up the pieces. It was a testament to his quick thinking and it happened to be the last executive order signed before he went silent. Our new President arrives tomorrow. A little bird tells me that we will employ the reinforcements ASAP and she is gonna let us take the gloves off and have a good old fashioned street brawl. Ladies and gentlemen, the United States might be down, but she is not out... by any stretch of the imagination." Shrill's resonant voice abruptly went silent, it was as if someone had hit the colonel's mute button; a hush fell over the room.

Brook looked around at the civilians assembled nearest her. The man in the back row slowly lowered his arm. His Adams apple bobbed up and down as he decided to keep his mouth shut and swallow his words.

"I'm in," Brook said, shattering the quiet. She was caught off-guard by her own voice, like some giant ventriloquist had uttered the words while its hand moved her mouth. Her motive was purely survival driven, not just for herself, but for Raven and Carl's survival too. Deep down though, she was ashamed to admit she had grown to like dispatching the dead. It was a strange sensation. After all, her husband Cade was the Tier-One operator and former Delta Force shooter. He was the alpha male and was supposed to be the protector, not her. Cade's whereabouts had been a mystery since she had talked to him last. Shortly after the outbreak, before the President declared martial law, she had spoken with him on her now long gone and useless Smartphone. Cade had instructed her to leave her parents' home in Myrtle Beach, South Carolina and seek refuge at Fort Bragg in North Carolina.

She had been successful at reaching safety with her daughter, brother and a little boy named Dmitri. They had saved the boy from the flesh-eaters in the small town of Aberdeen. So if she needed to be the alpha male - so to speak - then so be it. The only thing she could do now was protect her little girl and stay alive in the hope that they would eventually be reunited with Cade.

Slowly, out of peer pressure or basic herd mentality, one by one the rest of the civilians accepted the colonel's request.

"*Outstanding!*" Shrill boomed. "Follow me."

***

After leading them to the armory on the south side of the base, Colonel Shrill asked the others to sit tight while he pulled Brook aside.

"One of the operators involved in the airlift told me you acted courageously at Fort Bragg. He even went so far as to tell me your quick thinking saved some lives and one of the Night Stalker's Chinook helicopters. I wanted to say good job and welcome to Schriever."

Brook was speechless. She had expected the Bull Moose to tell her that she could leave if she had "mommying" to do. Instead his words enlivened her. She felt empowered and in charge of her own destiny. "My main objective is to keep my little girl from seeing any more bloodshed. We went through hell to reach Bragg and she is suffering from the ordeal."

The others were now intently watching the exchange.

"Ma'am, I fully understand if you feel the need to stay back and take care of your family. We *need* shooters and I am inclined to believe that you are one." He pointed his thumb at the other civilians. "We also need bodies to put bullets in the magazines and runners to distribute them." The base commander looked at the other men and women before he finished. "They... are not shooters."

Brook swallowed, and merely nodded.

He had her, but finished his spiel anyway, "The dead are following each other here and I fear if we don't act quickly, and decisively, then we *will* have another disaster like Fort Bragg on our hands."

***

That was how Brook ended up in the tower with the now empty sniper rifle and piles of decaying bodies scattered all around her.

While she waited for the ammo runner to exchange her empty magazines for full ones, she caught herself staring at one of the ghouls she had put down. The corpse lay sprawled fifty feet away. The entry wound in its forehead was as big as her fist; out leaked clumpy gray brain matter. The fully burned male stared back at her with dead open eyes, its black sooty maw peeled over ivory teeth in a final death grimace. *I wonder who loved him*, Brook thought dully.

Clomping boots jarred her from the moment of empathy. A fit looking soldier double-timed it up the ladder. Brook watched the top of his boonie hat until he reached the entrance to the guard platform. She was greeted by a wide country boy grin and an extended hand, "PFC Mark Farnsworth, I'm here to relieve you. Shrill sends thanks for your service."

Brook rubbed her shoulder, it was tender from the constant pounding. "It was the least I could do... considering the circumstances." She propped the Remington up against the wall, with the safety on and the bolt open.

"Thirsty?" Farnsworth reached into his pocket and handed Brook a silver and blue can of energy drink. "The colonel wants all of the volunteer shooters to stand down for now. Reinforcements will be on the ground any time now."

As he finished speaking, a landing C-5 Galaxy screamed overhead, rudely interrupting their conversation.

"Good timing, my eyes need a good rinse and *I* need some coffee." After inspecting the soldier's offering she handed the cold can back to him. "I can't drink that swill. No disrespect, I know it's the thought that counts," Brook said as she picked up her M4.

"Here, hope you won't need these, but just in case." The soldier handed her two extra thirty round magazines for the carbine.

"If those monsters get inside of here... these aren't gonna last long," Brook replied, stuffing the magazines in her pockets.

She about-faced and climbed down the ladder. Brook was looking forward to checking in on her comatose brother. She was praying for him, but the doctor's prognosis was not good. Brook had to keep a positive attitude. After all, over the course of the last few days Carl had already cheated death more times than she cared to count.

Chapter 5
Outbreak - Day 4
Forest Service Road 5543 West
Draper, Utah

The trees on both sides of the road clawed their way heavenward, doing their best to block out the brilliant blue afternoon sky. At ground level juniper and sagebrush prevailed, crowding the edge of the sun baked gravel road. Why it wasn't paved baffled Harry. Every kidney jarring impact with a pothole made him curse the person responsible for that decision.

He was only fifteen miles into the long trek back to Portland, Oregon. He had been awake for most of the last three days. The first two had been spent running and gunning, trying to escape the ever expanding undead outbreak. The constant adrenaline highs and lows had done a number on his old bones. Every nerve ending was aflame, yet his body begged for sleep. The feeling was akin to an out of body experience. The death and destruction seemed like something out of a nightmare, as if the person that had gone through the unspeakable horrors was someone other than him. The events of the last few days would be etched indelibly in his memory and tattooed on his psyche for the rest of his life. If he didn't redeem himself and at *least* attempt to find his wife, then the rest of his days wouldn't be worth living anyway.

The previous night had been spent attempting to sleep through the sounds of the undead assault on Camp Williams. The result was a scant few minutes of shut eye, disrupted by gunfire, shouting soldiers and the stress inducing racket of the ghouls outside the wire.

While Harry fought with the steering wheel, dodging the ambling walkers and canyon sized depressions in the road, he caught himself nodding off. Twice he almost put the Ford in the ditch. He was delirious and couldn't keep his eyes open, and in a moment of surrender he decided to rest them for a few minutes.

He drove on until a long stretch of zombie-free road lay in front of him, and for as far as he could see in the rearview mirror there was no sign of the walking dead. It seemed a safe place to take a quick catnap. His eyes closed without effort and sleep immediately followed.

In his dream, he was following a woman through very tall, swaying grass. It was a warm spring day and she looked every bit like his wife who he had abandoned the day after the outbreak. Every few steps she would stop and glance back at him and flash the smile that he had loved for the last four decades. After a few more strides she would pause, allowing him to get close enough to gaze into her azure eyes and feel her silky gray hair. Harry would let the strands glide between his fingers before inevitably she would turn and disappear, once again into the foliage.

***

Harry awoke with a start; he was disoriented and didn't know where he was. The one thing he was instantly certain of, it was night and very dark, the moonless kind of dark prevalent only away from city lights. His teeth chattered autonomously. A steady scuffing sound caused him to quickly forget his dream. The fatigue and stress accumulated since the dead started walking had taken its toll on the sixty-five-year-old man, culminating in nine hours of uninterrupted heavy sleep.

Harry remembered he had left his glasses on the dash before he closed his eyes. He groped around in the dark blindly trying to find them. The scratching persisted. Harry located his handkerchief, the type that most men of his age were required to carry by some unwritten rule; he ritualistically wiped the lenses of his second set of eyes. *It must be a tree branch brushing the side of the truck*, Harry thought, as he placed the glasses on the bridge of his nose and pushed them into their proper place. He looked to the right, still unable to discern the source of the sound in the inky blackness outside of his metal cocoon. His best thinking led him to turn on the dome light. The sudden assault on his retinas making his eyes snap shut; he had to squint first before he could fully reopen them.

The passenger window reverberated from a strong blow. Harry let out a yelp and fumbled to start the engine. Skittering and scratching, like fingernails on a chalkboard, came from somewhere in front of the truck.

Harry turned the key, the engine started and the headlights snapped on, illuminating several zombies. Somehow, even under cover of night they had sensed him inside the cab.

"Go to hell and leave me alone!" Harry screamed pointlessly at the milky eyes coveting his flesh. He was still shivering from the cold sleep he had been so rudely awakened from when suddenly it dawned on him he had been dreaming about his lost wife. Harry longed to slip back into the warm comfortable embrace of sleep and visit her again.

Harry slammed the truck into drive, jumped on the gas pedal and plowed through the group of undead. The Ford F-350 fishtailed left and right out of control the first hundred feet before he finally straightened it out.

Speed was his enemy on the unimproved, storm washed track of dirt masquerading as a road. *Slow down*, he told

himself. His fear wouldn't listen. The speedometer hit forty
and then pushed past fifty. Trees and scrub flashed by, Harry
felt compelled to drive faster by the unseen demons chasing
him. The F-350 started to shimmy on the washboard-like
ridges; it skewed sideways as the tires broke free. *Oh God.*
Involuntarily his eyes snapped shut. When they opened he
saw trees, road, trees and then road again. The locust cloud of
dust overtook and enveloped the Ford as it ground to a halt
in the middle of the road. Fine dust roiled silently through the
headlight beams. Heart racing and short of breath, Harry
started to recite the Lord's Prayer. "Our Father who art in
heaven..." Slowly the dirt curtain parted. He halted the prayer
and pried his arthritic fingers from the steering wheel.
Obvious indentations, where his hands had been, remained in
the rubber.

Marveling at the fact that he had somehow survived the
spinout alive, he looked up to see, not ten feet in front of
him, a disheveled pale woman in the center of the road. A
guttural sound exited her mouth as she raised her arms and
quickened her pace towards the truck.

Talking to himself, he tried to get his hands to work as he
fumbled with the box of shotgun shells. "Harry, you damn
fool. Why didn't you load this thing before you left the base?"
Like a clumsy running back, he fumbled the whole box of
shells onto the floorboard of the truck. They rolled the
farthest distance from him possible and pooled by the
passenger door. Stealing a glance over the dash, he saw that
the figure was still advancing. He made sure his door was
locked, popped out of his seatbelt and lunged across the truck
scooping up a handful of shells. Harry inserted the first one
backwards; the expletives flowed as he tried to right the
wrong.

Harry bobbed his head up. The pale walker was just inches
from his window when she spoke.

"He tried to kill me. My asshole of a husband tried to kill me."

She was in a frenzied state, but Harry was elated she wasn't one of them. "Slow down. Here, take this." He handed her a warm bottle of water and tried to calm her down. "What's your name?"

"Sally." Only a whisper came out; the woman exhaled a deep sigh and collapsed.

Harry got out and picked the woman named Sally up. She was petite and was very light - even to an old man unaccustomed to lifting anything except for an occasional pint of beer. With his head on a swivel, he worked his way around the truck and put the frail woman in the passenger seat. She was unresponsive, but still breathing.

Longest fainting spell I've ever seen. Granted the only time he had seen anyone faint was on television or in a movie.

Harry gave Sally a cursory inspection for any injuries, especially bite marks. Finding none on her exposed skin, he contemplated searching under her shorts and tee shirt, but decided it would be best to wait until the woman woke up and ask her if she had been exposed to the infected.

Harry had no intention of driving at night, but his little bout of narcolepsy changed that. He picked his way down the mountain, driving a moderate twenty miles per hour.

"*Oh no,*" Harry gasped.

The road was impassable. Illuminated by the headlights, hundreds of shambling zombies were blocking his way.

Sally stirred at the sound of Harry's voice. Risking a sideways glance as he worked the truck into reverse, Harry noticed the sheen of sweat coating Sally's face.

Rocks thrown from the spinning tires pinged off the undercarriage of the Ford as he tried to escape the dead. Harry found that steering while barreling backwards was nearly impossible. For the second time he lost control, and with a spine jarring impact the truck plunged into a yawning ditch.

"Oooh," Sally moaned. She had bounced off of the seat back and rebounded only to meet the dash with her nose and upper lip. She remained still with her eyes closed; red rivulets of blood streamed from her mouth and coated her splintered teeth.

The dead were quickly converging on the high centered truck. One wheel was completely off of the ground and the other three were useless as they spun in the gravel unable to get purchase. Once more pale hands started impacting the windows and body panels of the truck, trying to extract the meat within.

"Oohh."

Sally emitted a guttural moan; her eyelids snapped open revealing cloudy orbs.

Unable to get the truck moving, Harry began whimpering. The moment that he realized Sally had become one of them, his whimpers turned to screams.

The ghouls on the outside finally succeeded in breaking the glass, only to find Sally had already had her fill, and soon Harry would join them.

Chapter 6
Outbreak - Day 4
Camp Williams 19th Special Forces Garrison
Draper, Utah

The dead had been coming from miles around since the first days of the outbreak; most were drawn from Salt Lake City because initially the floodlights around the base were left blazing all night. A massive slit trench was cut into the earth with the tractors on the base, and then all it took was a boom box and loud heavy metal music to lure the dead over the edge where they were trapped and immolated.

Little did Major Beeson know the lights weren't the only draw. The dead were following each other like ants to a treat and once the steady stream started, it couldn't be diverted. By the time the base commander ordered the lights extinguished it was too late.

***

Corporal Litters blinked twice and then used the back of his hand to wipe the sweaty tears from his eyes. The damp bandana was tied tightly around his face but still didn't filter out the smell of death, but it was effective at keeping out the dust stirred up by the constant movement of the undead. They were never still, like meth heads on the constant hunt for the next hit, only it was human flesh they coveted and no amount could sate them.

For the third time in as many minutes he pressed the
scope to his eye to reconfirm his worst fear. She had on the
Sea World shirt, the one with the black and white orca he had
bought for her less than two weeks ago. Even though his wife
Carmen was out of work, with no prospects on the horizon,
Steve won out and convinced her to let him take them to Sea
World in San Diego. If he had known it would be their last
vacation together as a family he would have gotten her more
than just that goddamn shirt. Steve cursed God. *Billions of dead
walking the earth and you put her front and center pressed against the
fence.* With her sandy blonde hair still pulled back in a pony
tail, despite the pallor of her scratched and torn skin and
lifeless eyes, she was still his little girl. He had last kissed and
said good bye to Becca and Carmen in the kitchen of their
little house in Draper on the morning of the first day of the
outbreak. Now she was in his cross hairs and he couldn't find
it in himself to pull the trigger.

Litters was in charge of the back perimeter fence. It
abutted against the woods separating the two forest service
roads leading out of the back of the base. Until now there
hadn't been much activity; the few dead that did show up he
promptly put down. A pile of fifteen infected corpses littered
the outside of the fence, scattered randomly where they had
fallen, all having been killed by bullets from his M4.

Becca had been quietly swaying back and forth, both
numb hands gripping the chain link fence, for over an hour.
Her stare was getting to him. Inexplicably Litters stood up
from behind his blind of filled sandbags and put his rifle
down.

One last time, I need to feel my baby's soft hair, one last time.
Corporal Steve Litters didn't cry often. During the solemn
trudge towards the perimeter fence he completely lost
control.

Becca stopped swaying. A low guttural moan emerged
from the gaunt, stooped over ten-year-old. Behind her, like

wraiths, more of the dead materialized from between the gnarled trees.

"Honey it's me, Daddy." Litters wiped his nose on his fatigue sleeve. A long silver slug trail of snot remained behind.

Litters stood six inches in front of his undead daughter. In the far recesses of his mind a voice urged him to back away. If his little girl's catatonic gaze and eerie moaning wasn't deterrent enough, nothing was going to keep him from trying to fix her. He stammered, hot tears burning trails down his face, "Hold still, I won't hurt you."

He swallowed, a dry Mojave Desert throat cracking swallow, and reached his hand through the fence to comfort his Becca. Even though she only vaguely resembled the love of his life, her hair still had the same silky texture that he used to stroke while reading her bedtime stories.

For some reason the little ones were faster. Becca snatched her dad's hand and plunged her incisors into the soft flesh of his forearm; the bite was deep and violent and caused his hand to reflexively snap shut. The plug of flesh and tendons slid down her throat. Litters stared in disbelief as her second bite shredded the veins of his wrist. Hot blood surged from the jagged wounds. She no longer was Daddy's little girl.

What was I thinking? were his last thoughts before he blacked out. Corporal Litters' life pulsed into the soil, pooling near Becca's bruised and bloodied bare feet.

Chapter 7
Outbreak - Day 5
River Bend Campground
Wasatch Mountains, Utah

Sure enough, the thunderclouds hadn't been bluffing. Another low rumble, closer than the first, stirred Cade subconsciously. His eyelids twitched in response to the nightmare he was attending. When he was awake it was easy for him to separate who he was in the normal world, when there had been one, from who he had been trained to be when he was on a mission. The nocturnal thoughts were his brain's way of purging. His dreams and nightmares had been coming few and far between after standing down from active duty in the elite Delta Force. Now that he was thrust back into the throes of combat and in a constant state of hypervigilance, the midnight visitors had once again taken residence in his skull.

In his head Cade was back in Tora Bora, hunting Bin Laden, high in the mountains of Afghanistan. He watched the contrails of the circling B-52s. They were so high the occasional glint of sun off of metal or canopy was the only proof that a jet was indeed responsible for the chalky white lines. The explosions of the munitions falling from the silver specks boomed; the sound rolled and echoed across the valley. An Arc Light strike sounded like thunder, only on a grander scale.

The slight patter of rain drops didn't wake him; it was the second booming clap of thunder that had the honor. The storm had parked itself against the Wasatch front and was struggling to hurdle the craggy peaks.

Cade opened his eyes but didn't move his body; it was how he always woke up when in a hostile environment. Nothing moved in the dark but he was careful to remain statuelike, seated in the Jeep. A jagged fork of sheet lightning briefly illuminated the camp. *What was that?* Cade asked himself, hoping his eyes had been playing tricks. He caught a fleeting glimpse of a stationary figure, standing in the bushes twenty feet in front of the Jeep. *One one thousand one...* An explosive clap from the thunder cell followed. *That was very close.* He forced his body to remain still and not give away his position. The darkness was his friend. Turning on his night vision goggles could wait as well. Any movement in the 4x4 would rock the small vehicle on its creaky suspension.

He didn't have to wait long for the next lightning strike. Once more the surrounding camp site was revealed for a split second by the strobe effect of the lightning. The figure was no longer there. Cade's mind was trying to fool him into thinking it had been but a figment, a shadow or the moon and clouds fucking with him. His eyes and gut told him otherwise. Ever so slowly he reached up and swiveled the goggles down, letting them hover in front of his face. At the same time he retrieved his pistol from the passenger seat.

Being that he was still not under attack, he wrestled with the question: should he wait for Mother Nature to once again cast light on the subject or should he flick the night vision goggles on and go hunting?

The decision was made for him, when at once a pale hand penetrated the threadbare canvas top and a clenched fist shattered the glass inches from his head. The hand from above clutched the top of his helmet while the other groped

at his neck. In one motion Cade recoiled from the clawing
hands and discharged two shots, rapid fire through the
broken window. The night vision goggles were rendered
useless for a long moment, washed out from the muzzle flash
in the confined space. The zombie was flailing wildly and
thrusting its arms into the darkened interior. Cade scrambled
over the stick shift and popped open the canvas door with his
shoulder. His exit was less than graceful; he fell out of the
passenger side and barrel rolled before getting back on his
feet.

Cade moved away from the vehicle and flipped the goggles
up hoping that his own night vision would be of use. Though
his ears rang from the gunshots he could still hear the ghoul
shuffling around in the dark campground. The smell
emanating from the walker was much worse than that of the
rotting woman in the tent.

The next flash of lightning only allowed Cade two poorly
aimed shots at the approaching zombie. The first 9 mm slug
destroyed the lower jaw of the burly corpse, leaving it a
gaping black hole for a mouth. Shot number two sailed
harmlessly into the wilderness. The monster was so close
Cade could feel its presence. He flipped the goggles back
down only to find the jawless zombie two feet in front of
him, its head panning left to right, the green glow making it all
the more evil looking. Cade froze and held his breath,
partially because the odor made it necessary but also he didn't
want to give his position away. After a few seconds it lunged
at him without warning and its cold hands encircled his neck.
The zombie was much stronger than he thought it would be.
Cade used every ounce of strength to ward off the two
hundred pounds of dead weight with his free hand. He
inserted the Glock into the empty hole where the thing's
lower mandible used to be and squeezed off two shots,
resulting in a shower of glowing green brains splattering the
side of the Jeep. The zombie's lifeless hands still had a firm

death grip around his neck when the corpse sunk to its knees, dead for good. It took two back and forth sawing motions with the Gerber to sever the wrist tendons causing the dead fingers to spring open.

Cade inhaled deeply, willing the stars of near unconsciousness away and massaged his neck, feeling for broken skin. He had no idea if the Omega virus could be transmitted through an open wound and he hoped to never find out.

Cade's black Suunto read 6:15 a.m. The first light of dawn was weaving tendrils through the boughs of the trees and the rain had petered out. The full scope of the damage inflicted the night before wasn't evident in the flat green glow of the NVGs. Now that the sun was making an appearance Cade got a good look at the walker that had almost punched his ticket. The dead creature had on scuffed hiking boots, tattered and torn walking shorts and a light flannel shirt fully blackened with brittle dried blood. Cade found a wallet on the corpse and, feeling like a voyeur, he rifled through the man's personal things. His initial assessment appeared to be correct. Mr. Bob Kirkman of 2231 Glenhart Drive, Salt Lake City, Utah, had been carrying three thousand dollars worth of crisp twenties and ten ATM slips documenting their withdrawal. The dates on the slips indicated Mr. Kirkman had been in Salt Lake on the Saturday of the outbreak. Also in his possession was a picture of a woman that might have been the one in the tent, although Cade had no intention of attempting a positive identification. If he had to venture a guess, Salt Lake had been overrun with zombies early on and that was the reason the man and woman took to the hills. How Bob had become infected, and when the corpse in the tent had met her fate, was the real mystery.

Before he left the River Bend campground, Cade manhandled Bob's headless body and rolled it into the tent. The contents of the wallet had put a face on the dead couple,

and they were once like him. It seemed right to reunite them
in death.

Chapter 8
Elbert County, Georgia
June 6, 1979

Two muddy tire tracks snaked through the cow pasture in the middle of the Georgia sticks. It had taken an hour to drive here and, adding insult to injury, the client didn't even get his boots dirty. Peter let the engine idle for all of five minutes while the two ton limo sank into the muck. Apparently his passenger had seen all he needed. The man spoke through the intercom and instructed him to proceed to the next destination. Peter knew he had heard the man's voice before, but he couldn't place it.

When he finally managed to get the immense car turned around, he noticed the realty sign had a red "SOLD" sticker affixed to it.

The first ninety miles from Atlanta were blacktop heaven but the last twenty had been back road hell. The hired driver struggled to keep the big beast travelling in a straight line. The Lincoln Town car limousine swayed and shimmied, its springs loudly protesting each depression in the road. It wasn't much of a road. It was mostly gravel and potholes with washboard grooves scoured into it by the continual spring showers. The road would eventually dead-end at the Ellington quarry, four brutal miles from pavement usually only negotiated by large, high clearance trucks.

The brown cloud caught up with and enveloped the
limousine as it rolled to a halt. Peter waited for the cocoon of
dust to descend on the once black automobile before he
stepped out to open the door for his important passenger.

Peter helped the man out and stole a brief glance at him.
He appeared to be in his early forties. Blonde hair starting to
show hints of gray peeked out from under his black beret.
Wide rimmed black sunglasses and a thick moustache
camouflaged his true features. The face, combined with the
distinctive voice, still didn't help to pry the man's identity
from the recesses of Peter's memory. For sure he was a big
time player in the south, but it wouldn't do him any good to
dwell on his identity. Peter's personal rule was to never ask
questions or make small talk unless addressed first. It was
easier that way and honestly, the tips were better when the
clients sensed their anonymity was being respected.

He got back in the driver's seat and observed his passenger
approach the squat, windowless office building. The familiar
looking man carried a rugged aluminum attaché case in one
hand and a three foot long black tube in the other. Peter
watched him with idle curiosity until he disappeared into the
building.

***

The bell at the top of the door jangled, announcing the
possibility of a paying customer, few and far between these
days.

"Howdy." Milo Williamson looked over his bifocals at the
tall stranger. "How can I help you?"

"I'm Robert Christian, I represent a consortium of
businessmen and we are erecting a stone monument in
Ellington."

Milo looked the man up and down. It struck him as
strange that the fella didn't remove his sunglasses once inside,
but it truly was none of his business. "What kind of
monument and where will it stand?" Milo then realized, to his

dismay that he forgot to introduce himself to his visitor. "Oh forgive me. It must be the humidity messing with my brain. My name is Milo Williamson," he said, offering his calloused hand.

The man reciprocated, pausing for a heartbeat. "Robert Christian, the pleasure is all mine."

What soft feminine hands, he must be an executive, Milo thought. All of the bankers that had been turning him down for a loan lately had the very same buttery hands. Giving out notes for twenty plus percent interest sure was highway robbery. It definitely wasn't hard work. Milo was still sore the family business might fold. The economy had him in a bind and nothing was getting done... especially not in granite. "Sorry, I lost my train of thought. Refresh my memory, what and where?"

"It's a piece of modern art and the property is in Ellington, *like I said.*" Milo's potential client seemed annoyed. *Well, country bumpkin,* Robert Christian thought, "Do you have time to do the job or should I go elsewhere?"

Milo gestured to the cylinder on the counter. "May I see the plans?"

The man unrolled the blueprints, trapped one side down with his tan, brick-sized mobile phone and held down the other side with his free hand.

"Whoa... are these dimensions correct? Assuming they are, each of these slabs will weigh roughly ten tons each."

"The plans are to be followed precisely. One deviation and the celestial features in the design won't work."

"What do you mean by celestial features?" Milo said, scratching what little hair he had left on his head.

The tone of the man's voice suddenly changed. It was even more apparent his patience was wearing thin. *"Do you want the work... or shall I move on?"*

"Let me look at these for a moment." The old quarryman started making calculations. "Not counting the etching, and there will be a lot of extra time consuming work there..."

39

Robert Christian interrupted Milo by placing the attaché case on the counter and opening both latches. "We need it completed no later than March twenty-second."

"The timeline will be doable. It's going to cost roughly thirty thousand dollars though."

Robert Christian spun the case around to face the older man and opened the lid. Inside were neatly bundled stacks of twenty dollar bills. Andrew Jackson never looked better to Milo.

"There's fifty thousand dollars here. Get the job done on time and the difference is yours. Consider it a performance bonus."

Milo, not wanting to seem desperate, waited three seconds before accepting. "One thing though. What does the first line mean?" He had his finger on the blueprints. The first line that was to grace the monolith read *Maintain humanity under 500,000,000 in perpetual balance with nature.* "Is that some kind of cryptic warning?"

He never got his answer; the bell signaled the mysterious man's exit.

***

During the two hour drive back to Atlanta, Robert Christian contemplated his actions and the times he lived in. The world needed a wake up call. And it had to be something more than a thirty second commercial portraying a polluted landscape with a lone American Indian, in full authentic native garb, shedding a tear for Mother Earth. Any heart strings the spot might have tugged were quickly snipped by the next ad urging, *more*, *get it now*, *must have* and *consume.*

During the sixties, as a much younger man he tried to do his part. He went to rallies, marched and participated in sit-ins.

The seventies saw him get involved in politics, only to have his eyes opened to the realities of the military industrial complex and how the two were tightly woven together.

The monolith would not only enlighten the people that read the engraved words, but it would also stand as a tangible reminder to keep the Guild on task.

Although the writings etched into the granite obelisk touched on population control and leaving the earth better for the next generation, it wasn't a blatant call for eugenic action. Sadly, deep down Robert Christian knew that man would take care of that one way or another.

With the Soviet Union and the United States locked in a cold war, and a few hot wars by proxy, it was looking more and more like the *cleanse* might be accomplished through nuclear holocaust.

It didn't matter. The Guild would be ready and waiting, no matter the world changing event, to step in, pick up the pieces and send mankind onward in a good orderly direction.

The man in the back seat drifted off still thinking about the eventual ascension of his new world order.

***

Milo had the rock quarried and carved exactly as instructed. With the help of two cranes and scores of workers, the precisely placed formation of granite obelisks that would later be named the Georgia Guidestones was erected on time. The date was March 22, 1980.

Present Day
Outbreak - Day 5
Guild Headquarters. Jackson Hole, Wyoming.

The rising sun illuminated the Grand Tetons making them glow as if they had been gilded by King Midas himself. The massive mountains and pristine wilderness was a fitting backdrop for the meeting about to take place. Twelve of the most powerful and influential men in America were arriving from all points of the compass. They were about to set in motion a plan that had been decades in the making.

Their latest Manchurian candidate was now dead. Odero deviated at the end and it cost him his life; still they had to press on. The crisis that had fallen into their lap wasn't the one that they had strategized for, let alone could have ever fathomed. The United States of America was about to be drawn and quartered and each man would get their piece of the pie.

The mansion was the typical wood beam and stone construction that dominated in places where snow covered the ground the majority of the year. Sitting on a broad swath of land nestled up against the Grand Tetons, it was more compound than typical mountain McMansion. The first dead giveaway was the twelve foot tall by two foot thick rock wall ringing the perimeter of the property. Ubiquitous shiny black domes hung like bats from multiple locations. They housed the many video cameras and were strategically placed to provide overlapping visual coverage of the entire grounds. Security personnel, openly carrying automatic weapons, walked the grounds in and outside of the walls.

***

Armored SUVs of different makes and models began arriving at the grand estate, trickling in before dawn. The Escalades, Denalis and Hummers all entered through a remotely operated sliding metal gate.

Before the outbreak, the winter ski destination had been home to many Hollywood elites, CEOs of Fortune 500 companies and a smattering of billionaires and multi-millionaires. The majority of the resort workers lived on the other side of the Teton pass in Driggs, Idaho. During the summer months in Jackson Hole, Yellowstone National Park was the main attraction.

The security gate rolled away to let in the civilian model Hummer. Three men emptied from the vehicle, their big black carbines sweeping the circular drive seeking out any threats to their charge. Satisfied that all was as it should be, they escorted the back seat passenger from the Hummer. Even though the man wore a Kevlar anti-ballistic vest, the men formed a human wall that moved with him from his vehicle and up the flight of stairs leading to the huge wooden double doors that opened into the 28,000 square foot home. The mountain mansion had originally been owned by an A-list Hollywood actor and now belonged to Robert Christian. The flamboyant billionaire fancied himself as the most ambitious man in the world.

***

When the hidden door to the cavernous conference room opened, all eleven men seated around the dark mahogany table looked up from the documents they had been studying.

Robert Christian stood 6-foot-2. His presence dominated the room when he entered. "Stay seated, gentlemen," the newly arrived man intoned.

"I will," said the man still in his chair, directly to Christian's right. "I stand for no man."

The room broke out in laughter as, to a man, they all stood and greeted the deeply tanned, blonde haired, blue eyed man.

Each individual exchanged private words with the newcomer before taking their seats. Christian methodically worked his way to the head of the mammoth slab of polished old-growth.

"Gentlemen," he nodded his head silently and looked each man seated around the table in the eye. Pausing for dramatic effect he straightened his red power tie before addressing them. He had no reason to try and influence or impress these men; they were all equals here with the same goal. Soon they would be dividing the United States between them.

"As we speak, the first part of our global agenda has begun and is unfolding as planned." Christian cracked the seal and poured his bottled water into an ornate crystal goblet before continuing.

"I thank all of you for choosing me as the point man in New America."

"You have the biggest balls in the room," said the tanned thirtyish-looking man at the far end of the table. He was the youngest and yet the most outwardly confident man in attendance.

He had amassed his fortune in the dot-com bubble. An inside trader with tendrils in every boardroom in America had tipped him and all of the other men in the room off before the crash, allowing them enough time to park their money in safe havens offshore. Getting rich from the misfortune of the common man was a continuing cycle for the power elites. The first great depression had made most of these men's grandfathers fabulously wealthy. This latest depression transferred even more spoils into their coffers.

"Gentlemen, all of you have been informed of our esteemed colleague's untimely demise. I urged him to leave the White House and take his family to safety. Bernard Odero wanted nothing to do with our plan for this country after the fall. In fact, he told me in his very own words that he despised all we stood for. It pained him to go along with our plan and run for office."

"Why did he agree then?" asked the former President, John Cranston.

Robert Christian pressed a hidden button. At the opposite end of the rectangular table ornately carved walnut panels parted silently, revealing an eight foot wide flat screen monitor.

"I reminded Mr. Odero that after four short years he would be in his early fifties and could spend the rest of his life with his wife and daughters, taken care of and protected by us... *or* I was going to make sure that copies of these found their way into the hands of his strong willed wife."

The projector splashed picture after doctored picture of the young then-Senator, seemingly conducting an illicit affair. The woman had supermodel looks that would have given Heidi Klum a run for her money.

"Good God, those are brilliant. Whose work are we looking at?" Cranston asked.

Robert Christian couldn't tell if the randy ex-President was alluding to the woman's "assets" or the Photoshopped images. "It's not important now. The bottom line is he didn't follow protocol and now he's no longer in control and that means we are no longer in a position to *shape* things. Furthermore, he ordered the rest of his cabinet back to the White House with him, jeopardizing our plan further."

Griffin Blackburn spoke up. "Who's supposedly in control of the country right now?" The man was the heir to the Blackburn fortune. His family had built their wealth the same

way as all of the men in the room had: Gaming the system
and profiting from wars while being privy to information that
any inside trader would kill for.

Robert Christian promptly answered, "*Valerie Clay.*" His
voice dripping with venom, he drew out the words. "We have
never been able to get her in our pocket. We have sent
delegates from the right and the left. Anyone that we thought
might appeal to her sensibilities. It was all to no avail. Her
father was a decorated World War II pilot; he went on to
serve his home state of Washington for decades. Gentlemen,
her patriotism *will* get in our way."

Mark Buchannan, the newest made member of the
billionaire boys club, made his fortune in the dot com era. He
was the youngest American to amass such a fortune, at the
ripe old age of twenty-seven. Now in his late thirties he
thrived on power, competition and exclusivity - the reason
that he initially angled to become one of them. "We haven't a
clue where she is but we have people working on it."

"Gentlemen, the second phase of our plan is hurtling
forward. Soon the U.S. Navy will retaliate against China for
the sinking of the USS Seawolf. This should draw in the
Russians because the engagement took place near the
Kamchatka peninsula. It is one thing to lurk under their
waters, but it is an affront to their sovereignty to openly wage
warfare there. Getting the Eagle, Dragon and the Bear
fighting each other only accelerates our plan."

Captain of industry and big Texas oilman Hank Ross
asked in his thick southern drawl, "How long do we have to
keep our kin sequestered? It can't be too long because living
in Texas, they won't stand to being cooped up."

"The theory is the walking dead only have three to nine
months before the decay stops them from being ambulatory,
so don't worry about them. All we do is sit back, sip cognac
and wait for the infighting. Attrition is our friend." Robert
Christian leaned back and finished his water. "My good friend

Chuck Heston was a proponent of the Second Amendment. I held a different view. I wanted to have the guns for myself... but in hindsight an armed America is a good thing. Now, given enough time, they will kill each other off and also take a large portion of the infected with them."

Ross cleared his throat and drawled, "What will we do about the rest of the military, and the armed citizenry when we take control of the country?"

Ian Bishop spoke up. "I founded Spartan International and built it from the ground up for an event such as this. Men, we have a large private army built with funds paid to me by the U.S. Government." The former Navy SEAL, corded muscles rippling under his shirt, stood up and raised his deep voice a notch in volume. "As we speak, elements of Spartan are fanning out from different parts of the country. Our primary objective is to acquire as much of the unguarded United States arsenal as we can."

The oldest man in the room cleared his throat before addressing the young operator. "I know you well, Captain Bishop. You were on the tip of the spear the first time we had boots on the ground in Iraq. Is that right?"

"Yes, Mister President."

The ex-President from Kennebunkport continued his line of questioning. "With all due respect Sir, do you expect the United States Military to roll over and hand *us* the keys to the kingdom?"

"From what I have been told, most, if not all of the bases to the east of the Rockies have personnel problems. They either have skeleton crews that are lying low and waiting for orders to come from a nonexistent government or they are unmanned presently. The fact that this thing started on a Saturday is both a blessing and a curse."

The forty-third President of the United States entered the discussion. "Mr. Bishop, we haven't met, but if my daddy will vouch for you then you're all right by me. One question, what is the blessing and what is the curse?"

Bishop ignored the fact that two questions had been asked of him instead of the purported one. The ex-President had a penchant for double speak and butchering words.

"First the blessing. Since the United States has not been attacked by soldiers on our soil since the Revolutionary War, almost all of the military installations encourage their cadre to live off base, thus leaving very few behind to guard the henhouse. The curse is the fact that most of the civilian population was at home and not at work when the outbreak occurred. It would have been much easier to surround the population centers one by one and exterminate those things. Unfortunately, we're going to have to conduct the *cleanse* starting in the suburbs and working into the cities."

The former President belted out a wheezing laugh. "OK. Color me convinced."

Chapter 9
Outbreak - Day 5
Camp Williams 19th Special Forces Garrison
Draper, Utah

The zombies were amassed ten deep when Corporal
Litters reanimated. His daughter Becca was front and center
when the combined weight brought the fence down on top of
him.

Becca led the procession as hundreds of feet trampled
over her father's supine body. Soon after the throng passed,
the newly turned soldier arose and limped after, dragging his
shattered leg behind.

***

Major Beeson was forced to up the ante on the dead.
Initially they were luring the zombies into a slit trench and
burning them, but now there were too many arriving. There
were no longer lulls between the waves of infected. The two
heavy dozers they had employed in their earlier attempts to
bury and burn the walkers were now being used differently.
The dozers had protective cages and were fully armored. They
had recently returned from deployment overseas and had
been up armored there; the ingenuity of warriors on the
battlefield knew no bounds. Most of the vehicles at Camp
Williams had also been used in combat operations in Iraq and
Afghanistan and were up armored as well.

SOLDIER ON: SURVIVING THE ZOMBIE APOCALYPSE

The major had no shortage of volunteers to operate the bulldozers. Keeping the fencing clear of undead was fairly straightforward; the dozer operators simply plowed over the infected, the heavy treads churning up the corpses. It was a very messy job. Skulls popped, geysers of brain matter spewed forth, arms, legs and chunks of putrid flesh oftentimes clogged the treads.

Disturbingly the dead were beginning to show some cunning. Increasingly dozer operators had to engage zombies that were able to claw their way onto the tractor, sometimes using other zombies as a means to climb onboard.

It was Private Hector Vargas' idea to cut the slit trenches to slow down the first waves of zombies, and he was also the first to volunteer for dozer duty after that tactic had become ineffective.

Hector had become a United States citizen when his mom gave birth to him in Laredo, Texas. He spent the next eighteen years in the shadows. His family lived on various ranches and orchards all across the southwest. Working menial jobs for little pay was the norm for people like Hector's mom and dad who had entered the U.S. illegally in search of a better life. He watched the television whenever he had a chance; the exciting recruitment commercials weren't lost on the bored youngster. His dream was to see the world. He turned eighteen less than a year ago, and that same day he joined the U.S. Army looking forward to combat in a foreign land. The Iraq war slowed down before he completed basic training and to his disappointment he was eventually stationed at Camp Williams. To his chagrin he was nothing but a glorified maintenance man who happened to know how to drive a tractor. However, if it wasn't for the young man's ingenuity and bravery, the base would have fallen on day one.

***

Hector had a bandanna slathered with menthol petroleum covering his nose and mouth. Most of the walkers had been dead for days; it was July, the temperature had constantly been in the mid-eighties and the corpses were ripe with decay. Not only did the dead reek but they were also host to maggots, grubs and ants. Today Hector operated the only working tractor. Mechanics were tearing the other broken rig apart desperately trying to repair it. It was an uphill battle trying to keep the perimeter clear with only the one tractor. Before leaving the gate, the private gave his tractor the usual once over. It was full of diesel and running flawlessly. Hector maneuvered the dozer effortlessly as he pushed the growing mound away from the fence. If enough corpses were allowed to pile up the undead would eventually start to climb over their fallen and get into the camp. It was the reason the major had crews operating the heavy machinery around the clock. Now that Private Vargas was operating the only running dozer he was fighting a losing battle.

He knew that something was wrong when the multi-ton piece of equipment started responding sluggishly to his commands. Terror washed over him and a shiver of cold electricity started his adrenal glands pumping. Even though he had on bright orange heavy duty ear protection, the howls of the dead still found a way in. The tractor registered as a steady purr in his head and the lurching machine vibrated his bones. Abruptly the tractor died and Hector no longer felt the throbbing of the diesel engine under him. He found himself trapped in a sea of monsters with only the flimsy wire mesh cage to keep them at bay. With the tractor stalled and unmoving, the zombies swarmed onto the behemoth to get at the man inside. Rotting hands slapped against the sides of the metal cocoon groping for Hector. His situation was hopeless and he knew there was no way for the men inside to come to his aid without endangering themselves or letting the zombies flood in. He smiled and closed his eyes, thinking good thoughts about his Madre and Padre. Thankfully he had strapped the semiautomatic Beretta M9 to his hip before he left the base.

SOLDIER ON: SURVIVING THE ZOMBIE APOCALYPSE

***

Major Beeson had been summoned to the front gate the moment the last tractor quit running. *Goddamnit, why couldn't it have started acting up inside of the wire?* he thought, as he watched more of the monsters scramble onto the dozer. There were so many onboard that he couldn't see Private Vargas.

***

The safety of the base stood sixty feet away; it might as well have been two miles, for there were so many undead Hector knew there would be no escape for him.

In Spanish, Hector recited the Lord's Prayer. His sidearm held fifteen rounds of 9 mm and he used fourteen on the closest of the creatures; they were near enough to touch and touch them he did. Fourteen zombies fell from the deck of the tractor, dead once and for all. Private Hector Vargas made the sign of the cross on his chest, peeled the muffs from his ears and placed the hot muzzle firmly against his temple.

***

Major Beeson helplessly watched the scene unfold from his vantage point. Engaged point blank, the dead started to fall from the tractor. The reports from the gun were swallowed by the moaning of the undead. Finally Vargas placed the black pistol to his head, jerked in his seat and slumped forward.

The front gate was in danger of falling under the crush of the dead. Knowing full well his men were dangerously low on ammo and there were no reinforcements to call on, Major Beeson ordered the immediate evacuation of Camp Williams. The timing couldn't have been better. Thanks to Corporal Litters, the back door was also wide open.

Chapter 10
Outbreak - Day 5
Wasatch Mountains, Utah

The slot the road followed was a natural break in the long chain of mountains that started to the north in Idaho and ran all the way south to the Ogden valley in Utah. The rugged string of geological giants stretched for one hundred and sixty miles, bisected by only seven well traveled highways the entire way. The lightly used forest service road Cade had been following was forty miles equal distance between the two main passes.

He left the River Bend campground without eating, right after first light. Even though he had grown accustomed to the sight and smell of death, moving Bob's sun ripened corpse had spoiled his appetite.

The predawn fight with undead Bob was like a triple shot of espresso to his system. That had been two hours ago. Right now he was crashing from the adrenaline high.

Cade ground the bike to a halt in the shadow of a tall fir and pulled a soft Snickers bar from one of his many pockets. He slurped the hot candy bar and finished by rolling the wrapper up like a tube of toothpaste and squeezed the remnants into his mouth. A fleeting thought crossed his mind. He wondered what would happen after all of the candy bars had been pillaged or had far exceeded their use by date.

It was a silly thought at a time like this, but he had no idea
how chocolate was made or creamy nougat for that matter.
Oh, the things civilized people had taken for granted.
Everything changed forever a few short days ago.

Lost in thoughts of the mundane, he surveyed the country
directly in his path. The view from the apex of the
unimproved byway was majestic. The east side of the
mountains spilled out before him. Once again he consulted
the topographic map to get some idea of what lurked
underneath the lush, tree covered flanks of the Wasatch. The
Suunto watch on his wrist had an altimeter function; it put the
elevation at 6600 feet above sea level, and the map he held
confirmed it. He silenced the Kawasaki and rummaged in the
saddlebag for bottled water. Cade sipped the water and
listened to the mountain birds calling each other from the
tops of the pine trees. This setting reminded Cade of Mount
Hood, back in Oregon. It was hands down his favorite peak
and the place he and Brook spent most of their free time
hiking and skiing. The two of them had always marveled at
how the ever present mountain birds could survive in the
harsh environment. Their intrigue with the very intelligent
raptors was the reason they gave their daughter her name.
Whenever they were eating lunch on the tailgate of their truck
invariably one or more of the big black ravens would come
calling, looking for a handout or heckling all of the people
dressed for the cold and carrying their multi-colored skis and
snowboards. The setting and sounds caused Cade to
reminisce about his wife and daughter. As he finished the last
drops of his water he felt his throat begin to constrict about
the time the tears started to flow. He was alone on the dusty
road and let the emotion pour freely from his gut. In between
sobs he thought that he could hear engine noise. After a
couple of minutes, he heard it again, soft and a good distance
away. The sound originated from the side of the pass he had
recently emerged from. The road wasn't as wide and the trees

weren't as thick as they had been coming uphill. With the bike in neutral he coasted the silent motorcycle around the first switchback.

An old deadfall seemed like the best place to hide the desert tan Kawasaki. Cade took the M4 from its hard holster and placed the bike on one side behind the gnarled trunk bristling with dead twisted branches. For good measure he scattered some scrub brush on top of the bike to help break up its outline. With his rifle in one hand and the silencer in the other he melted into the nearest cluster of pines.

In the time it took him to fasten the silencer to the barrel of the M4, the engine noise drew nearer and more pronounced. Cade picked his hide thirty feet from where his motorcycle was secreted. He observed the big SUV through the magnified scope on his carbine, picking up flashes of the mint green Suburban between the trees as it slowed on the downhill and braked for the sweeping switchback. The unmistakable bass of reggae music thumped from the open driver's side window; behind the wheel was a light skinned black man with long flowing dreadlocks. His eyes were hidden behind mirrored sunglasses and his head bobbed to the pulsating beat, keeping perfect time. The man neither slowed nor looked anywhere but straight ahead as he passed Cade's position.

Now I have seen it all, Cade thought. It only took a few moments for him to uncover the hidden bike and kick start it. Cade slung the M4 carbine on his back where it would be much easier to access if he needed it.

Mister Rasta had a little bit of a lead but fortunately for Cade the heavy SUV left easy to follow tire tracks. Near the end of a long straightaway the gravel gave way to a single lane paved road. Cade slowed his pace so he wouldn't accidently run into the Suburban that he was shadowing.

He was torn. Should he make contact or not? On the one hand, if he let the man go along his merry reggae way then he might be letting the smallest scrap of useful information slip away. On the other hand he couldn't just walk up to the man, say "Hi" and pick his brain. That is unless he stuck a pistol in his face. At the very least, the man would likely have *some* knowledge about the shape America was in. Cade finally came to the conclusion that in order to have any chance of finding his family he was going to have to mine the man for any useful nuggets of information that he might have.

Cade slowed the bike to a crawl. On the shoulder of the road sat a gold, two door compact car. The small Mazda bounced on its springs. Unfortunately no one was getting lucky in the back seat; the tomb still held its trapped occupants inside. There was so much gore from the initial violence and the subsequent decomposition, Cade had to move closer to see inside. Three flailing corpses festered in the stifling heat of the closed vehicle. Opaque with greasy green bodily fluids, the window flexed against pressing palms as the swollen zombie in the front seat fought the locked door to get at the meat. The poor souls in the back seat had been young kids. Their faces pressing against the window almost seemed normal, except that they were both zombies. Thankfully he wasn't near enough to smell them but he could hear their howls over the idling bike. The car had Utah license plates with the rust colored rock arch splayed across the face. The cheap plastic frame held another clue; Saul's Salt Lake Mazda was printed in raised bold yellow letters. He wished mercy upon the trio but there was no reason to waste any bullets on them. He left the macabre scene behind, thankful that he didn't know anyone in Salt Lake. However, Duncan, the Vietnam era aviator that had stayed behind at Camp Williams, had a brother there. *God help him,* was the first thing that came to the former Delta operator's mind.

Cade thought it was about time to find a safe place to spend the night. A farmhouse or secluded commercial building would probably be best - anything would be better than the camp of the dead he had stayed in the previous night.

If his map was correct, then the town of Hanna was near. It appeared to be one of those *"blink and you will miss it"* kinds of backwater towns. Cade thought, *the kind where banjos dueled and polygamy was still practiced.* A brief smile crossed his face because it was something Duncan probably would have proudly said out loud.

Chapter 11
Outbreak - Day 6
Centers for Disease Control
Atlanta, Georgia

From the cockpit of the HH-60G Pave Hawk, the southeastern part of the country was beginning to look like every other godforsaken third world shithole that Chief Warrant Officer Ari Silver had had the pleasure of running ops in. Bodies littered the streets and sidewalks of every city they overflew. Stalled cars choked nearly every thoroughfare; the rare vehicle moving was inevitably being pursued by the walking dead. Everywhere he looked small house fires raged out of control. What troubled Ari the most was the fact that he had not seen any police or military trying to bring order to the chaos below.

Ari was pushing the helicopter hard and almost missed the people hailing them. Below on the starboard side of the ship was what appeared to be a small hotel or suburban hospital. The rectangular beige building belched fire from the ground floor up. Without thinking he throttled back the twin turbines of the black helicopter and brought it to a near hover at 200 feet AGL. The sign on the building was now readable; the Long Acre Retirement Villa was burning. The vivid scene was etched in his brain as the desperate elderly were jumping from the windows of the six story building. As the shadow of the Pave Hawk slowly arced across the building, a lady in a pink bathrobe, clutching a small poodle, jumped from the top floor. He watched her flailing body intersect with the aircraft's crossing shadow before bouncing twice on the ground. Oddly the zombies ignored her dead body but chased the seemingly uninjured dog around the green lawn. The geriatrics writhing on the ground that were not fortunate enough to die from the fall were being torn apart and consumed by the ravenous horde of undead.

For Ari the elderly jumpers conjured up flashbacks of 9/11. They were no different than those poor souls who were unable to hold on to the sharp twisted steel skin of the World Trade Center or the ones that simply chose to jump, escaping the inferno caused by burning jet fuel. He instantly remembered the man in a soot covered business suit performing the sign of the cross seconds before releasing his hold and freefalling backward one hundred stories to his death. It made no difference whether it was one hundred stories or six; it was still an awful way to go.

There was no way to help the few people that were still on the rooftop.

"I feel like a piece of shit," the pilot intoned, his voice seemingly about to crack.

"There's nothing that we can do for them Ari," said his co-pilot, Warrant Officer Bill Durant. The stress was also evident in his voice. "If only we could spare a few rounds from the minigun."

A third voice came through the intercom, "I think we have extra 7.62 for the mini as it is." The voice was the door gunner's and it was clear that he wanted them to intervene. "No one *has* to know."

Ari glanced back at the Delta Force operators that he was tasked with delivering to the Center for Disease Control in Atlanta Georgia. "General Desantos Sir, what say you?"

Without saying a word the emotionally detached operator put one gloved hand over his mouth and the other over his eyes. Out of solidarity the other D-Boys did the same.

CWO Ari Silver gave the door gunner thumbs up and held the helo in a perfect hover, upwind and out of the thick acrid smoke belching from every window in the building.

Sergeant Dean Hicks powered up the M134 and sighted on the undead orgy on the ground. The gun whined as it spit out three hundred bullets. Sod erupted in green and brown geysers as the bullets passed cleanly through the zombies and the doomed people underneath them. When the two second burst was finished nothing moved. Flames were now licking over the roof's edge. Several wheelchair bound people remained clustered together near the center of the smoking roof.

The gunner watched as elderly zombies began pouring out of the open rooftop door. *Please forgive me*, Hicks thought as he sighted on the trapped invalids. He caressed the trigger. Once more the minigun belched lead, but Hicks didn't see the carnage because he had purposefully diverted his eyes.

The mercy killing was over in seconds.

"Requesting permission to engage the targets on the ground," the gunner's voice crackled in Ari's headset.

"Negative, Hicks, save the ammo for a rainy day," Ari answered.

The black helicopter climbed, banked sharply and resumed a southern heading. Hicks's stomach violently churned from the combination of intense g-forces and mixed emotions over shooting fellow Americans. Jack Kevorkian he was not, but it would have been unthinkable to let the old folks be eaten by those things.

Ari knew deep down that the mission they were on could possibly mean life or death for the remaining percentage of the population; he twisted the throttle to increase their airspeed and make up for the lost time. Although Ari was not proud of the actions he and his crew had undertaken, he hoped that if he were in a similar situation someone would show him the same mercy.

"Look... on the deck," Ari said.

They buzzed an enormous traffic jam; sun glinted off of the multicolored metal and glass snake. It stretched for twenty miles. All of the vehicles were pointing away from the center of downtown Atlanta. There was movement among the cars. Some of the undead were shuffling between the tangled mazes, others were still trapped in the vehicles that they had died and reanimated in.

"*Whoa*. Look at all of those crows." Durant was talking about the black biomass feeding on the piles of corpses dotting the shoulder of the road. "It must have been madness down there trying to flee the city."

Hicks added, "No less than the poor people that heeded FEMA's advice and stayed behind in the belly of the beast."

Both men continued to stare at the carnage below as it whizzed by under the helo.

The Pave Hawk slowed to 80 knots, Ari gave General Desantos the five minute warning with his open hand, and Desantos passed it on.

The six Delta operators utilized the last five minutes readying their weapons and reflecting on the mission ahead. To a man, they prayed to whatever higher power they believed in before they had to face the walking dead again.

***

Mike Desantos thought that the mission to rescue the President and retrieve the football could never be topped in terms of difficulty. During the mission the previous night he had lost half of his twelve man team. They had breached the inner sanctum of the White House only to find that the President and his family were already infected, lost to Omega. He had personally put the bullet in Odero's brain and inherited the unenviable task of hacking off the President's arm to remove the briefcase containing the nuclear codes. For

his leadership, the rookie President Valerie Clay had
promoted him to the rank of Two Star General. It was
awkward to say the least. Generals rarely went out in the field
let alone did the shooting. Mike Desantos didn't question
orders, he merely followed them.

***

Today he was going to lead his team into the bowels of the
Center for Disease Control. There was no intel, no floor plan
and certainly no enemy strength estimates. His team was
loaded for bear but going into the den blind. He and his men
had been riding in the same helicopter for six hundred miles
nonstop. Thanks to aerial refueling, made possible by the
retractable probe on the helo's nose and one of the remaining
tanker crews, it wasn't necessary to sit exposed on an airport
tarmac or forage for fuel. He hadn't as of yet divulged their
final destination. These were the best of the best and they
would be ready to go even if their mission was taking them to
the gates of hell and they were tasked to bag old Beelzebub
himself. He would wait and break the news to them when
they were all safely on the rooftop.

Silver maneuvered the Pave Hawk around the sprawling
campus encompassing the level-four containment building. It
housed the Emerging Infectious Disease research arm of the
Centers for Disease Control. All of the bugs that could cause
a pandemic and kill a large swath of humanity were contained
deep underground.

"*That's encouraging,*" shouted Desantos over the onboard
comms as he stabbed a finger at the nearly empty parking lots
that dominated the grounds.

"Good thing for us the shit hit the fan on the weekend,"
added Durant.

"The Center for Disease Control is one of the best funded
operations in the United States. Outside of Plum Island in
New Jersey and a few smaller facilities... this is where the
dangerous shit is kept. Don't let the absence of a few cars

fool you. I shit you not, the place had to have had people working to sort out Omega around the clock." Desantos didn't want to take the wind out of the co-pilot's sails, but he was a realist. "Lock and load fellas."

Ari Silver finished the aerial recon of the grounds, noting the large amount of shambling dead. "General, we're going to have to take a chance with the aerials and put your team on the roof. It's way too hot to put her down on the grass, we'd be overrun the second the wheels hit the ground."

Avoiding the antennas on the approach to the LZ was front and center on the pilot's mind. Chief Warrant Officer Ari Silver had flown down Mogadishu alleys in a little bird, dropped SEAL Team Six operators on top of terrorist strongholds while under heavy fire and navigated the tight confines of dry wadis flying nap of the earth in both of the hot wars the United States had been embroiled in. It made no difference where he was flying; home was at the controls of a rotor wing aircraft. He deftly side slipped the big Pave Hawk around the array of antennas that bristled from the top of the modern multi-story steel and glass structure. Sergeant Hicks poked his head out of the door and called out the distance to the roof. Durant did the same from his seat. The antenna array was used to send and receive communications but it hadn't been utilized since the first days of the Omega outbreak.

Ari picked a path between two of the communication antennas, flared the Pave Hawk and gently put her down, being careful to avoid the air scrubbers and HVAC equipment scattered atop the roof.

Normally after an insertion the SOAR pilots orbited the target area in case the operators needed an emergency exfil. Desantos ordered Dooley and Rooks to remain behind and guard the Pave Hawk and her aircrew.

Even though the helicopter held enough fuel to transport them to the predetermined emergency refuel point, Ari made the difficult decision to remain on the roof with the engine

powered down. Another aerial refueling couldn't be
guaranteed, making the contingency plan necessary. Ari held
no reservations that his flying days might be numbered since
aviation fuel was not a finite resource and the people
proficient at refining it were probably dead. Ari sat in the
pilot's seat while the mission unfolded in the building below.

Chapter 12
Outbreak - Day 5
Schriever AFB
Colorado Springs, Colorado

Dirt and sand swirled in the air, kicked up violently by the dual cyclones from the aircraft's massive twin rotors. The flat black CV-22 Osprey settled lightly on the oft-used maintenance pad, the twin nacelles tilted into the full upright position before the pilot throttled back power.

Schriever AFB had been secure since the outbreak. Things here remained under control. Compared to the rest of Colorado Springs a few miles away, the sprawling base was a welcome sanctuary. Air force PJs with silenced automatic rifles were positioned at numerous locations around Marine One. Colonel Shrill thought it prudent to include the shooters as an added precaution.

The eight man Secret Service detail exited the hulking Osprey and fanned out in a full circle with their weapons at the ready.

The Commander of Schriever AFB greeted the new President warmly. President Valerie Clay was a tough as nails politician, all wrapped up in a petite package. Standing barely five feet tall, she was not what one would expect based on her reputation. The former Senator from Washington State knew how to gut a trout, could skin a deer by herself, and had the gift of disarming friend and foe alike with one glance of her hazel eyes. Clay's detail quickly hustled the two of them into the heavily armored MRAP (mine resistant armored personnel) carrier.

President Clay's eyes slowly adjusted to the dimly lit interior. Sitting directly across from her, wearing an impeccably maintained uniform, was the biggest man she had ever seen.

Colonel Cornelius Shrill snapped off a precise salute before he spoke. "Madam President, very pleased to meet you. But I wish it were under less dire circumstances." He held the salute, fully anticipating reciprocity on the President's part.

"Likewise..." the President said, before she finally realized that protocol dictated she return the salute. Her mind worked overtime as she struggled to determine his rank from the embroidered black insignia on his softcover.

Sensing her discomfort, the big man reached out his baseball glove-sized hand and spoke in a hushed tone, trying to convey to her his utmost respect. "Colonel Cornelius Shrill, I'm the highest ranking man left at Schriever. Omega got everyone else."

The President felt the man's grip loosen after his last statement. It hit her hard as well.

"May I call you Cornelius?"

"By all means ma'am, whatever you prefer."

The President disengaged her firm hold on the colonel's hand and flashed a rare brief smile. "Cornelius it is then."

"Madam President, with all due respect, may I ask you a question?"

The new President was still not comfortable with her "battlefield" promotion. She hoped that it was a question she could truthfully answer. Before speaking she pulled the heavy door shut, leaving only her and the highest ranking man in what would be the new Capital of the United States to talk in private. "What is it, Colonel?"

"Why are we *driving* from here to the base proper…? I would have thought it safer to land at one of the base's main heli-pads."

Colonel Shrill remained silent awaiting her answer.

"My secret service detail thought that other threats…" struggling to find the words, the President stared into the colonel's eyes before divulging what she knew. "There are elements in these United States that are happy the Omega virus has diminished the population such as it has."

The look on Shrill's face seemed out of place. He had seen and done it all during his fifty-two years on the planet. The news hit him like a ninety-five mile per hour fastball. "Let me get this straight, ma'am. We are at war against the walking dead and there are people that want you dead?"

Still struggling with how much she should disclose, the President answered in a hushed tone. "It's bigger than that, Cornelius. These very powerful men have been manipulating things from behind the scenes for nearly a century. We have reason to believe that they have followers serving in all branches of the military, and they may be willing to commit acts of espionage. As hard as it is for me to believe, I still have to be cautious. Of course the undead are attacking us from the outside as we speak, but it's the enemy that hides in plain sight that might do the most damage. These men are very wealthy, very powerful, and they belong to the ultimate "good ol' boys' club." Every one of them is used to getting *exactly* what they want, and what they want is the United States all for them. Colonel… this is the event that they have been waiting so long for."

Shrill gathered his thoughts, then went right to the heart of the matter. "What's their ultimate goal, Madam President?"

"After the fall of our government they will be waiting in the wings to divide up the United States. Goal number two is to subjugate the remaining populace by any means necessary.

SOLDIER ON: SURVIVING THE ZOMBIE APOCALYPSE

Someone has to do the dirty work in their new world order. In 1979 their leadership commissioned a massive granite monolith in Georgia. The locals call it the Guidestones. A lot of work went into making sure the stones stand precisely as to follow celestially the moon, sun and stars. GPS was in its infancy at the time it was erected. Given its build turned out so precise, it points to them having some help from within our government. Scariest of all is the last inscription on the monument."

"What was the message?" Colonel Shrill caught himself leaning in towards the President. He had been hanging on to her every word.

Valerie Clay ran a shaky hand through her brunette hair before she revealed what was inscribed on the 238,000 pound warning to humanity. "The first line reads *Maintain humanity under 500,000,000 in perpetual balance with nature.*'"

Colonel Shrill shook his head. "We failed that one long ago."

"All of the other lines have similar admonishments. The last one sums it all up succinctly. *'Be not a cancer on the earth- Leave room for nature- Leave room for nature.*'"

Colonel Shrill digested the story, his mind working it like a calculus problem.

"I hate to say it but fortunately the sheer number of undead may be the only thing standing in the way of them ultimately achieving their goal, and if luck isn't on our side I'm afraid the undead may be the final victors."

Chapter 13
Outbreak - Day 4
Stanley, Idaho

Richard Ganz increased the pressures on the shears. Tiny rivulets of blood poured from the cuts. The red was in stark contrast with the sheriff's pale white hands. Ganz had made sure the handcuffs were ratcheted as tight as they would go. "How does it feel, officer?"

An unintelligible word slipped between Blanda's split lips.

"What's the matter, cat got your tongue?" The redheaded biker followed through. With a horrible crunch the sheriff's finger separated from his hand. "You hang out here for awhile. I'm gonna go and do awful things to your little girl... I'll be back to finish with you though. Don't go anywhere, you hear?"

The battered lawman passed out, but not before Richard Ganz's words registered in his subconscious.

***

The bed springs screeched out a cadence of noisy protest as the fit young woman struggled under the weight of the huge biker.

Irene plead with the man, "*Let me go. I'll do anything you want.*"

"You already are. Now shut up or I'll cut your dad down so he can watch."

It was the third time in as many hours he had entered the
trailer to have his way with her. The redheaded pig was rough
and never did he look her in the eye. Each time it had been
the same. He kept his boots on, pulled his pants down and
then the frantic pumping started. She only remembered bits
and pieces of the horrific ordeal. While he defiled her he
would methodically choke her in and out of consciousness.
Another thing Irene noticed; he never took off the greasy
jacket adorned with the smirking Nomad Jester patch.

***

The scum was truly a one percenter. The ruthless biker
became a kingpin and learned to enjoy killing other human
beings in prison. Although there had been plenty of close
calls, somehow luck was always on his side. Not once did he
do extra time for a murder on the inside.

Richard Ganz served five years and was released with
nothing to show for his time but some battle scars and a new
found determination to grow his criminal empire and stay on
the outside.

The gang welcomed him back with open arms. The
association with the Aryan Brotherhood had seemed the
perfect fit. They all hated the same people and they all liked
the same things, money, guns, drugs and an obedient "old
lady" to hit the sack with now and again.

With the drugs selling steadily, money soon stacked up.
With money anything was possible. Ganz surrounded himself
with like-minded thinkers and moved his product and guns all
over the western United States.

The feeling he had had since the dead started walking was
second to none. Ganz fancied himself a modern day Billy the
Kid and he was approaching the same body count. He had
fulfilled his first order of business as soon as the President
declared martial law; Sheriff Blanda actually came to him and
asked for help with the walking dead. Dumbass Barney Fife
was trussed up with his own fucking handcuffs before he

70

knew what was going on. Richard Ganz hamstrung the only living man that stood between him and ruling Stanley, Idaho.

***

Stanley was one of the smaller alpine towns in the Sawtooth mountain range. The ease with which Ganz and the skins rounded up the meager population astounded him. He knew that a few of the town's hundred people were unaccounted for. His best guess was that they had gone to Boise and from eyewitness accounts very few escaped alive. Out of all of the women that the skinheads rounded up, only this nineteen-year-old remained. The rest had been either too old or too resistant for their own good.

Adolph Hitler would have been proud; the skinheads lined up all of the men and systematically put a bullet in each of their brains. Their bodies were heaped in the parking lot of the Stanley Police station.

The big redhead biker increased his grip on the woman's thin neck. *With the law gone the world truly is my oyster,* he thought, *and mine for the taking.* Even though he didn't like oysters the saying was his favorite, he had picked it up from some movie, but had no idea which one.

With her last breath, Irene uttered a curse upon her killer. Sheriff Blanda's only daughter died with the ruthless biker still on top of her.

Chapter 14
Outbreak - Day 6
Centers for Disease Control
Atlanta, Georgia

Sergeant Darwin Maddox once again had the honor of
breaching the door. He removed the small black nylon case
and worked the zipper. Inside were the tools needed to affect
a quick silent entry. Maddox placed the plain black box next
to the keypad and activated it with the flick of a switch. A soft
blue glow emanated from the liquid crystal display revealing a
series of rapidly changing numbers. It only took the device
twenty-five seconds to crack the coded lock. Maddox
deliberately keyed in the ten digit code necessary to disarm
the alarm. This alarm was like most, there was a window of
thirty seconds to make entry. There was extra time built in to
allow a security guard time to fumble with a set of keys,
maybe drop them once, pick them up and then unlock the
door before the alarm automatically rearmed.

Thirty seconds wasn't a lot of time to effectively pick a
lock but Maddox was left with no choice. With precision
honed by countless hours practicing on locks of all makes and
types, he deftly manipulated the pick and spoon in the
cylinder.

Desantos stood silently at his back, watching the man work while the sweeping hand on his Luminox wristwatch quickly burned through the seconds. "Six, five, four, three..." Mike Desantos counted down. With only a second to spare Maddox sealed the deal. The door unlocked with an audible click. Maddox moved aside, he wasn't eager to find out what waited on the other side.

Mike took Maddox's place. He aimed his machine pistol at the door and gave it a firm push. It moved quietly inward revealing a flight of stairs that disappeared into darkness. Mike powered up his NVGs and quietly entered the stairwell. Everything was bathed in a warm green glow. The Delta operator took deliberate sidesteps and worked his way down and around to the next landing. The other men followed him into the abyss.

Mike held his hand up, fingers clenched in a tight fist. The rest of the men froze in place. Mike found himself in front of a door identical to the one they had just thwarted. Still wanting to maintain noise discipline, he used the appropriate hand signals to summon his lock pick expert.

Maddox materialized without a sound next to Desantos and carried out the same routine as before. This time he had the lock popped in twenty-three seconds.

They were about to enter the third floor. Slivers of light worked their way around the door frame.

"NVGs off," Mike quietly instructed all eight men via their ear buds.

The operators stacked up. Mike was the first one through and found that he was at the end of a long hallway. Oak doors were spaced fifteen feet apart on both sides. Gray carpet covered the floor. The walls glowed soft orange, illuminated by the emergency lights positioned at each end of the hall. The drab colors made him feel like he was in a cut-rate motel, not a billion dollar federal building.

Mike Desantos, Sergeant Maddox and Sergeant First Class Lopez took the left doors while Sergeant Clark, Sergeant First

Class Haskell, Chief Warrant Officer Brent and Staff Sergeant
Calvin were spread out on the right.

Clark made first contact. The undead woman wore the
standard uniform: comfortable thick soled shoes, cheap
looking black nylon slacks and a flimsy cotton vest loosely
tied over her white cotton tee shirt. *Huffington Executive
Cleaning* was silkscreened in red cursive on the vest. She stood
silently swaying, gazing out the picture window, captivated by
a murder of crows feeding on the corpses that littered the
circular drive. Glacially slow, like an automaton at Disneyland,
the female zombie turned and faced Clark. Her alabaster face,
expressionless and devoid of intelligence, looked like it was
finished with paper mâché. The only evidence of injury that
Clark could see was a blood-stained compress on her forearm.
Her soulless eyes fixed on him. Invigorated by the sight of
prey, the zombie lurched into a cubicle wall and collapsed
face first on the floor, legs and arms still pumping.

Without pause, Sergeant Clark spanned the distance and
put his boot on the ghoul's neck. The thing bucked and
flailed, fighting against his weight advantage. The experienced
killer went to a knee and inserted the tip of his combat knife
where her spine and skull came together. Sergeant Clark
pushed the blade firmly into the creature's brain, forever
ending its struggles.

Mike Desantos was busy systematically clearing the rooms
on the left. Judging by the expensive sports memorabilia and
nicely framed degrees, they had to be the mid-level manager's
offices.

Clark wiped his blade on the cleaning lady's apron and
stepped back into the hall. *One tango down,* he relayed using
hand signals.

Desantos acknowledged with a quick nod.

The Delta Team thoroughly cleared all of the rooms
branching off of the hallway. Only an oversized set of double
doors remained. Emergency lighting escaped from beneath

the doors but there was no detectable movement or sound. Clark cautiously jiggled one of the handles. *Unlocked.* Next, he ever so slowly opened the door on the right while Clark covered with his H&K MP7.

The cavernous space beyond the double doors was unremarkable. Multiple burgundy filing cabinets, three copier machines and a water cooler stood like sentinels on the wall to their left. Row upon row of cubicles stretched the length of the room.

"It's a cube farm."

"A what?" Desantos asked.

"A room crammed full of workstations," Clark answered.

A slight stench hung on the air. Blood was smeared here and there on the walls. It was obvious someone had been attacked here.

Mike took the left, Clark maneuvered to the right. The emergency lights flickered momentarily but stayed on. Both groups of operators were at the midway point of the large room. Suddenly several heads gophered up from various cubicles around the room. The zombies began moaning and started moving about.

Mike came to the realization that both teams were cut off from either set of doors and, most ominously, each other.

Mike was advancing towards the far door when a ghoul emerged from the cubicle ten feet to his right. Apparently it had been casual dress day when the middle-aged man died. His Levis and pale blue knit Izod were caked with dried blood. Mike's suppressed machine pistol spit a quiet three round burst. The tight grouping punched a fist sized hole in the zombie's forehead, its bald cranium erupted, and blood and brain matter splashed the white ceiling tiles.

Haskell found himself cut off from the others; two of the creatures had him cornered.

"*Haskell, watch your six.*" Clark yelled into the comms. He was too late with the warning.

SOLDIER ON: SURVIVING THE ZOMBIE APOCALYPSE

They all looked on as Haskell fired a sustained burst point blank from his machine pistol. The bullets stitched the undead office worker across the gut. The resulting blowback showered the doomed shooter with putrid yellow guts and fecal matter.

Mike watched helplessly; both flesh-eaters had a hold of Haskell and were tugging him to the floor. The gut shot creature opened its jaws wide and took a mouthful of the sergeant's face, shook its head like a shark and came away clenching a hunk of the soldier's flesh in its yellowed teeth. Haskell put his hands on the pulsating wound. Hot copper smelling blood sluiced between his fingers. His uniform blouse was changing from tan to crimson from the neck down. Enraged, he found his MP7 hanging from its sling and with a sustained burst decapitated the gut shot zombie. Its head bounced away with the piece of his flesh still in its mouth. The other monster felt his wrath as well, two shots at point blank range sprayed bone and brains across the cubes and wall behind them. Haskell stood on shaky legs and continued to take it to the enemy.

Mike Desantos and the other Delta members looked on in awe as the sergeant went out on his own terms. The brave operator put down four more undead with clean headshots before a female zombie pounced on him. The man had lost a lot of blood from his fatal wound and his strength was beginning to ebb. Sergeant Haskell wrapped both hands around his attacker's thin neck and tried to roll out from under her frigid body. The dead weight pressed down on him; gravity was winning the battle as the ghoul's teeth inched closer to his neck.

Haskell had never smelled anything as stomach turning as the stench wafting from her open mouth. With the final bit of energy left in him, he thrust two fingers into its eye socket; the exploding eyeball showered his face with milky white fluid. Haskell drew his knife with the other hand and plunged the seven inch blade into her temple. It was his last act as a living breathing human being.

The six operators moved through the space, shooting and reloading as they wove between the work spaces. Sergeant First Class "Low-rider" Lopez kept an eye on their six. Cordite haze from the gunfire hung suspended in the air, diffusing the already dim emergency lighting.

The fractured team regrouped before the next pair of double doors.

General Desantos spoke to his team. "Check yourselves for bites, scratches or any wounds. Lopez, make sure Harvey can't reanimate, and pull his tags. We'll collect his body on the way out."

"He sure put up a hell of a fight," Clark intoned.

"Harvey saved a few of us for sure. I *will* put him up for a medal when we get home." Desantos peeled off his ballistic eye protection and rubbed his red-rimmed eyes. The pace of action during the last few days was taking its toll on him. As far as running hot ops went, Mike knew that he was getting close to the end of his shelf life. Before the dead started walking he had even confided in his wife Annie that this was going to be his final year going out with the teams.

Omega came along and changed everything. There would be no office in the Pentagon for him. There *was* no Pentagon. When President Clay pinned the two stars on him he asked himself why? Deep down he was coming to the realization that ops would never stop for him. As long as Annie and his kids were alive, he would stay as sharp as possible and continue to lead his men against all enemies - foreign or undead.

General Desantos felt it was time for a pep talk, something to spur them on. "Team, this building is meant to keep things in, very small and deadly microbial things. The door to the Level 4 containment area will be a very tough nut to crack. If we make contact, make your shots count. We don't need any extra bugs getting out. Our objective is to bring the scientists

and any hard drives and flash media we can round up, back to
Springs." He looked each man in the eye momentarily,
wanting to drive home the importance of the mission. *"The
man that we are going to retrieve...* is trying to figure out what
makes Omega tick. What little information that Springs has
received tells us Doctor Fuentes was making strides forward.
The problem with staying here is *security."*

"Seems super secure to me, Sir," Lopez noted.

"Sure it's secured *inside...* more so now that these ones are
dead." Mike pointed at the leaking bodies scattered about the
floor of the cube farm. "But this building is on the periphery
of Atlanta. There is no way to keep the enemy at bay, and
unfortunately there isn't enough ammo left to kill them all.
The more activity that takes place in here the more attractive
it becomes to those things out there. Already they're
swarming here, all because of our lone helicopter on the
roof."

"How many people lived here in Atlanta?" Lopez asked.

"More than five million," Desantos answered, letting the
number take its sweet time rolling off of his tongue. "I don't
mean to put any undue pressure on you men, but the fate of
mankind hinges on our success or failure today. We can not
fail. *We will not fail."*

Clark felt a chill trace his spine. *That was a General Patton
moment,* he thought, before he cracked the door and entered
the stairwell.

The Delta Team swiftly descended the remaining fourteen
flights of stairs to the sub-basement. On many of the
landings, behind the closed doors, things moved and bumped.
The sickly sweet smell of death was with them all the way.

The door at the bottom of the stairwell looked like it
belonged on a bank vault. The side facing the team was
completely flat and fashioned from a slab of solid polished
steel.

"Smile, we're on Candid Camera." Lopez poked the muzzle of his stubby weapon at the black dome suspended from the ceiling.

"If there's anyone left alive inside, there hasn't been any communication from them for two days," Mike said.

Sergeant Darwin Maddox inspected the door and came away looking concerned. He conferred with Desantos. "This one is a ball breaker. Eight titanium rods, the size of my wrist, are buried six inches into the jamb all of the way around. I have det cord, what I really need is an acetylene torch... or a couple of pounds of C4."

Lopez deadpanned, "What, no acetylene torch in your goodie bag?"

"*Quiet,*" Desantos barked. "Let's put our heads together on this one."

A whirring noise, followed by a series of loud clanks, echoed up and down the stairwell.

For a millisecond, to a man, they looked taken aback, and then the years of training took over.

Desantos and Maddox crouched in the dark, underneath the stairs, and covered the blind side of the door.

The other four men charged back up the stairs, climbing them in big strides. Once they regained the high ground they trained their machine pistols on the blast door.

The team watched as the massive slab began to swing slowly inward. Suddenly the air pressure changed. Desantos opened his mouth and worked his jaw trying to pop his ears. He wasn't very concerned who emerged... because as far as he knew the dead couldn't open doors. Especially not a two foot thick hermetically sealed one.

Chapter 15
Outbreak - Day 5
Hanna, Utah

Cade gave the bodies of the three boys a quick inspection. Someone had taken the time to line them up side by side. The oldest of the three had a deep gash that split the top of his cranium from ear to ear. Gray scrambled brain matter sloughed out of the horrific wound. The other two appeared unscathed until he leaned in closer. Each body was minus one eye. The entry wounds were small and Cade didn't see any obvious exit wounds. It was apparent that the coup de grace on the kid with the Grand Canyon in his dome was committed during a fit of rage. Whoever had to kill these boys a second time didn't like the imposition.

Although the three boys were no longer a threat, it was obvious that they had at one time reanimated and pursued the flesh of the living. Now, despite their hideous appearance, they were still and seemingly at peace. The bodies had been bloating in the sun for awhile and Cade was grateful that the wind was blowing the smell of death away from him.

Cade crouched silently in the shade of a Douglas fir and surveyed the two story weather-beaten home. It was in need of cosmetic fixing but seemed otherwise well taken care of.

There didn't appear to be anyone in the house, or at least no one that was moving about. Before approaching, he looked around for any walkers. Satisfied he was alone, he sprinted across the brown grass and bounded up the stairs. One of the treads creaked loudly under his weight; the nails used to secure it had been exposed to the elements and had long ago worked loose. Cade froze and craned his neck, focusing his right ear in the direction of the closed front door. Suddenly the wind picked up, setting the branches of the white aspens clacking. The sound reminded him of the bamboo wind chimes his wife Brook had brought home from the Oregon coast.

After a few ticks, it was evident the noise had not piqued anyone's curiosity. Cade finished his ascent of the stairs and crouched on the porch to the right of the front door. He tested the patinaed door handle. *Unlocked.* Before he did a little breaking and entering, Cade checked his six for any approaching threats.

With the exception of the rotting corpses at the end of the drive he was still alone. The wind abruptly changed direction, bringing the stench of the dead with it.

Cade pushed the door inward, revealing an ornate mahogany foyer; beyond, a beautifully carved banister followed the curve of the stairs to the second floor. Apparently the owner paid more attention to the interior of the house than the outside.

Cade knew that the dreadlocked man was close by. His vehicle was hidden, as good as a large mint green Chevy Suburban could be, between the back porch and a garage only big enough for a truck half its size.

Another clue someone was in the house was the unmistakable smell of marijuana. In his youth he had only smelled the stuff once or twice. It was a drug he had never ingested into his system, he preferred to be of sound mind and body at all times. Occasionally Cade would enjoy a sip of bourbon or a cold beer. In everyday life some people relied on substances to take the edge off. In Cade's line of work the edge was expected to be present and honed razor sharp at all times.

He made the landing at the top of the stairs without as much as a creak coming from under foot. The pot odor was getting stronger. It appeared to be coming from the room at the farthest end of the hall.

Arranged on the wall, individual photos of three boys faced him; their unnatural smiles conjured up by some photographer's inane words. All three were attired in Boy Scout uniforms and appeared to be in their teens. The corpses on the front lawn were undoubtedly the same young men whose pictures Cade was staring at.

His memories were like ghosts and it pained him that it took someone else's family pictures to extract them from the ether. He reflected fondly back to his time in the Eagle Scouts. The graduation ceremony was special. He remembered how very proud Mom and Dad were on that warm spring day.

Lately he found himself withdrawing. Retreating inward was an effective tool that he utilized when he had to be away from Brook and Raven, either on deployment; or later running special ops with Delta Force. He was more efficient at his craft when his mind wasn't wandering to places it shouldn't. The skill had proven itself very useful these last few chaotic days.

Stealthily, he pushed the first door open with the silencer affixed to his M4. From the looks of the room it belonged to a teenaged boy. A cream colored wooden dresser, of the cheaply made Scandinavian variety, stood in the far corner; the drawers were half open and bursting with unfolded clothes.

A large poster of some teeny bopper girl with jet black hair, dark lipstick and much too sultry of a look for her age dominated the wall over the bed. Cade suddenly wondered what had befallen the Hollywood and entertainment set when their fans had become hungry for more than just a glimpse or an autograph. Oh to be a fly on the wall on Rodeo Drive when the dead started their army ant-like march. The dining must have been to die for in front of the white marble storefronts displaying their super expensive marked up merchandise. It wasn't in his nature to wish ill will on anyone, but even he had a threshold of tolerance, and when it came to the whiny ungrateful bastards on television, he was fresh out.

The room was vacant, its only residents being the girlie poster engaged in a stare off with a long retired NBA player wearing a gold and blue uniform.

Room number two was also devoid of anything living or dead. It must have belonged to the youngest boy. Transformer posters covered every square inch of the once blue walls. A bare mattress sat atop the wood framed twin bed. Everything he had seen so far pointed to the occupants having tried to make a hasty exit.

Cade stepped in front of the open door, the silenced M4 pressed firmly to his shoulder. Peering over the top of the scoped weapon he noted that the small bath was also empty. Subway tiles smeared with bloody handprints and a shredded shower curtain hanging askew ruined the once spa-like serenity of the room. Given the evidence of a violent struggle in the bathroom, Cade's alert level ratcheted up a notch.

One final closed door remained at the end of the hallway. It was streaked with black dried blood, and visible scratch marks ran vertically from top to bottom.

Creeping on the balls of his feet, without making a sound, he hurriedly closed the distance to the last door. He let the silenced carbine hang from the sling, and removed his Glock 17 from the thigh holster. In one hand he held the polymer pistol, it was aimed at the center of the wooden door, and with his free hand he tested the knob. *Unlocked.*

Cade Grayson had been entry man many times, usually with a team of highly trained shooters to get his back. This time he had an uneasy feeling. Not only was he alone, but so far the entry had gone perfectly. On nearly every operation that the Tier-One operator had taken part in good old Mr. Murphy had made a guest appearance. Sometimes the Intel was bad. One time the target had been tipped off by a corrupt Iraqi government official, for a few thousand dollars U.S. On that particular operation Cade had been the tip of the spear and took two rounds from an AK-47 at point blank range. Thankfully, the tactical ballistic proof vest kept him alive and in this world. However, it didn't keep his ribs and sternum from shattering from the double mule kick of the 7.62 x 39 mm projectiles.

In the back of Cade's mind he was waiting for Murphy's Law to once again come into play.

To provide as small a target as possible, Cade went into a combat crouch. Ever so slowly he turned the doorknob and then gently gave the door a push. He crept in, sweeping the large master bedroom from the left to right with his pistol; the first thing to catch his eye was a machete with a bright neon green handle. The long blade was propped up, handle within reach, next to the headboard of the king sized bed, and laying on the hardwood floor, near the machete, was a wicked looking crossbow, bristling with extra bolts.

He kept the muzzle of the Glock trained on the motionless body sprawled face up on the bed. Cade noticed dreadlocks spilling out from underneath the white sheet. It was all the evidence he needed. Cade had the driver of the mint green Suburban right where he wanted him.

Like a ninja, Cade padded deeper into the room and reached for the corner of the threadbare sheet. He was about to wake the man from his pot-induced slumber when the low guttural moaning commenced from somewhere outside.

Sitting bolt upright, the light skinned black man let out a startled gasp and stared cross-eyed, first at the Glock and then directly into the hard eyes of the man behind the weapon.

"Are you proficient with those things?" Cade said, nodding in the direction of the machete and crossbow.

"I ain't no Rambo, but I'm still here," the man said as he stood up with his hands still in the air, the obvious discomfort from the pistol pointed at him evident on his hawkish face. The high cheekbones, sharp pointed nose and brilliant gray green eyes looked out of place under the tangle of tightly braided dreads.

Cade noted the well worn cork logging boots on the man's feet and that he had on long pants and a long sleeve thermal shirt even though it was summer. "First things first, is there anyone else in the house with you?" Cade knew the answer but wanted to test him by looking for the betraying micro expressions associated with deception. Without looking away or displaying any of the telltale signs, the man answered the question.

"Not any longer." He bowed his head; his dreadlocks covered his face like a funeral veil.

"Those things must have followed one of us here, and where there's one, there will soon be many more." Cade looked at the pipe and baggie full of what he assumed was weed. "Are you still high?"

The man peered at Cade between dangling strands of knotted hair. "Not anymore."

"You sure are a man of few words..." Cade said as he slid the pistol back into the holster, and out of habit, checked to make sure the magazine was seated in the M4. "But I believe you. We better move it, grab your weapons."

Without hesitating, the stranger snatched his crossbow and machete, and hustled towards the window at the opposite end of the hall.

Cade formed up next to him and while they looked on, a half naked walker crashed through the trees that separated the property from the road. Like she had been here before, and still belonged, the creature stumbled up the walkway towards the front porch. Before her first death she was probably some lucky guy's high school sweetheart. Scraps of clothes hung from her body. Trudging through the woods and underbrush had left her pale skin crisscrossed with ugly gray lacerations.

The man cocked the compound crossbow; with a firm click the bolt was seated. He glanced back. Cade couldn't help but notice the lack of concern on his face.

Cade squeezed in and grabbed one side of the window. Working together they hauled the window up in its tracks. The hefty lead weights used to counterbalance the wooden window banged in the sash, capturing the walker's attention. At the sight of the men her clumsy gait quickened.

"There are two more walkers moving along the hedges at your three o'clock..." Cade said, acting as spotter. "And four more close behind," he added.

With only a whisper of sound the bolt left the bow and found a home in the creature's right eye socket. The barbed titanium tip shredded everything in its path before becoming lodged in the thing's brainstem. Her pasty body collapsed like a marionette whose strings had been severed.

With adept precision the man quickly reloaded the compound crossbow. The next walker, a boy of about ten with a mop of brown hair, took one through the septum. The bolt split the dead kid's nose and lodged firmly in his atrophied brain. Like a crash test dummy, the abomination went limp and smacked the sun-baked lawn, liquefied gray matter oozing from its nostrils and open mouth.

The moaning intensified as soon as the other zombies noticed the ruckus.

Cade eased his 5-foot-9-inch frame through the open window, planted his combat boots on the shingled roof and sat down cross legged. Now with a solid base to shoot from, he shouldered the M4 and found his first target.

The right ear of the young boy disappeared in a fine spray of white cartilage and rotting flesh. Without as much as a flinch the cadaver kept up its quick forward march. Cade was disappointed his first shot missed its mark but he made no excuses. He already found out the hard way, the younger the walker the faster they moved. In a group they all seemed to pick up the pace, no matter the age, gender or condition of the walking corpse. Cade figured it must be because of the inbred human desire for competition, so he had come to the unscientific conclusion that when an infected victim reanimates, in addition to the overwhelming urge to consume living flesh, some of the other innate drives remained hardwired. Some of the zombie swarms he had come across resembled a Black Friday crowd storming a Walmart. Another looked like the Bataan death march - a slow moving procession following a leader.

A few days prior he had gotten to see firsthand the speed that an undead toddler possessed. He and a handful of fellow survivors had had to contend with a large throng of them. Not everyone survived the encounter at Wakeena Falls. He shook his head and cleared his mind, bringing himself back to the present.

Cade's second shot was precise, the bullet struck the top of the ghoul's head above the right eyebrow and exited, propelling flesh and vertebra from the back of the walker's neck in a fine pink spray. The kid's body fell near the front stoop. Cade was certain the corpse wouldn't be walking again.

In quick succession, the bowman put down three more ghouls. The black bolts protruding from their heads made them resemble castoff voodoo dolls.

Cade scanned the woods across the road through the ACOG scope. "I don't see any more where they came from. Mind if I ask you a couple of questions?"

"Ask away."

"I saw you on the forest road earlier today, where were you coming from?"

"I was returning from a little city outside of Salt Lake... It's where my parents live - or lived."

"Did you find them?" Cade asked. Merely saying the
words caused him to think about Brook and Raven whom he
hadn't even spoken to for far too long.

The man answered Cade's question while he continually
scanned the tree line for more undead. "No, I got as far as
Provo before the monsters got too thick and forced me to
turn around and hightail it out of there." Reaching out to the
operator with his free hand, he introduced himself as
Daymon Bush. "You can call me Daymon or D for short. As
long as you're not gonna put that pistol in my face again."

"My name is Cade but I won't guarantee you anything."

Daymon quickly sized up the man named Cade. He was
fully clad in desert camouflage, his dark hair wandered from
under the tactical helmet. A medium length growth of black
facial hair worked to conceal his chiseled facial features, but it
was the eyes that revealed the man. This man had cold dark
eyes that projected a supreme air of confidence. It only took
him a second to process all of the information, in that time
Daymon decided Cade was not someone he wished to tangle
with.

Cade continued. "Nothing personal, but I've had a few
encounters with fellow breathers that didn't end so well. It looks
like we're on the same side." He offered a dusty gloved hand
to Daymon. "One more thing..." Cade asked. "Who taught
you how to shoot a bow like that?"

"Mr. Lawson, my Scoutmaster. I made it to Tenderfoot
before I got bored and quit."

"Hell of a teacher," Cade said admiringly.

Chapter 16
Outbreak Day-5
Sawtooth Mountains
Stanley, Idaho

The first rays of sun were encroaching on the edge of night. The denizen of Mount Stanley had been hiking down the talus- and scree-covered flank of the alpine peak for three and a half hours. Dan had timed his descent so he would be near the outskirts of the small town of Stanley, Idaho before dawn. The sixty-five-year-old retired Marine paused on a small finger of rock and turned off his tiny Petzl headlamp. Dan pulled out his armored binoculars and quickly glassed the large compound.

***

The Aryan Brotherhood, after having been asked to leave Coeur D'Alene, chose Stanley to be the epicenter of their intended Fourth Reich. Dan had had little contact over the years with the rejects that considered themselves patriots. Until recently the group had done little to disrupt the peace in idyllic Stanley, short of a few parades in full Nazi regalia, followed by vitriol filled speeches, which were unfortunately allowed under the First Amendment.

Two days prior, Dan had come down to this very same finger of rock. It was his favorite place to rest up before the final leg of the long trek to town. While surveying the camp

89

with his binoculars he watched young skinheads, the foot soldiers of the Aryan Brotherhood, gun down three men in the center of the compound. Dan looked on in disbelief as the man he knew by the name of Richard Ganz committed the final heinous act. He pulled his chrome Desert Eagle and blew a woman's head off. All in all Dan witnessed four murders that day, and they were all committed in cold blood.

Dan had an overwhelming urge to do what was right and tell the sheriff what he had witnessed, but determined for his own safety he couldn't risk going anywhere near the scene of the murders. However, Dan's conscience finally got the best of him and he decided to turn in the murderers so they could answer for their crimes.

***

The high powered Bushnells made the compound look like it was near enough to touch. There was no sound coming from within. He guessed the hangovers would take all day to sleep off.

Dan had listened to the raucous party taking place during his three and a half hour trudge down the mountain. Strangely, more gunfire came from the compound than all of the previous New Years parties combined. More troubling was the absence of Sheriff Blanda. He usually let the gang get a *little* rowdy before taking action; knowing when to pick and choose his battles was one of the man's best skills.

Something else was afoot. The total absence of passenger jets or commuter planes during the last few days piqued his curiosity.

Dan was resigned to the fact that he had at the least a day's worth of interviews in front of him. He also had a feeling there was going to be a face to face with Richard Ganz at some point. He knew that fingering Ganz and the skinheads wasn't going to be as cut and dried as picking them out of a mug shot lineup. The Stanley jail wasn't equipped with a two way mirror like the one on *Law and Order*.

Dan had a sinking feeling that the accused were going to get to see their accuser, and then Sheriff Blanda was going to read them their rights and call the Feds... he *hoped.*

If everything went as planned Dan was going to get to see his lady friend before the day was over.

***

Elizabeth Paxton and Dan had been schoolmates and then a couple when they were in high school. The Vietnam War and the draft shredded all of that. While Dan was away fighting for his country, the local football hero Randy Tolliver started making nice with Lizzie. Dan failed to keep up correspondence, therefore the months and miles apart made it easier for Lizzie to forget about him. The lowest point in his first tour was that damn Dear John letter. Dan almost ate his Colt .45 to erase the hurt; instead he took it all out on Victor Charlie. Dan had really taken it to the enemy during his three tours in Nam. He was a highly regarded member of Marine Force Recon. After Dan received the world altering letter, MACV-SOG became his life and every Viet Cong wore Randy Tolliver's ugly mug.

Dan returned from the Vietnam War in 1970 and worked mostly odd jobs. Lizzie and Randy had a long lasting marriage. Over the years Dan remained alone and mostly kept his distance.

Randy Tolliver made a widow of Elizabeth two years ago. Dan was still fond of Lizzie and helped her out when he came down from his cabin in the Sawtooth Mountains. Although the spark was no longer there on her part, the man known as Mountain Man still was compelled to check in on her.

***

Dan kept still and listened. Nothing moved in the Aryan's compound. Considering the amount of empties lying around, the party had been as wild as it sounded.

Dan was aware that two vicious brindle Pit Bull Terriers normally had the run of the fenced-in grounds. Stealth was

his first priority; he didn't want to give them any reason to
bark.

Dan heel and toed it past the entrance and hurriedly
crossed the open road, becoming one with the shadows again.
The man still knew how to move silently. You could take the
man out of the Marines, but the learned skills remained. The
Colt .45 rode high on his hip, concealed by a black lightweight
nylon wind breaker.

He paused mid-step. Someone was stirring inside the
cheaply constructed dwelling to his three o'clock. *Go back to
sleep Nazi boy.*

The rusty screen door made a long drawn out screech
when it opened.

Dan froze instantly mid stride.

A squat, shirtless man stood framed in the doorway. He
stretched, yawned and scratched his billiard ball head before
crossing the threshold into the crisp morning air. He clearly
forgot he had three steps to navigate. A surprised look
crossed his still drunk face when his foot didn't contact terra
firma instantly, the sudden bone jarring contact with the
ground making him curse.

"*Motherfucker, shit...goddamnit.*"

Dan suppressed a chuckle and remained statue still.

It appeared to Dan that the man was having problems
with his fly as the expletives continued. Finally he extracted
his shriveled manhood and left the contents of his full
bladder steaming on the ground. After fumbling to put things
away, the man put his suspenders back over his shoulders,
scratched his ass and limped back to the shack. The groaning
screen door once again tried its best to wake the camp before
slamming shut with a resounding bang.

The stars dancing in front of his eyes alerted Dan that he
was holding his breath. A slow exhale and a greedy gulp of air
later, things were back to normal. Dan willed his body to stay
still for another five minutes. Satisfied that the coast was as

clear as it was going to get, he continued past the cluster of one story dorms.

The dogs were sleeping in plain sight, right on the same spot where the executions had taken place days prior.

As silly as it seemed to him, he still recited some words in his head. *Do not open your eyes. I am not here. Keep sleeping.* He wouldn't admit it, but deep down he was a superstitious man. The words did the trick, Dan was sure of it. The truth was, the dogs had been slurping up spilled beer all night and were as hung-over as the Aryans.

The main road snaked from the base of the mountain and ran straight through the town of Stanley. Dan walked along the shoulder. A few times he noticed the smell of death lingering near the road, but quickly dismissed it, assuming it was nothing more than road kill in the ditch.

It was a twisting three miles before Dan arrived in front of the sign reading, "*Welcome to Stanley, Idaho. Population 100.*" He was parched, sore and had been walking on the two lane road for ninety minutes. As remote as the mountain town was, he still expected to see the early morning delivery drivers. A refrigerated truck usually brought fresh seafood and meat a couple of times a week from Boise. Dan also thought the absence of the white Econoline van, that without fail delivered daily newspapers to the sleepy town, was a very bad omen.

Chapter 17
Outbreak - Day 5
Hanna, Utah

Rapid fire banging resonated from somewhere downstairs, followed by the tinkling of breaking glass.

Cade followed in Daymon's footsteps, down the dimly lit hall to the head of the stairs, while leaving a few feet of separation between the two of them. Daymon padded down the stairs, crossbow aimed over the handrail, cocked and at the ready.

Somewhere in the house a door slammed, followed by the metallic snick of a deadbolt being thrown. The sound echoed off of the plaster walls, amplified by the narrow confines of the downstairs foyer. Cade noted the focused look on Daymon's face, locked eyes with him and raised his carbine as a show of readiness.

Even over the muted moans from outside, the sound of someone or something breathing heavily downstairs was unmistakable. The gasps for air were interspersed with grunts and groans of pain. It instantly reminded Cade of his class of Ranger hopefuls, sucking wind between evolutions, during the qualifying course at Fort Benning. His intuition told him one or more people were downstairs seeking sanctuary from the walking corpses. The two story house was situated prominently near the entrance to town, which made it an attractive place to hide out.

Cade noticed Daymon cautiously poking his head around the door jamb. He was positioned at the far end of the hallway which ran from the front door, dissecting the expansive house. Cade kept watch on both Daymon and the locked front door behind them.

Another loud crash, followed by more breaking glass resounded from the rear of the old farmhouse. Instantly the smell of death invaded the house. With a flurry of motion Daymon raised his crossbow and sent a missile flying down the hall towards the commotion.

Daymon was in the act of reloading when he was knocked to the floor. The blur of blubber hurdled over him and scrambled down the hall, screaming as he went. The man was severely overweight, yet exhibited speed that belied his girth. He was obviously being propelled by adrenaline, a basic human instinct for survival and a heavy dose of sheer terror. The shirtless man scrambled a few more feet, fingernails clawing and scratching on the hardwood floor. He came to an abrupt halt eye level with Cade's combat boots. As if in slow motion, the big man swiped a curtain of sweaty hair from his eyes, slowly raised his fleshy head and peered up the barrel of Cade's M4.

Between gasps for air, the pasty man begged. "*Nooo... Don't shoot. I don't want to die... please help me.*" It was an embarrassing display. The man grabbed the banister and shakily pulled himself up from the floor. Cade looked the man over, searching for any bite marks or wounds. The big man was now on his feet with his back against the wall, his head hanging like a spent marathon runner.

"*Oh my God...* I came around the corner thinking your friend here was going to put one of those barbed arrows in me. The thing nearly parted my hair."

"I'm going to put a few rounds in you if you don't move it," Cade shot back while manhandling the sweating middle-aged man out of the way.

From his vantage point, Daymon could see an undead mob surging onto the back porch. All at once they came to an abrupt halt.

Momentarily repulsed by the closed door, the bloated beings began to amass on the back stoop. It groaned and creaked, sounding like it was close to collapse.

The wretched odor of decay wafted into the house. Like the tentacles of a giant squid, it sought out and displaced every last pocket of fresh air. Rotten arms flailed in the broken window, sending the few remaining shards of jagged glass onto the tile floor.

The full pressure from the jostling corpses made the sturdy door flex inward. Daymon knew that eventually the press of flesh was going to splinter the door jamb. He shouted a warning without removing his eyes from the path that the zombies would eventually flood, "There are at least twenty of those things on the porch and the door is about to fail!" Daymon backpedaled down the hall in the direction of the stairs, keeping his weapon trained on the kitchen entryway.

The crack of splintering wood, followed by the sound of sliding furniture, resonated down the hall.

The frantic intruder screamed into Cade's face, "We'd better run man. Those things, they never quit and they don't tire. *I've been running for blocks.*" His jowls swayed and his bloodshot eyes bugged out. He was the poster boy for *losing it.*

Cade recoiled from the man's sour breath. "It looks like you've been running for *miles* not blocks," Cade replied coldly.

The man had on expensive slacks and leather wingtips that were once highly polished. Cade passed quick judgment and pegged him as a politician or lawyer before the Omega virus rendered those titles obsolete.

Before the outbreak Cade could find little sympathy for people who let themselves get morbidly obese. Sure there were the "medical" situations, but Happy Burger didn't force the grease bombs down their gullets.

Even after he had been home and out of the harsh environment of Afghanistan for more than a year, at thirty-five-years-old he still found the time to run a few miles to keep trim. *Maybe some people didn't possess the discipline needed to keep fit. It was a totally different ballgame now, run or be eaten was a hell of a motivator. Pretty soon,* he thought, *there aren't going to be very many like this guy left alive.*

Cade ceased the one sided conversation with an open palm to the man's face. He raised the rifle, aiming down the hall past Daymon.

The first moaning zombie filled the opening. One of its eyes dangled and bobbed, swaying to and fro by its useless optic nerve. The remaining good eye was intently focused on the meat it so hungered for. Its pale arms were outstretched, straining to reach Daymon.

Both men fired at the same time. The crossbow bolt embedded four inches into the ghoul's remaining eye. A millisecond later a triple tap from the silenced M4 punched the crossbow bolt the rest of the way through the zombie's head. Tumbling lead, shredded fiberglass, bone and brain matter splattered the cupboards.

Daymon shouted, "*Hurry*, get up there and look for anything big and bulky to fill the stairwell, anything to slow them down."

The shirtless man labored up to the second level close on Daymon's heels.

Cade stayed behind for a moment to provide rear guard. He hoped the two men wouldn't get overzealous and start raining antique furniture down on his head.

There were twenty-seven rounds of 5.56 left in the magazine. Cade was used to keeping a mental count, it was an invaluable lesson learned in basic training and later perfected in combat. The need to conserve ammo was real, so he switched the selector from burst to single fire. Making all of his rounds count would be tantamount to surviving the day.

It was a humorous but deadly scene as the crush of walking dead jammed through the four foot wide hallway. The two ghouls at the head of the pack were tripped up by the fallen zombie Daymon and Cade had double teamed. The undead pileup provided Cade with clean kill shots; he popped off two rounds at the prone monsters. *Five downrange, twenty-five rounds remaining,* Cade's inner voice told him. The impacting 5.56 lead split their heads wide open, showering the rest of the ghouls with hair and rank cerebral fluid.

More undead filled the far doorway, blocking out what little light there was. The horde clamored over the three carcasses, moving much too fast for Cade's comfort.

About to be trapped downstairs Cade grabbed the banister, careful to keep his weapon from banging in his wake, and hauled ass up the stairs three at a time. He was halfway up the stairs when something heavy grazed his heel.

Daymon watched with concern as the piece of furniture shattered with an ear splitting crash on the stairs right behind Cade. The old bedside table, built a century ago, bounced all the way to the bottom of the stairs.

"Look out below!" Daymon cried.

"*A little late*," Cade countered.

The second wooden missile was much bigger and sturdier. The ladies vanity, Edwardian in origin Cade guessed, came crashing down on top of the moaning swarm. One of the ghouls took a direct hit. The two hundred pound piece of furniture pinned its body to the stairs, its head protruding from underneath while its arms and legs flailed in a futile attempt to get to the meat upstairs.

"Sorry dude, that was close. If it wasn't for the incredible Hulk here," Daymon said gesturing at his large companion, "that thing wouldn't have gotten over the hand rail."

"No worries. No blood no foul," Cade replied.

"Then what's the situation Sarge?"

Since Cade was still wearing his desert camo it was obvious that the question was directed his way.

"I have a sinking feeling there are way too many of those things for us take down."

As soon as he finished his sentence, the stained glass inlay on both sides of the ornate front door burst inward and fell with a heavy thump onto the wood floor.

Tattered zombie arms probed the new breach. Soon multiple heads, their lifeless eyes darting about, explored the openings. One of the creatures squeezed its body into the small gap next to the door, sacrificing both breasts in the endeavor before becoming hopelessly stuck.

The big man exited the master bedroom with three bronze lamps clutched in his hands. After depositing them over the side he went back into the room for more to add to the mound.

"Give me a hand," he called out.

Cade followed him into the room where he had apparently been trying to rend the footboard off of the sleigh bed. It only took one kick from Cade's boot to finish the job for him. The dovetail joint failed and the side rail of the bed broke free. Cade was pleased to hear the loud crack, especially since it wasn't the front door failing.

It only took the big man two stomps before his weight shattered the second bedrail letting the massive King footboard fall freely to the floor. The two men pushed the curved footboard through the doorway and muscled it over the railing. The slab of mahogany sailed into the throng of walkers, all of whom were already having a difficult time navigating the growing pile of corpses and broken furniture.

"How many people live in this little burgh?" Cade asked as he poured accurate rifle fire into the moving wall of dead flesh.

Over the increasing moans, he could have sworn that he heard someone say two hundred.

"Come again?"

The obese man yelled to be heard over the grunts and groans of the stinking corpses. "*I said*, two hundred, maybe more, because it's summer and the lake draws vacationers here from the big city."

"That's bad news; I only have two magazines left. The rest are in the saddlebags of my bike." Cade changed the magazine and charged the gun in one fluid motion. The former Delta Operator was back to dropping undead before the empty clip clanged to the floor.

Their situation seemed to be going from bad to worse. Cade thought about the satellite phone tucked in his pocket and decided he would use it as a last resort.

Their garage sale-sized barricade was growing larger. The footboard served as a good foundation for the other assorted crap that Daymon was heaving onto the mound.

The big man was sweating profusely while he worked on freeing the headboard. Finally, after breaking off the long side rails, he was ready for assistance once again.

"Sarge, Skinny... help needed."

Daymon was out of ammo for his crossbow so he hefted the machete and went to lend a hand. It took a lot of grunting and dragging from both men but they finally succeeded in carting the headboard to the rail and hefting its weight over the top. Three undead were crushed flat and immediately stilled by the falling chunk of old growth.

The remaining zombies thrashed about, tangled up in the bedding that Daymon had ingenuously floated over the railing.

There was only a few feet of open headroom left in the stairway. Cade went looking for a cherry to put on their sundae. "In here big guy, and grab those bed rails!" Cade bellowed to be heard over the moans of the dead.

A brilliant white, cast-iron claw foot tub sat against one wall of the master bathroom. Cade decided that it was going down the stairway even if it killed him. The long boards preceded the big man as he entered the bathroom.

Cade stepped aside to make room.

"Put yours here," Cade pointed at the six inch gap between the tub and the wall and then he inserted his the same way at the foot of the tub. The added leverage of the bed rails allowed the men to easily uproot the clawed feet from the tiled floor. Cade lithely moved out of the way as the tub crashed over onto its side. The big man was not so fast. He howled out in pain while jumping around on one foot and holding onto the injured one, all the while his pale white flab jiggling with each hop. The tub left a deep indentation on his wingtip shoe.

"It's broken... broken! Owwww."

"Suck it up and help me or I'll break the other one," Cade hissed.

Whimpering, the big man helped push the weighty tub out the door. It took them a little bit of finessing to get the vessel's feet to cooperate allowing them to wiggle it through. Cade kicked five of the carved balusters out of the railing and then returned aft to help push the tub over the edge. It barely squeaked through, fell six feet and lodged upright fully blocking all access to the second floor.

"We're effed now," Daymon grumbled, looking at Cade, while trying to ignore the panting, sweating, shirtless mound of flesh standing next to him.

"If we're going to die here together, we might as well be on a first name basis. I'm sorry I called you Sarge and Skinny." The fat man extended one sweaty mitt towards Daymon, hoping to forge a detente.

Daymon's hesitation was obvious.

After wiping his right hand back and forth on his black slacks, the man extended his hand once more. "My name is Hosford Preston, Attorney at Law."

"*I knew it.* Let me guess, they call you Hoss... right?"
Daymon joked with the man.

"Only my friends," the lawyer replied as he rubbed his
ruined toes, "and I'm sure they're *all* dead now."

Daymon couldn't hold back. "Newsflash... nearly everyone
in this town is dead and currently banging on the pile of shit
that's clogging the stairs."

"You can call me Cade, Sarge is a little below my pay
grade."

"Tell me then *Cade,* where *is* the rest of your army? I've
been holed up in the attic of my law office for days and
haven't seen any authorities. Those freaks had me treed until
they heard you and that other guy roll into town. That's when
they began wandering away from my practice. I waited for
them to leave the front door area and then I made the dash
here."

Daymon was seething mad and fingering his green
handled machete. "So you *led* them here?"

"It wasn't my intention; they spotted me leaving the
building. One of them started that fucking moaning and it
escalated from there. The next thing I know there are twenty
of them dragging after me. I barely made it here alive."

Cade sensed the mass of dead crushing against the
improvised obstruction. Groans and creaks from the stressed
staircase and handrail comingled with the nonstop moaning.

The Gerber combat dagger slid from the sheath with ease.
Cade cut a long swatch of fabric from the bare box springs
sitting amongst the splintered remains of the antique sleigh
bed. After dividing the single piece into six smaller swatches
he passed them to the other two men.

"What the hell am I to do with these?" asked the insolent
lawyer.

"They aren't big enough to silence that pie hole of yours,"
Daymon said as he pushed a piece of the cloth into each ear.

A light bulb illuminated in Hosford's skull and he proceeded to plug his ears as well.

Cade removed two packages of MRE crackers from his cargo pocket, tossed them to his fellow prisoners, and then retrieved the satellite phone. He powered the device up and deployed the stubby aerial. The little technological marvel was developed solely for the military. Cade was familiar with its workings and used one like it during operations in Iraq and Afghanistan.

The device didn't work the last time he powered it on, so Cade crossed his fingers and hoped he'd be able to get an uplink on this attempt. Cade searched his other pocket; it contained a flare gun and a canister of purple marking smoke. Duncan had slipped them to him before he left Camp Williams.

"Daymon, hold the fort down. I'm going to try to get us a ride."

Daymon interpreted it to mean Cade wanted him to keep an eye on the loose cannon named Hosford Preston.

Chapter 18
Outbreak - Day 5
Stanley, Idaho

Beauregard Hampton was one of the most important men in the city of Stanley. Of the hundred or so residents, he was the only one with keys to open the only grocery store in town. If the lights weren't on at Hampton's Mercantile, you weren't getting your milk - or beer for that matter.

Bo, the octogenarian owner of the store, was there every morning before 6 a.m., without fail, except for Sunday which was *his* holy day.

Where are all of the people? Dan looked at his watch, it was after 7 a.m. The main drag was deserted save for a dusty, brown Dodge Power Wagon parked awkwardly away from the curb. He was hearing the niggling voice in his head, the one that had saved his ass many times.

With an air of caution, Dan walked toward the darkened general store.

A shiny brass shell casing skittered and bounced in front of him, accidentally propelled by his scuffed leather boot. Recognizing the spent cartridges scattered on the sidewalk and what they probably meant, the voice inside of Dan's head suddenly started screaming, *"Danger, get the fuck away!"*

Dan knelt down, exhaling from the stab of pain in his bad knee. He retrieved one of the spent shell casings and examined the markings. *7.62x39mm, Wolf brand, probably from a Kalashnikov.*

Once he was in front of the store and adjacent to the abandoned truck, he noticed there were multiple bullet holes punched into the fender and driver's side door. Given the way the puckered indentations walked along the sheet metal Dan deduced it was from a full auto burst.

A shiver ran through his gut while a sense of dread washed over him. "I better check on old Bo," muttered Dan.

The retired Marine released the strap with his free hand and withdrew the black Colt Model 1911 .45 caliber pistol from the holster on his hip. A bullet was already in the chamber. Dan cocked the hammer before he tested the doorknob. Finding it unlocked, he nudged the door inward gently with his forearm. The bell above the door jangled. Already tense and on edge Dan jumped, his heart rate quickened and beads of sweat erupted across his forehead. Fear in small doses was necessary, but unchecked it could get you killed. This, Dan was well aware of. *You'd better be careful old man. It ain't your first rodeo... but remember, the last one was a long time ago.*

The bell finished its alert, replaced by a noise barely audible over the hammering of his heart. Faintly, from a darkened corner, came the sound again.

The old vet's ears weren't deceiving him, a raspy wheezing emanated from somewhere beyond the empty shelving. Dan imagined his friend Bo incapacitated or seriously injured, waiting alone through the night for someone to come to his aid, and how frightening that would be for an eighty-five-year-old man.

His first impulse was to barge in, hand cannon leading the way while calling out the proprietor's name. On the other hand, rushing in would be damn foolish. Dan thought that if Bo wasn't dead yet, then a couple more ticks of the clock's big hand probably wasn't going to kill him. Dan still had no idea who had shot up the turd brown Dodge or if they were even still around, but he had to assume that they were most likely still in the area and most definitely armed. Discretion would have to be the better part of valor, because there was no doubt his .45 was no match for the automatic rifle responsible for ventilating the Dodge.

Head swiveling, Dan took in the sights and smells inside of the store. The stench of rotting meat first assailed his senses. Trying his best to breathe only through his mouth, Dan extracted a handkerchief and covered his nose.

An antique bronze cash register dominated the prime real estate on the counter; it was older than Bo and usually more cantankerous. The drawer was open and still contained a fair amount of cash. *Strange*, Dan thought.

The sound of his footsteps shattered the shroud of stillness and echoed off of the empty shelves. He stopped in front of a row of darkened glass doors; every last ounce of beer and wine was gone, yet bulging gallon containers of warm spoiled milk remained.

Once more, like the rattle of a dying man's last breath, the panting sounded from the rear of the store.

The kerchief went back in his pocket as he withdrew the tactical flashlight, switching it on with a press of his thumb. Dan held the pistol in his right hand, the barrel resting over the top of his left wrist, ensuring that the flashlight beam and muzzle moved as one.

His Marine Corps training kicked in, this was no tunnel in Nam, but the unknown danger was still real. Dan edged his head around a display of Gatorade capping the end of the aisle, waited and listened for a few seconds. *Nothing*. He then crept further into the semi-darkened produce section.

Shit. The wheezing resumed, louder than before, from somewhere behind the plastic slats that separated the front of the store and the stock area in back.

Dan had no idea what was going on in his little town. The shell casings and the pockmarked vehicle added a strange twist to the deadly mystery.

The blued barrel poked between the hanging slats, allowing the brilliant white beam from the flashlight access to the storeroom.

Dan swept the room from left to right. Boxes and plastic crates were piled high. A rolling recycling bin full of crushed and flattened cardboard boxes succeeded in further blocking his view.

The eerie noise was repeated, much louder and much nearer. In the windowless storeroom the carrion odor was overpowering. He fought the urge to vomit, but instead hacked a couple of dry heaves. In response, the mysterious sound repeated anew, louder still.

The former tunnel rat deliberately knelt down on his good knee, the bad one protesting with a loud pop. The ray of light from the tactical flashlight probed the area under Bo's oak roll top desk. Still half in the shadows, something moved. Dan recognized the mangy tail as it swished a slow, steady, half arc on the floor. Champ wheezed again. He was older than Bo, *in dog years* Dan thought, and looked worse for the wear.

Dan recoiled, a gasp escaping his lips as the source of the retched odor was revealed by the cone of light. Beauregard Hampton, stiff with rigor mortis, lay stretched out beside his beloved Collie, one stiff arm around Champ and the other clutching an obviously fatal stomach wound. Bo's wizened eyes, cloudy and dry, were still open. The store owner's face wore a slack, pale, scowl, frozen in death. Maggots teemed inside of his abdominal cavity; the sickening wet symphony of the squirming larvae made Dan wince.

Champ's fur was glued to the floor in the long dried blood that had pooled around both man and his dog.

Dan spent a moment wondering what kind of shitbags would shoot an old man in the gut and leave him to bleed out. The kind came to mind immediately, reminding him why he had come to town in the first place. Finding Sheriff Blanda was more important than ever, now that he saw what the fringe element was really capable of.

The grizzled vet sat and comforted the skinny old dog while reflecting on the last time he was in his friend Beauregard Hampton's company. One hot afternoon a month ago the men sat on the porch of this very store and discussed the past, present and the future; neither one of them aware of the tragedy about to beset the Nation. Bo had given him a book a mile thick, covering all anyone would want to know about the last Great Depression.

"Read up and get ready," was the wise advice that he received from Bo that June day. He told Dan that he had barely survived the first financial crash and he hoped he wouldn't be around for the one he knew was looming on the horizon. The entire population of Stanley, Idaho knew of Bo's beliefs. Most people brushed them off as the rantings of a cynical old coot. It was also common knowledge that he was ready for "eventualities" as he put it. Bo owned a sizable cache of weapons and ammunition and stored some of them in the cellar of the hundred year old general store. Dan feared that Bo walked in on a robbery and got himself killed, *all over some guns and beer... what a shame.* Old Bo was a fixture in Stanley. The man was a treasure and would be missed.

Dan switched off the flashlight. While he sat cross legged in the impenetrable dark with only Champ and Bo's cold corpse for company, he tried to think of all the scenarios that would leave Stanley empty and deserted.

Chapter 19
Outbreak - Day 5
Hanna, Utah

Long shadows stretched across the unkempt yard. The lifeless eyes of the three boys glowed orange, the setting sun reflecting off of them. Night was coming swiftly and the dead didn't have an opinion, they only wanted upstairs.

Cade spent the better part of an hour trying to think of a way out of the mess he and his two new acquaintances were in. His call to Duncan at Camp Williams went unanswered. It appeared aerial rescue wasn't in the cards.

The green Suburban was in back of the house, but so were most of the zombies. Cade watched for an hour. The SUV was a no-go. It never had less than twenty flesh-eaters surrounding it. He contemplated the idea of jumping on top of the rig and quickly slipping inside. It was a good twenty feet to the roof of Daymon's Suburban. Even if he did clear the gulf, from this height he was sure to rupture a tendon or break something, and coming up lame in the middle of a pack of undead would be a death sentence. While deep in thought, Cade detected movement from the corner of his eye. A toddler-sized zombie had wormed its way through the jumbled maze. Reacting instantaneously, Cade delivered a boot to the juvenile's sternum. The awful sound of breaking ribs echoed off of the ceiling. The blow sent the thing sprawling across the floor and it screeched to a halt on the white tiles in the adjacent bathroom. Undeterred, the ghoul grabbed onto the pedestal sink, hauled itself erect and resumed the attack, hissing and clacking its teeth at the three survivors.

Daymon was first to intervene, playfully egging the thing on. "What's the matter, miss the preschool bus?" Tracing a barely visible green arc Daymon's machete flashed through the air, and with a hollow thunk cleaved into the center of the undead boy's forehead. Daymon put his boot on the ghoul's scrawny neck and wrenched the blade from its skull.

"That was fucking awful," Hoss whined.

"This is fucking awful..." Daymon displayed his weapon, brains still clinging to the steel.

At the first sight of bloody gray matter, Hoss began to dry heave.

"Where'd you learn to swing that thing?" Cade already had a hunch it was Daymon who had taken care of the three on the lawn, and after what he had just witnessed there was no doubt.

"Fighting fires, cutting brush for back burns and such. Put so many hours in using the thing it's a natural extension of my arm," Daymon replied.

"I was hoping that you didn't say the Boy Scouts taught you. I didn't remember there being a machete merit badge anyway. Please... remind me not to get on your bad side," Cade said jokingly while he unceremoniously tossed the small body on the barricade below while taking every precaution to keep from coming into contact with the chunks of frontal lobe dribbling from the zombie's head.

Leaving the two men alone, Cade went into the master bath in search of water. He splashed his face and then drank his fill. When he gazed into the mirror he was taken aback by his own reflection. Through red-rimmed eyes the thousand yard stare had returned.

In the days since the outbreak he had had little time to sleep and even less time for personal hygiene. His sideburns were now merging with his black goatee, which was on the way to becoming the full beard that he always wore on deployment in the Middle East.

Cade rifled through the medicine cabinet and found what he needed. Wasting little time, he smeared the viscous black eyeliner on any exposed skin. The dead had poor night vision but he needed every advantage he could get to escape the house alone, unseen and unscathed.

"Daymon, I need to borrow that sword of yours."

"I've got *zero* ammo for the crossbow and there's no way I can go downstairs and look for an extra butcher knife... why, you gonna leave me high and dry?"

"We're trapped up here and we're not going to be able to shoot our way out..." Cade had already made the decision, was standing on the ledge, and nobody was going to talk him down.

"What do you have in mind then?" Daymon asked.

"The Cliffs Notes version, I'm going to slip away from here, hopefully undetected, and then find another Suburban or something bigger."

Hosford couldn't resist. "Sounds pretty elaborate to me," he chimed in.

"I'm just trying to keep it simple."

"We'll hold down the fort for you then," said the usually quiet Daymon, thrusting the green handle in Cade's direction. "Don't forget about us."

Cade took the blade. "Don't worry, I'll be back."

In the one of the boy's rooms Cade found a dark blue tracksuit. It was a size too small but the material stretched easily. He thought that since the moon was still in a very full phase it would be stupid trying to evade a town full of walking dead wearing light tan digital camo. Cade removed all of his weapons and his combat harness before he donned the nylon two piece exercise outfit over his fatigues. *I'm going to*

broil in this getup, was his first thought, but he was confident
that wearing it would allow him to move stealthily and attract
less attention from the zombies.

***

The path of least resistance appeared to be the front of the
dwelling. The door was still keeping a handful of zombies at
bay while the majority of them were swarming around the
Suburban and crushing into the house via the back door. By
his estimation there were fifteen to twenty milling about the
walk and porch.

The window remained open making it easy for him to get
out onto the roof while keeping the noise to a minimum.

Cade wanted to go as fast and quiet as humanly possible.
He had the M4 at the ready strapped to his chest and had
decided to use it only as a last resort. Even though the carbine
was silenced it still produced a muzzle flash, especially at
night. It would have to be a knife and machete affair only.

Cade's Suunto read 2 a.m. He remained on the roof until a
series of clouds masked the nearly full moon. Reluctantly he
plucked the fabric from his ears, letting the voices of the dead
fully assault his hearing.

Peering over the edge of the roof, Cade took a headcount
of the ambling zombies. Four patrolled the porch and another
five traipsed around the shin high grass flanking the walk. For
some reason they seemed less agitated. Their moans and
groans had subsided somewhat; Cade guessed it was because
he and the other two trapped men hadn't shown their faces
for a couple of hours.

While lying face down on the roof Cade grasped the rain
gutter firmly and gave it a wiggle. There was a little give, but it
would most likely hold his weight without tearing off of the
house while he lowered himself to the ground.

Cade waited until the zombies on the porch were facing
away from him before he committed and rolled off into
space. The gutters flexed but held fast. The only noise, a

112

muffled rattle from the rifle, failed to reach the zombies' ears. Cade held his breath and gradually lowered his one hundred eighty pound frame to full extension, let go, and dropped the remaining eight feet to the ground. He absorbed the impact with his knees; the dull thud from his weight meeting the soft bark dust was masked by a gust of warm wind smelling of carrion and earth.

Cade sat nestled between two cat piss smelling shrubs, alone and exposed, fighting the impulse to break and run. Doing so would have been disastrous. Two heartbeats after landing in the bushes a bloated creature ambled by, its chalky legs close enough to touch; the thing's bloody shredded feet slapped a rhythm on the cement walk. He contemplated burying the dagger in its brain but grudgingly resisted the urge.

Cade knew that he would have to be methodical and patient if he was going to slip by without prompting a chain of moaning zombies. He had a lot of ground to cover, and hoped that the undead weren't as thick the farther he got into town.

Cade thought about Brook and Raven, who were his first priority. A selfish notion wormed its way into his brain, urging him to abandon the strangers and go on solo. Cade shook off the thought. He had given his word to Daymon, and he would return to get them. Dad always said a man is only as good as his word. It was sage advice that he took to heart.

With the ten inch Gerber dagger in his left hand and the two foot long machete in his right he steeled himself, ready to run the gauntlet. Three walkers patrolled the ground between the house and the presumed safety of the tree line. There was no way to know what lay beyond. The trees were a natural buffer separating the house from the road. Since the NVGs were stowed on the bike, and the bike was surrounded by undead, he would have to navigate the foreign surroundings by moonlight.

Picking his order of battle came naturally. Cade slowly stood up and calmly padded in the direction of the first zombie. Judging by her garb, in life the middle-aged woman had been a waitress. A bloody uniform hung in strands from her withered body, a greasy apron still encircling her waist and riding above her short skirt. The nametag pinned near her left breast confirmed his suspicion. Her name was *Vera*. A towering blue beehive hair-do bobbed with every footstep and it was gradually losing its fight with gravity. Vera's dead eyes noticed the meat coming towards her. Thin bloodless lips curled over yellowed teeth as her mouth parted.

Cade noted the bite marks all over her exposed skin. Vera had been someone's blue plate special; chunks of meat were missing from both sides of her thin neck. On the ends of both arms, strands of flesh and tendon dangled where Vera's fingers used to be. Before a sound escaped, Cade plunged the matte black Gerber deep into her eye socket. It was a successful silent kill, the dry brown grass serving to muffle the hollow sound her husk made striking the ground.

Daymon and Hosford looked on from the upstairs window as Cade took the war to the dead.

The next walker had a badly mangled leg, its white femur bone fully exposed. The lack of muscle rendered the appendage virtually useless. Cade stepped over Vera and shadowed the limping zombie. The thing was half a head taller than he, but that would be to Cade's advantage. Focusing on the bone directly below the ear, the operator cocked his arm and swept the machete in a deadly arc.

Daymon kept a very sharp edge on the blade. The zombie's head separated from its body cleanly. Cade watched it spin through the air like an extra point kick, bounce two times on the lawn and come to a stop, upright against the mailbox post. Inexplicably the eyes longingly tracked him as he crossed its path.

The only obstacle between Cade and the road was the pudgy, flesh-eating teenager tromping through the colorful flowers planted along the walk. Like a dark wraith, Cade approached from behind and slipped his dagger effortlessly between the first and second vertebrae into the creature's brain. He wrapped an arm around the thing's waist holding onto the limp body before gently placing it on the ground. He wiped the Gerber dagger on the ghoul's *Beastie Boys* tee shirt and continued moving.

Cade forced his frame into the relatively thin cover of the tall row of hedges lining the front of the property and took a moment to catch his breath and assess his situation. For now he remained undetected, but the three ghouls that he had dispatched were promptly replaced by more of them, ambling from the back of the farmhouse.

In the open window, illuminated by pale moonlight, he could make out the portly lawyer's silhouette. He wasn't certain, but it appeared the *Chris Farley* lookalike was flashing him the thumbs up.

Chapter 20
Outbreak - Day 5
Schriever AFB
Colorado Springs, Colorado

Brook opened the door to the metal Quonset hut she
would be calling home for the unforeseeable future. Her eyes
were still transitioning from the brutal Colorado sunshine to
the mineshaft-like gloom inside the prefab metal dwelling
when she was attacked around the waist by her diminutive
eleven-year-old Raven.

"Mommy!" the pigtailed girl squealed in delight. Brook
scooped her up and squeezed her tight. It had been many
hours since mother and daughter had been together.

"Wow, you look like *shit*," said Annie Desantos, who lay
sprawled uncomfortably on top of a lumpy well-used
mattress, nine-plus months of pregnant woman belly
gloriously on display.

"Says the beached whale to her friend," Brook replied,
tight-lipped, suppressing a grin. Both women laughed after
the exchange.

Annie's daughters Serena and Sierra came running with
sunburned Dmitri in tow.

"Have you heard anything about *our* Dad?" the twins
inquired in unison.

"And what about *my* Dad?" Raven asked, her brown eyes relaying anxiety and sadness. It was enough to make Brook want to cry. She held back the tears and looked away, covertly wiping her eyes before looking back at the kids.

"Well girls," after putting on her positive face, Brook bent at the waist so she was speaking directly to Serena and Sierra at their level, "I haven't been told anything yet, about your Daddy or Raven's, but I'm sure we'll hear inbound helicopters any time now." Then the girls received a comforting hug from Auntie Brook.

Raven continued to cling on to her mom, trying to acquire her undivided attention.

"Raven, we've already talked about this - but we can revisit it if you wish?"

Nodding her head in the affirmative, Raven's gaze bored into her mom's until Brook acquiesced and reassured her anew.

"If I know your Dad as well as I think I do, he's looting a Toys "R" Us as we speak so that he has something special to give you when we *are* reunited." Brook made sure to end the conversation on a positive note, because Raven had a tendency to only remember the last words spoken. Brook chalked it up to her daughter being eleven. "Your Dad is on his way as we speak and I wouldn't be surprised if he returns with Mike in the same helicopter."

Serena and Sierra beamed at the mention of their Dad, and jumped up and down in a display of giddy anticipation.

Brook gave the kids her best comforting smile and told them to go play. Then she turned her attention to Annie. Brook's voice took on a more serious tone as her nurse's training kicked in. "Have you had any contractions?"

"No, not today, I did have a spell of Braxton Hicks before the outbreak. Thank God the little guy didn't come before the outbreak happened. I would've probably been at the hospital fighting those things off with a scalpel in one hand and a newborn in the other... thank God for small miracles."

"Refresh my memory, when was your due date?"

"One week ago." Annie arched her eyebrows.

"*Shit.* Pardon my French, kids."

"No prob Mom," Raven smartly retorted.

Brook asked Annie, "Do they have any obstetrics-related
medical equipment here?"

"Nope, the doctor said that the infirmary is only for
inpatient stuff, small emergencies. Even though this is a big
base, everybody went to the Air Force Academy north of
Colorado Springs to have their needs met."

"That's not gonna fly," Brook said, a trace of concern
creeping into her "work" voice.

"I don't think we need to worry anyway. The girls were
delivered without complications." Annie's glass was usually
half full no matter the situation.

"All it takes is one little rupture on the uterine wall and
you could bleed out. Besides, this is a boy we're talking about
and you know as well as I do how much of a pain in the ass
our boys can be," Brook said, winking at Annie.

"What can we do? I sure as *hell* don't want to go to a
hospital... not with those things walking around."

"I'm going to go and talk to Colonel Shrill and try to get
us the basics, at the least. If I have to, I will go off the
reservation on this one." Brook gave Annie a pat on her leg,
gently rubbed the boy in her belly and made direct eye contact
with her, communicating what couldn't be said aloud with the
kids near. "Keep an eye on Raven until I return...?"

Annie nodded, fully aware that Brook might be away for a
while.

Chapter 21
Outbreak - Day 5
Hampton's Mercantile
Stanley, Idaho

Dan was pulling himself up off of the cold cement floor when he first detected the distant engine. Champ kept his tail swishing steadily back and forth, the only sound in the pitch black store room.

Dan knew better than to initiate a skirmish he probably wouldn't win. Always an honest man, especially to himself, he knew full well his commando days were behind him. The idea was to lay low and let whoever was driving the vehicle go on their merry way.

It wasn't Dan's day in more ways than he yet knew. Squeaking brakes announced that the vehicle was stopping directly in front of the store.

A door opened and heavy metal music escaped into the street. It sounded to Dan like only one person had exited the vehicle, and then quickly slammed the door shut, leaving the engine running. The door to the store opened noisily. This time Dan anticipated the jangling bell that had caused him to jump minutes ago. Determined footsteps pounded up and down the aisles. Cooler doors opened and closed.

"*Greedy bastards*, motherfuckers left not one can of beer."

The male voice was of the nasally variety. Dan had heard it
before, but couldn't quite place whose it was.

"Everyone fucks me over. The end of the world, and *I still
get no respect*," the man whined.

The absence of other voices and the fact that the grown
man was nearly crying out loud, told Dan that *Rodney
Dangerfield* was probably the only other person in the store.
There may be others in the vehicle. Patience Dan, patience, he thought,
while he listened to the temper tantrum.

The voice abruptly ceased, replaced by the steady swishing
of the old dog's tail.

"Who's back there?"

Whoever it was, he sounded like a little kid, alone in the
house and trying to summon up enough courage to enter a
dark room.

"*There are three of us and we got guns. Show yourself... now and no
one gets hurt.*"

The next thing the disembodied whiny voice said both
baffled and amused Dan.

"*Come out, come out*, wherever you are, I ain't afraid of no
zombies."

The man was obviously deranged. Dan remained silent,
pistol firmly gripped in hand with the flashlight ready to blind
the interloper or interlopers, whichever the case may be.

Leading with the barrel of his sawed-off shotgun, the man
parted the plastic barrier and surveyed the room. A beam of
light swept the floor, found Bo's body and wavered for a
second before it settled on Champ, illuminating the old dog
and his noisemaking tail.

Placing the shotgun to his shoulder, the skinny man aimed
at Champ. "Some fucking watchdog you are."

"*Woof.*" Dan's best big dog imitation elicited a yelp from
the skinny silhouette framed in the doorway. Dan finally
placed the voice; he couldn't let the good old dog die at the
hands of Mikey Connell, the town's resident Jeffrey Dahmer

in training. The piece of work had been known to mutilate animals, dead ones at first. Later he graduated to his neighbor's live cats and dogs. Every time someone's best friend went missing, Sheriff Blanda knew whom to talk to first.

A .45 caliber slug is about as big as they come. The hole it made when it struck the side of Mikey's ribcage wasn't evident, but the gaping exit wound was a sight to behold.

Little Mikey Connell went into shock before his shotgun clattered to the ground next to his twitching body.

Dan didn't even have a chance to chastise PETA's most wanted before a frothy last breath bubbled between his bloody lips.

Chapter 22
Outbreak - Day 6
Centers for Disease Control
Atlanta Georgia

Doctor Sylvester Fuentes was compact and wiry, so much
so that his white lab coat actually wore him. A pair of reading
glasses were perpetually perched on his forehead and a
second pair dangled from a leash around his neck; in a
drawer, next to his last half eaten bag of Oreos was a third
identical pair - *just in case*. He was a brilliant microbiologist;
forgetfulness and a penchant for inhaling Oreo cookies were
his main flaws. Forgetting wasn't a dangerous thing for a
scientist, every step of an experiment had to be documented
and Sylvester was always in the act of scribbling down his
every thought. Sylvester's life had become one continuous
sticky note.

He popped an Oreo into his mouth and savored the dark
chocolate as it melted in his mouth down to the sweet layer of
white frosting. Currently he was hunched over, face pressed
firmly to the eyepiece of the powerful electron microscope.

"Come on... stay dead... *Damn.*" The doctor, normally
calm, cool and collected pounded his fist on the stainless
counter. *"This beastie cannot be tricked."*

The Yin to his Yang, Jessica Hanson always had a way of putting things into perspective. "At least... Doctor. We've got all the time in the world to sort this mess out. Unfortunately we *do not* have all of the Oreos in the world."

Fuentes glared at his cohort for mentioning the impending emergency, and put his face back onto the scope.

The cells in the dish were from a biopsy he performed on himself. Every time he introduced bodily fluid from an infected cadaver into the dish, so far without exception, Omega immediately attacked and began to assimilate the living cells.

Fuentes' latest attempt was to see if the unaffected cells extracted from around his thalamus would protect other healthy tissue. If he could replicate the chemical reaction that spared the thalamus in the infected, then it would be the first step towards engineering a vaccine that might be able to fool the immune system into thinking all of the body's cells were of the same type surrounding the thalamus.

It was a billion to one longshot with seven billion people's lives at stake. Fuentes was no optimist when it came to this nasty bug. This was mankind's extinction level event and from the outbreak's start, he had tried to warn anyone that would listen.

The outbreak had started on a Saturday and almost immediately the President declared martial law, ordering everyone to stay home. The facility was virtually abandoned; most of the staff went home to see if their family was safe and secure. Fuentes didn't have the heart to try to keep them here; nor did he have the authority.

Now it was only the two of them: Doctor Sylvester Fuentes and the civilian Scientist Jessica Hanson. All communication was down, even the director of Health and Human Services hadn't contacted them in two days and the President was at a secure and undisclosed location - or so they said before the world outside went silent. The many civilian

contractors working at the Center for Disease Control failed
to return on Monday.

To make any progress Fuentes needed to have more
scientists working with him. His goal was to try and
understand how the Omega virus worked. It was very simple
how it killed the host, but how it enabled the host to
reanimate and restart certain functions in the body was the
mystery. Upon introduction into the host, the virus began
spreading throughout the body and replicating exponentially.
If the patient didn't die from a major wound, trauma or rapid
blood loss, then the virus would work its way through the
body and shut down most of the organs necessary for "life"
as it is universally defined. For some unknown reason Omega
left the part of the brain related to basic function unharmed.
The thalamus, which is the relay station of the brain, was
mostly unaffected. It processes visual, auditory, and
somatosensory systems. Most of these sensory signals still
traveled through the infected body, with the exception of the
somatosensory which relays signals from skin and internal
organs. Most importantly, also located in the thalamus is the
part of the brain that enables motor control, allowing the
dead to walk. The synapses were muddied - so to speak - and
didn't fire like normal living humans. Unfortunately the
remaining function was enough to keep the infected moving
and hunting for food.

So far, in the big scheme of things, Doctor Fuentes didn't
know jack shit. To fully engineer an agent to block and or
fight off Omega was the logical first step. The big issue was
the fact that once infected, the victim had only seconds
before the virus began replicating in the bloodstream. Once in
the bloodstream it was only a matter of time before it reached
the brain. Fuentes theorized that his only chance for success
was to develop a proactive immunization and not an after-
the-fact antidote. It was a known fact that most people, once
infected, were past the point of no return anyway.

The first carrier detained in Washington D.C. was a Chinese male, mid thirties, who carried no form of identification. Because all of the airports in the states now used powerful facial recognition software to screen all passengers, the man was quickly identified. It was determined that he entered into the U.S. from China on the day before the outbreak, posing as a diplomatic courier. The man was no government pencil pusher, he had the physique of an athlete and scars that one only obtained from being gunshot. The doctor had a hunch that the Alpha was Chinese Special Forces or a member of the MSS Chinese intelligence services.

Curiously enough the man had two needle marks on his left arm, and Fuentes strongly doubted that the infected Alpha specimen was a junkie.

"*Doctor*, something's agitating the walkers outside." The waifish woman delivering the warning was a longtime member of the civilian staff at the Center for Disease Control. Jessica Hanson hadn't yet decided if it was a good or a bad thing but it happened to be her weekend rotation at the lab. Before Omega, the entire staff of the Level Four Containment wing had been working diligently trying to figure out the origin of a new strain of the hemorrhagic fever that had popped up recently in the Congo. It had already been knocked down, but during the week their focus was on preempting another flare up. That was before the vicious Omega virus was introduced into the population of the United States.

Doctor Hanson continued to monitor the action outside. The ghouls were looking skyward, fixated on something in the sky, out of the camera's range.

Probably a flock of migrating birds was Hanson's first thought. The woman in the lab coat swiped the touch screen. The picture changed and started to cycle through all of the different live views streaming from the outside cameras. Scores of walking dead dominated nearly every camera shot.

Nothing out of the ordinary presented itself, until the rooftop
image flashed on the screen.

"*That's* what the infected were interested in... and I *assumed*
they were salivating over some birds."

Doctor Fuentes sounded very impatient. "Don't hold
back... what *were* they watching? Enlighten me *please*."

"There's a Black Hawk helicopter on the roof."

"Are you sure it's not a news chopper?" Fuentes asked,
hoping that it was. After all he could handle a news crew. A
group of gung ho soldiers was a whole 'nother can of worms.

"No sir. I've had the displeasure of being a passenger on a
helicopter like the one upstairs. I've never been so sick. Those
pilots think anyone can handle high g-forces." Jessica
shuddered, remembering how much time her face had spent
buried in the air sickness bag. If she remembered right, the
maneuvers got more extreme when it was apparent to all on
board that she was a "puker" as they had so fondly labeled
her.

Fuentes looked up from the experiment he was
performing on the squirming cadaver strapped to the stainless
steel table. "Are there any markings on the chopper: Air
Force, Army, Marines...?"

The image from the rooftop dome was a little grainy and
in the low light Hanson couldn't read the markings. "No,
Doctor." In her best spooky voice, "*It's a black helicopter.*"

Doctor Fuentes was known as the resident conspiracy
theorist and he always caught hell for it.

Matter-of-factly, as if he were in his own home, the doctor
said, "We had better tidy up if we are going to be receiving
guests."

Optimistically Hanson added, "On the bright side. It's
good to know there are still people alive out there, even if
they are from some government organization."

Always the consummate smart ass, Fuentes chimed in,
"And I thought that I had filed my *last* tax return."

"That's not even remotely funny. Millions, maybe even billions are dead and they are the lucky ones. Unfortunately a huge percentage of the population is like him, dead and walking around hunting for any living thing to eat." She nodded her head at the zombie writhing on the table. "Doctor, don't you forget for one second... we still have family somewhere out there."

Jessica Hanson was no idiot; days ago both she and the good doctor had come to the same conclusion. They probably had a better chance of being struck by lightning than finding their loved ones still breathing.

"Doctor Hanson, please cycle the cameras to the south stairwell." The image of the helicopter was replaced by the south stairwell view; three men clad in combat gear, brandishing stubby machineguns now filled the screen. Even in the dim cone of light emitted from the emergency lamps, there was no mistaking the men with guns for the undead.

"Open the door, *they're heeere*," Doctor Fuentes said, mimicking the little girl from the horror movie Poltergeist.

Chapter 23
Outbreak - Day 5
Schriever AFB
Colorado Springs, Colorado

The man Brook sought was nowhere to be found. The few
Airmen that gave her the time of day instantly clammed up
and sent her packing at the mere mention of Colonel Shrill.
She knew, from being the wife of a soldier, when she was
being sent up the chain of command.

Only an hour into her search, she found herself standing
in the empty office belonging to the woman in charge of
every satellite in the U.S. arsenal. Cold air buffeted Brook,
causing goose bumps to form on her exposed skin. The heat
outside was pretty intense so she didn't mind the ten minute
wait standing directly in front of the government issue air
conditioner. It was apparent that this small space belonged to
a career Air force Officer. All kinds of plaques and certificates
graced the institutional brown walls.

Brook had almost always been the smallest woman in the
room, which changed the moment Major Freda Nash walked
into the icebox of an office. Brook's jaw nearly hit the floor
when the woman, a full inch shorter than she, strode
purposefully in, looked her in the eye and sat down behind
the clunky metal desk without saying a word.

The Major didn't speak and since Brook didn't want to start her unannounced meeting off on the wrong foot, an uneasy silence ensued. It was like two Chihuahuas caught in a staring contest.

Against her better judgment, Brook spoke first. Too much was at stake. "With all due respect, Major..." Brook attempted to read the nameplate cloaked by the clutter on the desk top. "Nash, did I read that right?"

"That is correct," the intense Major replied, "and you are?"

"Brooklyn Grayson, my husband Cade was very active in the Special Operations community until a year and some months ago - but he's not the reason I need to speak to you."

Before she could continue, Major Nash interrupted. The diminutive officer spoke in rapid-fire sentences, barely stopping to breathe or let Brook get a word in edgewise.

"I knew the name sounded familiar. Your husband did good things for this country. His name was spoken in high regard, albeit in hushed tones, in the halls of Congress and the Pentagon. In case you weren't aware, your man, either directly or indirectly, was involved in killing or capturing a good chunk of the deck in Iraq. I know for a fact he was there when the Aces were taken out."

Brook hadn't been privy to the classified stuff. She had no idea that the Ace of Hearts and the Ace of Clubs Major Nash referred to were in fact, Saddam's sons, Uday and Qusay Hussein. Cade would never tell a soul, but he had actually put a bullet in Uday's brain to make his brother talk. Uday was on his way to paradise anyway. Qusay spilled his guts but unfortunately the impromptu interrogation didn't lead to Saddam's capture. Before anyone left the destroyed compound, Qusay was allowed to bleed out, alone on the dirty living room floor on the second story of his "safe" house.

Finally the Major paused long enough for Brook to continue on and plead her case. "I was actually trying to get an audience with Colonel Shrill and that's how I come to be standing in front of you. A wife of a soldier in the "Unit" is here on the base and she is very close to going into labor... in fact she's days past her due date. To make a short story long..." Brook's attempt to break the ice with a little play on words was totally lost on - or intentionally ignored by the hyper major.

"Continue, I'm listening."

"Annie Desantos is the wife of Mike Desantos. He operated out of Fort Bragg..."

Once again Major Nash butted in before Brook could finish her thought.

"I never would have fathomed that Bragg would cease to exist. That place was supposed to be impenetrable. Short of a suitcase nuke, nothing could touch it. Especially like that Fort Hood crap. To answer your question, yes, I know Mike. As a matter of fact we have been assisting him on his current mission... but that is *need to know information*."

Brook's eyes widened. "Mike is on an Op then? *That is great news*. I'll let Annie know as soon as I see her; it sure will lessen her stress level." Brook tried to speak to the major so that she would follow and hopefully not interrupt again. "I'm a nurse, and I'm going to help the doctor deliver Annie's baby. I need a way to get to Saint Francis Medical. We need the proper equipment to deliver *Mike's* first son safely into the world."

Nash answered, as if Brook were a neighbor asking for a cup of sugar and it was no big deal. "Saint Francis has..." Nash caught herself mid sentence, "had a top notch neonatal center. If the place hasn't been overrun by the dead then you are good to go. At any rate, anything you need, Mrs. Grayson. I will personally make the necessary calls."

"Thank you, Major." Brook was stunned. After their icy introduction, she had no reason to expect this positive of an outcome, but feared that she was going to have to fight someone for assistance or at the least, twist some paper pusher's arm. It was a blessing that she had found a woman who saw things eye to eye with her - *literally*.

The door had barely closed behind Brook when Freda Nash picked up the phone and punched in a number.

Chapter 24
Outbreak - Day 6
Centers for Disease Control
Atlanta, Georgia

As soon as the mechanical sounds from the door ceased, Clark moved closer and rapped twice with his free hand, silenced weapon at the ready.

"Come in." The disembodied voice sounded from the far side of the thick door and echoed around in the stairwell.

Clark took out his collapsible mini mirror, extended it halfway and used it to inspect what awaited beyond the door. Dressed in white lab coats, a man and a woman stood a few feet from the entrance, waiting to greet the intruders.

A man's voice said, "It's safe to come in, we've been waiting for the cavalry to come calling."

The door was easier to open than it looked. Desantos estimated that it weighed at least a ton. "Back away and keep your hands where I can see them." The doctors complied while Desantos kept his weapon trained on them. In a blur of motion the other five operators fanned out and cleared the room.

"*Don't go near the patient on the table*," the woman shouted.

"We know full well what your *patient* is capable of. If I get any closer to that monster I promise you it won't be to make friends." Clark had long ago stopped feeling empathy for who the undead used to be.

"*Take it easy*... this one has to be studied. You're looking at the Alpha carrier." To protect it, the doctor stepped between the soldiers and the undead creature.

Clark bristled, "No better reason than that to put two in its brain."

"*Stand down soldier.*" Desantos turned his attention to the scientists and started asking questions. "Tell me doctor, how did he get infected?"

"Judging by the track marks on his arm, he injected himself with the virus. I believe someone with a security clearance much higher than mine is calling it the Omega virus... or something like that. At any rate, it is aptly named. We may be looking at the end of the human race as we know it."

"How did the infection spread from Alpha to the population? Does anyone know what happened?"

"We were only privy to the police report. Alpha infected two people at an Italian restaurant. They both received minor bites..."

Desantos interrupted, "Why weren't they rounded up and quarantined?"

"That's the sixty-four thousand dollar question. The first two refused to be taken to the hospital. They didn't even care that he could be carrying hepatitis and might have given it to them. There was apparently a little bit of a language barrier, which may be why they refused."

"Illegals?" Lopez asked.

Fuentes took a swig from his bottled water and replaced it on the stainless steel autopsy table. The alpha specimen intently eyed his every move. "We will never know. They left as soon as they were bandaged up, a little boy and his mom."

"So they took the bug with them." Desantos processed the information for a second. "What happened next?"

"Well... one of the waiters held him down until the
ambulance crew arrived. After a little more of a struggle -
during which time the ambulance drivers were infected - they
strapped him to a gurney and transported him to Bethesda."
Fuentes stopped at that, he had a feeling that the General
knew the rest of the story.

Mike rubbed his tired eyes. "I heard that the hospital was
like a war zone. Seven SF operators died getting this monster
out of there. That was where the shit really hit the fan. It was
the beginning of the end. Washington D.C. was teeming with
tens of thousands of deranged flesh-eaters before nightfall."
Mike stared at a spot on the floor. "I saw Washington from
the air with my own eyes... the city was on fire. It all still feels
like it never happened... like I'll wake up any second and find
the world back to normal."

Fuentes waited until he was certain the General was
finished and then continued his account. "I was here when
the soldiers, led by a Captain - I think he said his name was
Gaines - delivered the Alpha. We received the police report
and a top secret folder containing instructions from President
Odero to drop everything, study this one and find a way to
stop the spread of Omega. The Captain had me destroy both
of the documents as soon as Hanson and I had finished
reading them. I've never even seen a burn bag before - pretty
effective."

Desantos was done reflecting on the past. He issued
orders for his men to collect any and all documents pertaining
to the outbreak. "Doctor Fuentes, will you please help my
men properly prepare the specimen for transport?"

"Yes sir." Fuentes fetched the straightjacket and hood the
Alpha was wrapped in when it arrived.

"Hanson, please help my men collect all of the flash drives
and remove the hard drives from the computers."

"Consider it done." Hanson hurriedly peeled off her lab coat and immediately went to work. It was apparent that she was eager to get some fresh air.

***

Lopez held onto the ghoul's restless legs, he couldn't stand to watch as the thick burlap sack moved and undulated on Maddox's shoulder. He and Maddox lugged the Alpha specimen up the seemingly never-ending flights of stairs. Lopez was a very religious man and he found it unsettling to be so close to one of the demons without putting a bullet in its brain.

"It's a shame we can't just cut the bastard's head off. It would be easier to hump up the stairs, that's for sure," Lopez said, as he shifted the moving bag to a different pressure point on his shoulder.

"Hey Doc, have you seen one of these things lose its head? It's eerie how the eyes still follow, even with no body attached." Clark shuddered at the mental image.

"I hate to break it to you, but we need the whole package," Fuentes said, brushing off the initial question. If only Lopez could have seen the experiments they'd conducted on other infected, people they used to work with, as well as walkers they plucked off of the street. The things that he had done in the name of science would haunt him for the rest of his life. *The soldier doesn't know what he was missing*, Fuentes thought, *and his ignorance truly is bliss.*

Desantos issued an order. "Calvin, take point. I'll watch our six. Clark, you and Brent collect Haskell's body when we get to the fourteenth floor."

Clark was honored to carry his fallen team member to the helicopter. He would walk through lava for "Cowboy" and he certainly was glad that he hadn't been ordered to carry the hissing, bagged and gagged monster to the waiting helo.

Chapter 25
Outbreak - Day 5
Stanley, Idaho

Stanley was quiet, way too quiet for Dan's liking. Even if the state fair was going on in Boise, with its draw of games of chance and greasy food, there would be some people out and about at this hour.

Mountainview Boulevard was usually festooned with colorful flags and banners year round, advertising upcoming holidays, bazaars or festivals. Dan hoped that the person strung up alongside the vibrant "Summer Days Classic Car Cruise In" banner wasn't his old friend Sheriff Blanda. The closer he got the tighter the knot in his gut constricted.

Dan stood at the base of the light standard and shed a tear. The man's leather boots, spit shined at all times, were directly at eye level, swaying from each gust of wind that rolled off of the mountains warming flanks. Dan caught fleeting glimpses of his own bearded face reflected in the brilliant hand buffed sheen. Someone, probably the Aryans, had hoisted him off of the ground, tightened a coiled noose around his neck and left the city's only lawman to be eaten by the crows. Dan considered shooting the feeding opportunists but decided that he didn't need the unwanted attention gunfire might bring. If he could talk to the animals, like Doctor Doolittle, he would tell the noisy birds where they could find Mikey Connell's cooling corpse.

Dan had no way to reach the rope to cut his friend down, so he reluctantly left him swinging and trudged up the narrow street towards Lizzie's house. All of the houses on both sides of the side street were still dark inside. *Strange*, no kids watching cartoons and not one lady of the house cooking breakfast at this hour. The pieces of this puzzle were still scattered all over the card table in Dan's mind. He was baffled. A few times he detected shadows flitting by closed drapes, but not one person came out to offer a greeting. Dan was no social gadfly, but neither was he a pariah in Stanley.

As he walked, he found himself deep in thought rehashing the events of the last few days.

He was a little troubled that he felt no remorse about killing the Connell kid. His dad and mom had been nice enough and Dan wondered to himself where they went wrong. It had been more than thirty years since he had killed another human being and he had a feeling Mikey Connell wouldn't be the last; Sheriff Bob Blanda's murderers were the perfect candidates.

The years of outdoor activities had left the man a minor case of arthritis that made it necessary to stop every so often. Elizabeth Paxton's house was one block ahead on the left. The Victorian era painted lady shone in the morning sunshine. The old three story house was painted in yellows and oranges with dashes of purple thrown in. It truly matched Lizzie's personality.

Dan pinned his hopes on her being up and willing to talk to him. God was he feeling lonely, and after what he had been through at Bo's store he really needed to talk to another human being.

Gosh darn steps. Three flights meandered up from the street to Lizzie's purple door. If knees could talk, Dan's would have screamed, "No way." Finally standing in front of the door, Dan wiped the perspiration from his face. After taking a much needed breather, he stood and listened for movement inside the home. *Nothing.* Dan rapped on the door three times. Given the stillness of the town the knocks sounded like he used a baseball bat. There was still no movement from inside.

He wrestled with the decision to turn around and go home or test the door and see if it was locked. The latter won out.

"Elizabeth, it's me, Dan..." in mid sentence the sickly sweet odor hit him full in the face. He flashed back to Nam and the smells and sights he could never purge from the deepest recesses of his mind. Dan silently vowed to himself that when the day was done he was going to call the VA hospital in Boise and see if he could have his head examined - so to speak.

Crossing the threshold into the parlor of Lizzie's home was the hardest thing he had done in years. Fully afraid of what he was going to find, he forced his legs to propel him deeper inside the dimly lit residence.

Dan knew the layout of the house from previous visits. He went directly to his lady friend's bedroom. The disgusting odor intensified the closer he got.

Hundreds of loudly buzzing houseflies ambushed Dan when he set foot in the bedroom. His worst fear was realized: Elizabeth Paxton's corpse was the source of the throat constricting stench. Lizzie was dressed in her Sunday best, an empty bottle of pain pills sitting on the bureau next to a half empty glass of water. There was no evidence of foul play, but what really troubled Dan was the absence of a suicide note. *Why in the hell would the old gal want to go out like that?*

Dan was trying to make sense out of it all when he noticed the rifled through Idaho Statesman newspaper. From where he was standing he thought the headline read, *"Dead Walk."* *Impossible*, his eyes had to be playing tricks on him. Dan worked his way around the bed and fetched the newspaper and found he had, in fact, read it correctly. Even more troubling, the paper was dated days ago, not April 1.

Sitting down, he read and reread the article. Dan could only fathom the editor of the Statesman allowing something this outlandish to be front page news, as a prank maybe, but only on April Fool's day or Halloween.

The remote control for Lizzie's Zenith sat atop the comforter which was tightly wrapped around her bloated legs. Dan fanned away the flies and grabbed the remote, intent on seeing what had happened that was so catastrophic which warranted having all of the passenger jets grounded. Dan pressed the power button. *Nothing.* It finally dawned on him that he hadn't seen any lights on in town, interior or porch. He had assumed that Bo's store was without power because of the foul play. Dan didn't profess to be a detective, but he didn't often miss details like these.

Dan turned his head and craned his neck in the direction of the main drag that cut through town. He noticed the distinctive sound of Harley Davidsons; the loudly throbbing motorcycles approached from the west. Dan parted the yellowed lace curtains and took in the spectacle passing by a block away.

Bikes of all types careened through town, followed by dozens of civilian SUVs, mostly Suburbans, Cadillac Escalades and Hummers.

Soon the air was filled with hoots and hollers. Rebel yells, cat calls and war cries sounded from the passing procession of black leather and gleaming chrome.

United States military vehicles brought up the rear of the convoy. The people manning the turret mounted armament on the passing Humvees looked nothing like soldiers. An M1 Abrams main battle tank played caboose for the Mad Max parade. It lurched along, slowing down and speeding up like a drunken sailor on liberty. The thing that made the scene all the more maddening was the black and red Nazi flags flying from many of the vehicles - including the military hardware.

Revulsion washed over Dan followed by a searing white
hot rage that invaded his every cell. It felt like he was in the
midst of a Twilight Zone episode and he knew Rod Serling
wasn't going to bail him out of the surreal nightmare.

Chapter 26
Outbreak - Day 6
Hanna, Utah

Cade paused between the hedgerows listening for any movement. Satisfied all was clear, he stepped out of the foliage and dashed across the two lane road, using every shadow for cover.

Before venturing out of the farmhouse, Cade had noticed the small cottage from the upstairs window. All of the curtains facing the street were drawn tight. There was no sound or obvious movement coming from within, so Cade worked his way around back, on guard for random walkers lurking in the dark. Nothing was stirring here and so far the block and a half that he had already covered had been zombie free. It seemed too good to be true. Cade was left waiting for the other shoe to drop.

He needed to find an RV or similar vehicle, and it had to be tall enough so the two men could get on top without the walkers making a meal of them.

Cade waited in the shadows for a heartbeat, then he one eyed it around the corner. There was only an old beat up Volvo station wagon in the drive, and it wasn't what he was looking for. He side stepped up the drive with his back against the wall, dagger in one hand, the machete in the other. Cade went around the garage and stole a look in the dusty window; the place was empty, nothing but shadows and cobwebs inside, so he moved on.

Cade heard shuffling and scraping coming from the front of the house, and melted into the dark, between two thorny bushes, adjacent to the car.

When the nosy walker reached the top of the drive it stopped, head lolling back and forth, and stayed in one place for a moment. Cade wondered if the thing was aware of his presence. As far as he knew he hadn't made a sound. Mysteriously, the monster staggered in his direction. A shaft of moonlight illuminated the creature's face revealing two empty eye sockets. Not only were the eyes gone, but so were both ears and some of its fingers. It was pretty ripe and probably was one of the first to be infected days ago. The thing stopped two feet from where Cade knelt and appeared to be looking directly at him.

Cade felt the first tingle of adrenaline caress his brain and surge into his extremities. He had a growing suspicion that somehow the zombie's other senses remained intact - maybe even enhanced. *It knows I'm here.* Cade knew that if push came to shove, he could hack its head off and be on his way, but with noise discipline being high on the list he held back.There was no telling how many more were nearby, and he sure as hell didn't want to be pursued by a pack of the things.

Patience, Cade, he admonished himself.

The ghoul spent five minutes standing still as a statue, and then shambled between Cade and the car. *He must have remembered this place from when he was still alive*, Cade thought.

Strangely, as if this whole area was memorized or ingrained into some deep abyss of its memory, the eyeless walker abruptly turned left and reached for the door. The nubs that used to be fingers couldn't find purchase; they only left a slimy sheen on the door knob.

Cade watched the struggle taking place inches from his head. It took all of the patience that he could summon to remain still while marinating in the rotten stench.

After fumbling with the handle and getting nowhere, the corpse abruptly turned away and wobbled around the back side of the house.

It was the perfect opportunity to beat feet in the other direction, and Cade took advantage. Once he was away from the small cottage and the walker, he continued along the street. There were no streetlights and the moon hid behind clouds, leaving everything cloaked in darkness.

Cade estimated he had travelled roughly three-fourths of mile from where he had started. No joy, it appeared that everyone had left town in their RVs. He was about to settle for the first SUV or big truck he came across and improvise from there, when lo and behold, wedged between a ranch style house and a chain-link fence, he spotted a medium-sized motor home. The big white hulk was probably a 1960s model and appeared to have been sitting for some time. A thin layer of mottled green mold spackled its boxy exterior from the roof on down to the under-inflated tires.

***

In the hour since Cade left, the creatures had been successful, by sheer numbers alone, in shifting the furniture blockage.

"If that thing fails... I'm feeding you to them first," Daymon yelled at the top of his lungs. He wanted to make sure that Hoss heard him. After being under full assault for hours by the undead house party downstairs, his ears were beginning to ring; adding to it was the incessant braying of the motor mouth lawyer. *This dude should bill by the word*, Daymon thought, *not by the hour*.

"I had a *feeling* that G.I. Joe was going to leave us here." Hoss's voice wavered; it seemed that he was on the verge of panicking.

Daymon couldn't find a shred of sympathy for his cell
mate. The fat fuck had led the horde directly to the house and
he was going to pay.

Hoss yelled from the bedroom, "I could use a hand in
here."

It took both men to move the antique armoire, the heavy
piece leaving deep gouges in the hardwood floors. After
pushing it through the doorway and severely damaging both
sides of the jamb, they sent it tumbling below. Almost
everything upstairs that wasn't nailed down now teetered
precariously on the zombie dam.

Daymon sat on the floor, hoping the obstacle would do
the job while he cursed himself for stopping at the house to
rest in the first place. *If I ever get out of here, I'm going to make
Hoss wish he had never crossed paths with me,* he thought, as he
tried to ignore the big man's labored breathing.

SHAWN CHESSER

Chapter 27
Outbreak - Day 6
Hanna, Utah

Cade held in place for a few minutes observing his surroundings before sprinting to the Winnebago. Pressing his back to the skin of the RV he reached for the door handle, which happened to be unlocked.

Once inside, the only smell to assail his nostrils was that of your garden variety mold and mildew. The interior was as dirty as the outside: food wrappers, beer cans and articles of clothing, both men's and women's, were strewn about. It appeared someone had been using the vehicle for their "play" house.

Cade planted himself in the driver's seat and scanned the instruments; they looked no different than the ones found in any U-Haul he had ever driven. He had a choice to make: It would take him a couple of minutes to hotwire the vehicle or he could search for the keys, which would only take a few seconds. Cade chose the latter, because when running from zombies, every extra second counts.

His first inclination was to check the glove box. It was empty save for some maps, an ice scraper and miscellaneous paperwork, but no keys.

It was a hunch, he'd seen it on television and the movies a hundred times, there was no way that they were going to

145

actually be there, but he was compelled to look anyway. The
vinyl sun visor on the driver's side was stuck in the up
position and wouldn't budge. Cade took off the kid gloves
and manhandled it, finally getting it to flip down. Deposited
on Cade's lap, like Manna from heaven, was a fob full of keys.
"I'll be damned," he said out loud. Incredibly, whoever
owned the vehicle was a fan of cliché.

Cade didn't have high expectations for the worn down
Winnebago. He turned the key in the ignition. *The planets must
be in alignment*, he thought. First the keys and now the whining
starter did what it was designed to, and with only a little bit of
complaining. Black smoke billowed from the tailpipe until the
engine decided to turn over. A gunshot-like backfire
beckoned the dead to come and get it. Cade had a visual of a
cowboy cook, banging on a triangle, calling all hands to
dinner.

Cade found he couldn't see a thing through the grimy
windshield; it was obscured with an opaque brown coating of
tree sap, dirt and who knows what. After finding the wiper
control, Cade liberally spritzed the glass with windshield
cleaner. The crumbling wiper blades beating a rhythm,
swishing back and forth reluctantly, only made things worse.

Cade snatched the ice scraper from the glove box and
cautiously left the idling land yacht. With his M4 in hand and
his head on a swivel, he began furiously scraping away at the
glass.

The sun would be making an appearance very soon, the
first rays of light were slowly revealing the details of his
surroundings, and for the first time in many days Cade was
aware of the faint chirping of the early birds.

He was working at cleaning the windshield when the
moaning started. He had already heard the eerie sound a
hundred times, yet it still caused the hair on his neck to stand
at attention.

A number of walkers abruptly appeared, emptying from the open doors of the Handy Pantry food mart a block away. The surging wave of pale walking corpses quickly homed in on the RV.

Cade shouldered the M4 bracketing a female walker in the Trijicon ACOG crosshairs. Her face bore the marks of a violent attack. Waxy skin and purple muscle sloughed from one side of her head, the torn cheek bounced up and down with each lurching step, and the bared orbital bone and mandible caused a permanent half smile.

Cade caressed the trigger, sending the 5.56 hardball downrange. The bullet struck the exposed part of her skull below the eye socket, sending a fan of razor sharp bone and tooth fragments into the trailing walkers. He expended half of the magazine on the first few ghouls, buying him a little more time.

Turning his attention back to the window seemed foolish considering the encroaching mob, but hanging his head out the window and trying to drive the ungainly Winnebago through a throng of undead seemed even more asinine.

He risked five more quick passes with the scraper and jumped back into the driver's seat. Without hesitating, Cade put the RV into gear and mashed the accelerator to the floorboard. The Winnebago lurched forward when the underinflated tires jumped the wheel chocks meant to keep it in place.

Cade kept his foot to the floor and heaved the rig into a sweeping right-hand turn, intent on getting back to the house before sunrise and the cover of darkness was totally lost.

Fifty feet in front of the RV Cade noticed the same ghoul from earlier. He couldn't believe the tenacity of the blind zombie, it was in the middle of the road, head panning side to side, totally oblivious of the speeding motorhome. Rooted in place, the walker met the grill face first. The dual rear tires cleaved the creature in two. The monster's severed lower extremities did a strange looking cartwheel and rolled into the

gutter, while what was left clawed across the asphalt, trailing
blood like an injured animal.

Chapter 28
Outbreak - Day 5
Stanley, Idaho

Dan was at home with death. He had dealt it. He had come face to face with it many times in Vietnam. None of that made it any easier to sit with Lizzie's corpse and wait for darkness to come.

Lizzie had taken her own life, Dan thought. *What could have been so tragic and devastating to make the woman take the cowardly way out?*

The power was out, but the afternoon light was enough for him to read the entire article in the Boise paper one last time. Something clicked, even though there was no mention of the grounding of the entire commercial airline fleet; Dan knew that he had to give credence to the Omega story.

Bang.

It sounded to Dan like the screen door was opening and closing with some help from the wind. Strangely he didn't remember the wind blowing during his walk to the house.

Bang. Bang.

Now it seemed like someone or something was smacking the back door. Dan pulled his Colt from the holster and out of habit pulled back the slide to make sure a round was in the pipe. He skirted the bed and in passing, gave his old friend Lizzie a pat on her cold foot.

Bang.

"All right, all right, *I'm coming - keep your shirt on.*" Dan had no problem talking to himself. As long as he had lived alone, up in the Sawtooth Mountains, he had made a habit of talking to himself. It was his way of conquering the loneliness.

Dan navigated the shadowy dining room, careful to watch where he put his feet.

Bang.

He entered the kitchen and waited a moment for his eyesight to adjust to the bright light streaming in the glass pane. All he could make out was a man's silhouette peering in through the window. He was over six feet tall and nearly filled out the doorway; probably a drunken Nazi biker, Dan theorized.

Bang. Dan put the pistol behind his leg. If the man was high or drunk, he didn't want to make matters worse by openly brandishing a firearm.

Bang.

Dan had never seen a person so determined... yet so out of it at the same time. The guy's skin tone reminded him of those monsters that were featured in the old Boris Karloff movies - he couldn't remember what they were called. *Damn, getting old is for the birds.*

"*Stop, I'm armed and will use deadly force.*" Dan raised his black pistol and aimed it at the crazed man. It didn't deter him; it seemed only to further fuel his rage. The door frame splintered a little more with each blow. *I am not going toe to toe with this yahoo,* Dan told himself. For some reason the famous Revolutionary War quote, "*Don't shoot till you see the whites of their eyes,*" popped into his head the moment he locked eyes with the intruder. Dan noted that the guy's pupils were fixed and the "whites" were yellow and jaundiced. *The lights are on and there's no one home,* he thought, as he summoned the resolve to shoot the seemingly unarmed maniac.

The door blasted from the frame and caromed off the small breakfast table, landing lengthwise partially blocking the doorway. A normal human would try to step over the obstruction - the mindless druggie tried to bull right through it.

The man smelled rotten, worse than Lizzie. Like the tumblers in a lock everything instantly fell together and started making sense. *The Boise Statesman was right,* Dan thought incredulously, *the dead really are walking.*

Dan leveled his weapon point blank at the struggling man's head; the pistol bucked twice in his hand. The Colt's report was thunderous in the confined kitchen, momentarily deafening him.

The abomination collapsed over the splintered door.

The Colt .45 is a very effective man stopper, not much skull was left from the eyebrows up. Dan watched the dead man's brain dribble out in slow motion, clumping in a mound on the black and white checkerboard linoleum.

He prodded the body with the still smoking muzzle and then rolled it over with his free hand. The fact that the unmoving corpse was already ice cold to the touch further confirmed what he had read in the fish wrapper.

His newfound knowledge of how his world had changed around him dictated his next move.

My daddy fought the Nazis, he thought, *and I sure as hell ain't gonna let them repopulate the town I was born and raised in. There has got to be someone, somewhere, upholding the rule of law.*

With Sheriff Blanda swinging in the wind and Lizzie gone for good, there was no reason for Dan to remain in Stanley.

Dan searched the cupboard where Lizzie kept her car keys; he found them after moving around countless bottles of prescription medicines.

Over the course of the ensuing three hours, two more large groups of brigands roared down the main street in the direction of the Aryan's fortress-like compound. For good measure Dan waited until half past two in the morning, with only the two corpses for company. He wanted the thugs to do their usual and get good and shitty before he attempted to sneak past them.

Dan stepped over the shortened corpse, steering clear of brain matter, and warily trudged into the obsidian black night.

***

The garage doors were closed but unlocked. In a city as quiet as Stanley, where everyone knew their neighbor, there was no need to batten down the hatches. The simple fact that the doors remained shut told Dan the old gal's car was still parked inside. The unoiled hinges shrieked in protest when Dan yanked them open. He had his pistol trained on the shadowy interior; the only thing taking up space was the midnight blue Dodge Aries.

The rarely used four door started after a few cranks. Dan maneuvered the car from the cramped garage and let it coast down the driveway to the street.

Before leaving, Dan turned in his seat to look at the charnel house. A very important part of his past had died there. Her name was Elizabeth Eloise Paxton and he would always love her.

With a heavy heart and a lead foot he intended to put Stanley, Idaho behind him forever.

***

Well before he got to the Aryan compound Dan extinguished the headlights, hoping the occupants inside were all passed out or too drunk to notice the darkened car creeping past.

His hopes were dashed when he noticed the one man roadblock. Two fifty-five gallon metal drums with a length of yellow police line tape strung between them served as the only barricade.

Nobody said this lot had any brains.

Dan stopped five feet shy of the barrier; the lone man stood up from a plastic lawn chair and drunkenly sauntered to the driver's side of the car. He looked like your garden variety skinhead, spider webs and skull tattoos adorning every piece of skin that Dan could see. Why they only posted one sentry, when the dead were supposedly walking all over the place, troubled Dan.

"Where are you goin'... and wish no lights?" the man slurred suspiciously. He was obviously three sheets to the wind.

With as many newcomers as Dan witnessed streaming into town, he thought it might be easier to masquerade as one of them than try to explain who he really was, so he tried to bullshit his way past the inebriated guard. "I was in town trying to find another fifth of whisky. The whole world is our liquor store now... right brother?"

"Thish afternoon we went on a raid two towns over - lotsa booshe. Ganz did stash away the besht stuff for himshelf." The skinhead took a step closer to the car, trying to get a better look at Dan. "You wash yourshelf. Someone push shome big holes in Mikey Connell. Hish car was still running when they found him dead thish afternoon. What I'm tryin' to get through that thick head of yours... what'd you shay yer name ish anyway?"

The kid was falling out. Had himself a little too much sauce. Dan pulled the lock blade knife from his belt and covertly flicked it open. "They call me Grady." Dan was winging it and hoped the kid didn't know who he was. "Since Ganz is keeping the high end stuff for himself, you want a nip of this Louis the Thirteenth cognac? I found it in some old broad's closet... after I waxed her ass." He hoped he wasn't pouring it on too thick.

The skinhead instantly perked up. "Thaths the shit, thaths like, three thousand bucks a bottle ishnt it?"

Fish on; the Nazi put his elbows on the door and his face in the open window.

"Give it up old man." The Nazi's breath smelled like cigarettes and stale beer.

Fully expecting a mouthful of fine spirits, he instead
received six inches of tempered steel buried deep into his left
eye. The skinhead died with shit in his pants and shit for
brains.

Dan left the Nazi where he fell, with the knife still stuck in
his head. The wily old mountain man was thirty miles away
before anyone discovered the dead sentry.

Chapter 29
Outbreak - Day 5
Schriever AFB
Colorado Springs, Colorado

Word got around about Annie Desantos' situation. Captain Gaines needed to round up eleven volunteers to go on the mission. Mike Desantos was so loved in the Special Operations community that there were no less than fifty other operators wanting to get on board the two Little Birds.

A chalk of Army Rangers and everything else that they needed for the mission was loaded onto a lone Chinook.

***

Brook finally found Captain Gaines holding a clipboard and fine-tuning his mission plan. She asked if she could accompany him on the mission, even implying that it was what Mike would have wanted.

Gaines saw right through her line of bullshit. "*Under no circumstances*," the Captain told her when she insisted on going. When it was apparent that her pleas weren't going to work, she resorted to telling him he couldn't possibly know which equipment she needed. Captain Gaines took a deep breath and let her have it with both barrels. "Young lady. I will personally bring back the whole goddamned baby factory, anything to bring Mike's future shooter into this world.

Because the Lord knows, the human race is going need all of
the help it can get."

After his egotistical speech, the big man left Brook
standing speechless and walked directly to the flight line to
brief the SOAR aviators.

***

Brook stalled for a few minutes, letting Captain Gaines get
a head start. She knew that he was leading the mission
personally and would have his hands full getting his ducks in a
row.

***

While Brook hid in a shadowy recess beside the Quonset
hut used by the pilots for preflight briefings, a pair of C-130s,
no doubt bringing more troops home from the sandbox,
landed noisily nearby.

A man's booming voice projected through the flimsy
double doors. She was certain that it was Captain Gaines
spouting the same puff up piece that he laid on her minutes
ago. While Brook was fully aware that her friend Annie and
her unborn child's life might well be in jeopardy, the reason
for getting the natal equipment was purely insurance against
any complications. The Captain made it sound, to anyone that
would listen, like they were saving the baby Jesus.

***

The two MH-6 Little Birds sat empty and unattended on
the flight line. Brook knew it wouldn't be feasible for her to
covertly hitch a ride on one of them. There really wasn't
anywhere to hide onboard the smaller helicopters. They were
favored by the Delta boys for insertions. The Night Stalkers,
who piloted the nimble birds, always dropped the operators
right on target.

Brook turned her attention to the monstrous Chinook
sitting idle beyond the smaller choppers. It was identical to
the one that had spirited her and Raven to safety from Fort

Bragg. The slight woman nonchalantly walked between the two smaller helicopters and made a beeline for the transport.

Only one person was working inside the CH-47. He entered and exited the craft several times before Brook finally worked up the nerve to make her move. After sprinting to the side of the helicopter, she drew even with the open side door and poked her head inside. Half expecting to get caught, she was delighted to see that the loadmaster had his head down, busy feeding a belt of ammunition into the M240 machine gun.

Brook slithered into the open door and crawled to the inner bulkhead, where she covered her small frame with the nylon straps that would eventually be used to keep the medical gear from jostling around during their return trip.

***

The two loadmasters and the eight man Ranger chalk had no idea that there was a stowaway in their midst.

Brook's mind was going a mile a minute but she kept still. She had no idea when to show herself, but when she did she would exercise extreme caution so as not to startle the men with guns, *because these days everyone seems to have an extremely itchy trigger finger.*

***

From her seat amongst the greasy straps, Brook could feel the vibrations from the thumping twin rotor blades transmitted through the Chinook's thin hull. Even though the flight was supposed to take less than an hour, Brook still fought to stay awake. *Well,* she thought, *no better pick-me-up than an instant jolt of adrenaline.*

Brook slowly and deliberately, so as not to alert the soldiers sitting nearby, tried to worm from under the heavy gear that had been her hiding place. She suddenly sensed that she was being watched, prompting her to look up. Brook read his nametag. Vasquez had the death dealing end of his black rifle pointed directly at her head.

SOLDIER ON: SURVIVING THE ZOMBIE APOCALYPSE

The Ranger's intense stare was unnerving. The noise inside the helicopter prevented Brook from hearing the words that were coming from his mouth. She was, however, able to somewhat read his lips. The message was unmistakable - *Move and you are dead.* Brook took the weapon aimed at her very seriously. Nary a muscle twitched for the rest of the flight.

***

The forty-three-year-old Captain "Ghost" Gaines and his boys sat on the outside of the Little Birds, combat boots dangling in the slipstream, and endured the constant buffeting of the cooling mountain air.

For a newbie to high altitudes such as the mile high cities of Colorado Springs and Denver, which was ninety miles to the north, breathing could be difficult at times and headaches were a frequent occurrence. For Captain Gaines the clean, thin air was a welcome relief from the smog he endured as a youth growing up in Southern California.

It was in the city of Compton, hanging out in a friend's garage, when he held an AK-47 for the first time. Ronnie Gaines was an impressionable youth and he loved the war movies that were constantly being pumped out by Hollywood at the time. The Rambo movies were his favorite. Longing to fire the gun, he begged his friend to take him along so that he would get a chance to pull the trigger. Juwon told him to go home and maybe when he was older he could hang with the "fellas."

That night Juwon Castle went out, got drunk and fired the very same gun on a crowd gathered after a high school football game. The young banger fully intended to hit some rivals. Instead two random bullets found a freshman cheerleader and her father.

As far as Gaines knew, Juwon was still in prison - he received twenty-five to life. The events of that day forever changed Ronnie Gaines. In a way he owed his military career to his childhood friend.

For the next three years he shunned the gang lifestyle and focused his energies toward school. Although he caught a lot of shit for studying, he was big enough to defend himself.

Ronnie enlisted in the Army and shipped off to basic the week after he graduated from Crenshaw High.

By the end of the summer he was out of basic. Little did he know that in a few short years he would be a full-fledged Ranger chasing the enemy from Kuwait to Basra.

Special Forces training came next and then, a day he would never forget, he was selected for the 10th Special Forces Group. Ronnie Gaines had arrived.

***

Gaines took note of the other two helos. They were flying tight, in perfect formation. He had a hard time deciding who were the more disciplined operators, the SOAR pilots or the men they delivered into the shit. It didn't matter, for the hospital loomed and he had to get his game face on. From his vantage point he could see dozens of infected looking skyward. The Omega virus had started jumping from infected to healthy citizens only days ago. The ones that reanimated early on were getting riper by the minute. Gaines marveled at the human mind. His was already filtering out the obscene stench wafting up from below. The worst hovels in every third world country each had a unique and different smell associated with them. It had been the same everywhere he deployed; you eventually got used to it.

A voice crackled in his headset. "We have an unwanted passenger onboard Badger Three. How copy?"

"Copy that, this is Captain Gaines, is the stowaway a female?"

"Affirmative."

"She's one of us. Keep her onboard for the duration."

"Copy that, Badger Three out."

Goddamnit, Gaines thought, *that woman is a persistent one*. It didn't surprise him that Mrs. Grayson took after her husband,

after all Wyatt had been known to push the edge of the
envelope himself from time to time.

"Five mikes." The call sounded in everyone's headset.

The Little Birds hovered in front of Saint Francis Hospital
while the snipers onboard thinned the mob of walkers with
their long guns.

Gaines stared at the biggest pile of occupied body bags
that he had ever seen; quite a few of the thick rubber bags
undulated, enclosed in each, a trapped zombie struggling to
get free.

***

In the rear of the hovering Chinook, Brook noticed the
men start to check their loadouts. Magazines were inspected,
a firm rap in the palm made certain the rounds were seated
before the soldiers jammed the mags home and charged their
weapons.

A chorus of *hooaahs* preceded the tail gunner's covering
fire. His M240 emitted a distinct ripping sound as he poured
the tracer rounds into the walking dead. Down below, undead
bodies jerked and shuddered; the creatures' skulls exploding
like festering boils.

Brook was pissed. She had been told to stay put, in no
uncertain terms, by the bigger of the two crewmen, who
parked himself near the side door, manning the pinnacle-
mounted M240 machine gun.

Although she didn't have a rifle pointed at her any longer,
the threat was definitely implied; furthermore, the loadmaster
kept shooting glances her way. It was going to take a hell of a
diversion for her to get past him.

Brook strained to see out the open rear of the helicopter.
Her line of sight was obscured by the Rangers getting into
position to deploy. On the starboard side, facing the modern
cement and glass hospital, the crew chief let loose again with
his weapon. Brook heard the droning M240 abruptly go
silent, followed by a salvo of colorful language. While the

crew chief struggled with the jammed weapon, Brook took full advantage, melted into the crowd, and followed the Rangers into the fray.

***

The snipers on the two MH-6s, Badger One and Badger Two, were putting very effective lead downrange. On approach the ramp gunner on the Chinook, designated as Badger Three, was decimating the creatures below.

The five minute mark struck and the CH-47 touched down. Gaines watched the Ranger chalk pour from the back and proceed to fan out, then a small figure in civilian attire scurried from the chopper and formed up behind the last Ranger.

The Captain continued his observation as each Ranger began clearing their sector with precise fire; walkers were falling fast under the constant barrage from the 240s on the CH-47.

Gaines observed a knot of zombies flanking the Rangers' positions. Focusing on the threat to the chalk, like a football coach with a bird's eye view, Gaines started calling out plays. He would have to deal with Mrs. Grayson later... if there was indeed a *later.*

"Chalk leader, be advised you have Z's at your two o'clock, directing fire your way."

"*Roger that,*" Staff Sergeant Todd answered, making himself as small a target as possible.

The SOAR pilots rotated the Little Birds to afford the snipers clean shots. The flanking walkers were systematically cut down by the sharpshooters.

One lone crawler inched closer to the prone soldiers. "*Chalk leader check your six. I repeat enemy at six o'clock.*" Gaines watched helplessly, realizing that the warning was too late for the man on the ground.

Sergeant Vasquez felt something wrap around his legs and he instinctively rolled onto his back. The creature fell to the side and then continued clawing its way on top of him, its raw femur bones scrabbling against the asphalt. The Ranger's rifle was pinned by the ghoul's weight. All he could do was put one hand around the creature's shriveled neck and squeeze its vertebrae in his strong grip. In a fight for his life, the young Ranger searched for his sidearm.

Vasquez was struggling to keep the monster's snapping teeth away from his face when his fingers finally found the butt of his pistol. Before he could bring the gun to bear, someone kicked the legless zombie off of his chest sending it flying through the air.

Vasquez sat up and squeezed off three rounds, rapid fire, into the crawler's head, and looked at his savior. He couldn't believe who was standing in front of him; it was the woman from the chopper.

"Lady, how the hell did you get off that helicopter?"

Brook had saved the same Ranger who only minutes ago had his rifle trained on her. "*It doesn't matter... but I'm not getting back on,*" she said defiantly.

"Do you know how to use this?" Vasquez asked, as he handed the Beretta to her.

"I think I can handle it..." she answered.

"Keep close to me... and thanks for stepping in when you did."

Brook shot him a quaint smile. "You owe me one."

***

The Army Rangers leapfrogged around a white and orange ambulance, one at a time each man moved forward with the rest of the team providing cover. One by one they formed up under the covered circular drive directly in front of the emergency room drop off area.

A badly decomposed, half eaten, human body wedged open the pair of wide sliding glass doors; the look of terror on the corpse's face retold its last moments alive.

A score of undead moved about the lobby. Shell casings littered the tile floor; the walls and ceiling was pockmarked with puckered bullet holes. Long dried blood trails criss-crossed the waiting room heading nowhere in particular.

Taking it all in, Brook thought it must have been hell on earth when the infected descended on the hospital. From her experience as an ER nurse, patients were looking for first-aid, comfort, answers and to have their fears assuaged. Judging from the signs of violence and mayhem, those needs had not been met here. She shuddered and then marveled at the hand fate had dealt her. If she had been home in Portland instead of visiting her folks at the apex of the outbreak, she would have been smack dab in the middle of a catastrophe such as this. The whole macabre scene, eerily illuminated by the emergency lighting, would surely haunt her for the rest of her days.

"*Engage at will,*" Staff Sergeant Todd ordered his men over the squad's comms. Todd aimed for center mass, as every professional soldier was conditioned to, and placed a three round burst into the nearest ghoul's chest. The impact launched the walker off of its feet. The undead boy crash landed, limbs askew, on a row of folding chairs, scattering them across the waiting room floor.

Vasquez watched the boy immediately get back on his feet; the hole in the kid's chest was the size of a volleyball.

"Goddamn." Vasquez never took the Lord's name in vain, but the sight in front of him was a worthy exception to the rule. His hands shook as he shouldered his M4 and put the kid out of its misery.

The noise from the discharging weapons was deafening indoors. It was amplified greatly because of the low dropdown ceiling. The cordite haze hovering in the air reduced the visibility somewhat.

Moving in from the left, Sergeant Stanley Loomis engaged the threat nearest him first; the undead woman was clothed only in a bloodstained hospital gown, split down the rear. Her naked backside was colored with dark black and purple post mortem bruising; she had apparently been positioned face up shortly after her first death. With a determined deliberate pace the flasher lurched in his direction. Her hissing and moaning was the most evil thing he had ever heard.

Sergeant Loomis had the woman in his sights and pulled the trigger. There was no recoil, no report and no shell casing pinging on the floor. The round in the chamber had failed to fire and the ghoul was almost on top of him.

Brook squeezed off two shots from an oblique angle, three feet to Loomis' right. The walker's face disappeared in an explosion of flesh, bone, and dark gray brain matter. Brook brushed past the ashen faced soldier and took cover behind a chest high nurses' station.

The remaining Rangers had their hands full fighting the zombies as they pushed deeper into the lobby of Saint Francis Hospital.

***

The SOAR pilot held his ship in a hover directly over the Life Flight landing pad. It was situated on the ground level so that the incoming medical crew had direct access to the trauma center through a set of wide sliding glass doors. The landing pad was ringed with seven foot tall fencing to prevent anyone from accidentally wandering into a spinning tail rotor.

Captain Gaines planned to catch the zombies in a classic pincer. The Rangers would close on them from the front. The Delta Team, consisting of Gaines and five other shooters, would fast rope from one helo at a time and form up before venturing into the bowels of the trauma center. For insurance, Gaines left one sniper on each of the Little Birds to provide over watch security as well as relay any Z movement to the teams on the ground.

***

"Go, go, go!" As soon as Captain Ronnie "Ghost" Gaines gave the order, the three Delta operators from Badger Two hit the fast ropes. In seconds they were on terra firma, silenced SCAR rifles at the ready. Badger One side slipped into position, the rotor tips passing dangerously close to the hospital wall. The Night Stalker pilot hovered in place while Gaines and the other two operators quickly rappelled to the ground.

The Delta Team moved as one, each man watching a specific sector. Gaines abruptly went to one knee and signaled for his men to follow suit. A throng of undead shambled past, directly in front of the six motionless operators. Captain Gaines initiated contact, his SCAR silently spitting lead missiles head high; ribbons of flesh and shards of cranium plastered the stark white walls. The spent brass bounced and tinkled on the floor.

In unison, Sergeant Jackson engaged the ghouls on the left and Sergeant Yates targeted the zombies on the right. In seconds nine undead, in various stages of decay, lay heaped on the floor, their ravaged bodies intertwined in a final orgy of death.

Gaines ejected the nearly full magazine and replaced it with a fresh one. The other men followed suit.

The NICU was near the rear of the three story facility. Gaines felt very fortunate that the equipment they needed was on the ground floor, meaning there were no stairs to negotiate. In a moment of absurd clarity Gaines remembered how much he had hated moving before the shit hit the fan and a real life *George Romero* movie became his new reality.

"*Clear!*" Gaines yelled after looking through the glass windows inset into the swinging double doors labeled "NICU."

Once in the neonatal intensive care unit, it became obvious the widespread horror spawned by the Omega virus had been taken to a new level. The entire room looked like a set from one of those *SAW* movies.

Usually unaffected by the violence he encountered in his line of work, Captain Gaines involuntarily froze in his tracks and took in the carnage. It was the first time in days that he had felt empathy for the dead. The infected had already gotten to the helpless newborns unfortunate enough to come into the world during the hellish outbreak.

If there were any reason to question God's existence, Captain Gaines thought, *this is it.*

Most of the incubators contained bits and pieces of tiny corpses. Inside one, an underdeveloped hand scratched at its plastic coffin, the tiny undead brain instructing it to feed.

At the first sight of the dismembered miniature bodies, Sergeant Yates, a father of two, nearly fainted. His knees hit the ground first, followed by a torrent of hot vomit.

Sergeant Jackson registered the movement first but couldn't react quickly enough. An undead nurse sprang from a darkened supply closet and pounced on the kneeling Yates; her weight propelled him face first into the floor shattering his teeth into jagged shards. Instantly the monster latched onto the side of his neck and drew back with a mouthful of skin and carotid artery. Yates let out an anguished howl and bucked the infected woman off of his back; blood cascaded from his horrific neck wound and mixed with the puke on the floor.

Reacting to the attack, Gaines leveled his SCAR and delivered a double tap to the rear of the ghoul's head.

"Medic!" the Captain bellowed as he probed the rest of the room for lurking zombies. He was physically ill because they had let their guard down and failed to check the small closet.

Except for Yates fighting to live, it was eerily silent in the hospital, even the raucous shooting in the ER had ceased.

"This is Chalk Leader, how copy?"

Gaines ignored Staff Sergeant Todd and withdrew his Beretta. After he was certain there was a round chambered, he made the sign of the cross over his fallen comrade with slow deliberate motions. Yates had passed and was now starting to reanimate. "Sorry friend," Gaines whispered before shooting the fallen man behind the ear.

The Captain processed his deed for a moment before answering the Ranger's radio call. "This is Ogre One. The objective is clear; bring your squad forward, over."

"Copy that, Chalk One out."

In an instant the NICU was overflowing with soldiers.

Gaines noticed Brook file into the room amid a knot of Army Rangers. "Christ, lady, how'd you bribe your way onto that helo?"

To Brook it almost sounded like a compliment. "I've acquired a few new survival skills."

Gaines arched his eyebrows and started issuing orders. "Gentlemen, grab any and everything this pretty lady tells you to and load it onto Badger Three. ASAP, *the enemy knows we are here... and he wants to eat.*"

As Brook passed by the tall Captain, he stopped barking orders for a tick and quietly whispered into her ear, "Now don't go and get yourself bit. I wouldn't want a can of Cade "Wyatt" Grayson whoop ass opened up on me." He let loose a suppressed version of his infamous cackle.

***

To a man, every soldier disregarded the undead preemie thrashing about in the grimy incubator. Being a mother herself, the sight was too much for Brook to ignore. There was no way to tell for sure due to the advanced decomposition, but judging by the pink wristband the poor thing was a little girl. Ignoring reason and listening only to her instincts, Brook grasped the thing's stick-thin wrist and read the name on the plastic band. "Well Hanna, sweetie, it's time to go to sleep now. I'm sorry it had to be like this..." Brook placed a small pillow over the hissing baby's shriveled face. A muffled report followed. The pillow absorbed the gunshot and any blowback. Brook looked at the pistol in her shaking hand, and wondered how many more "yets" this new world would hurl at her.

***

SOLDIER ON: SURVIVING THE ZOMBIE APOCALYPSE

The large Chinook shuddered slightly and lifted into the air. She was a bit heavy due to all of the medical gear stuffed in amongst the crew and passengers.

Before the bird was fully loaded, Brook wheeled two mobile med carts out of the ER and had them shoehorned onto Badger Three. The carts were stuffed full with every type of medicine; hopefully there was something in there that might help her brother Carl.

Sergeant Stewart Yates' body was secured in a black rubberized body bag and rode home one last time with his Ranger chalk. The twenty mile flight back to Schriever took only a few minutes. Sitting next to Yates' body was very uncomfortable. Brook had been desensitized to killing and seeing the infected on a daily basis had ceased to faze her, but the death of someone that she had just been interacting with was a different story. During the entire flight back, Brook grieved for the man and his kids... if they weren't dead already.

***

As soon as the bird full of med gear crossed over the perimeter fence, Brook watched the two Little Birds carrying Captain Gaines and his men peel off and head for Fort Carson. The Chinook started to slow, prompting her to look out the front canopy between the pilots. The horizon dipped, along with her stomach. Out of the port side bubble, Brook watched the reason for the abrupt maneuver glide by, followed by the roar of its four huge turboprops. As soon as the C-130 touched down on the end of the runway, the Chinook pilot nosed the big beast down and darted for a suitable landing spot.

***

A cadre of soldiers rushed to the chopper and began unloading the medical gear. Brook wheeled the medicine carts to the tarmac. "These need to go along with the other gear," she said to one of the men scurrying about.

The base was foreign to her; not to mention the fact that she was loopy as hell from sleep deprivation. It took her a few moments to get her bearings.

After a few wrong turns, Brook found the infirmary. Annie Desantos looked peaceful with her eyes closed. The only discernable movement was the rising and falling of her distended abdomen. *She's still pregnant,* Brook thought, *that's a good thing.* "Big momma, we need to get you and Mike Jr. on a baby monitor," she said softly.

Brook pulled the sheet up around Annie's neck and exited the room as quietly as she entered.

***

Carl's condition hadn't changed since the last time Brook checked in on him. His scab covered face was slack, his breathing seemed normal and judging by the digital numbers on the heart monitor, his was still beating.

"Carl, it's your sis, Brook. Can you hear me?" She took hold of her comatose brother's hand and gave it a firm squeeze. Brook started; Carl had squeezed back. "I know you're in there. You squeezed my hand." Brook did it again but got no response.

Brook held Carl's hand while caressing his hair. Using a wet washcloth, she dribbled water on his forehead and dabbed at his oozing wounds.

The shotgun blast sure did a number on your face big brother.

After taking care of the most pressing matters on her plate, Brook groggily walked back to the Quonset hut that was her temporary home.

***

Another transport plane roared overhead but she was so spent that she couldn't summon enough energy to even look up. Brook opened the door and was instantly mobbed.

Raven clung to her waist clamoring for her attention. Sierra and Serena shouted for Auntie Brooklyn to fill them in on how *their* mommy was.

169

Overwhelmed was an understatement. After the girls were
sated and had their questions answered, Brook started the
bedtime stories.

While she read the girls a book about *the bear that kept
snoring on*, she silently marveled at the resiliency they displayed
in the face of the horrors that had been heaped upon them.

One by one the kids conked out. Brook shortly joined
them.

***

Chapter 30
Outbreak - Day 6
Stanley, Idaho

Dan travelled without the benefit of headlights to show the way. Twenty miles an hour was as fast as he dared go in the total dark.

A few miles outside of town the reason for Stanley's lack of electricity was evident. Dan had to slow the Dodge to a crawl in order to slip by a tangle of downed power lines near a jumble of wrecked cars.

Movement in a compact Toyota caught Dan's attention. He stopped Lizzie's old car and got out to investigate. Dan used his tactical flashlight to fully illuminate the wreck. The driver's glass was shattered, and the entire front of the vehicle was buried under the back bumper of a white Ford Excursion. It was a miracle that the accident didn't culminate in a huge fireball. *Maybe*, Dan thought, the *truck had run out of gas first.*

The Toyota's engine block had been pushed into the passenger compartment. Even though the zombie was pinned in the driver's seat from the lap down, the infected female still thrashed about, reaching her chalky white arms through the shattered window in his direction.

Dan stayed out of the zombie's reach and walked to the rear of the car. He wiped a portal in the road grime covering the rear window so he could safely look inside.

In a rear facing car seat, an infant arched its tiny body fighting against the restraints holding it down. Its dried lips silently opened and closed in anticipation of a meal. Slowly, the infected baby turned its head to face Dan, and stared him down with cold dead eyes. It was all too surreal; he still couldn't believe the sight directly in front of him, even after his first encounter with the zombie in Stanley. He acted without thinking. As if on auto-pilot Dan put each of the creatures out of its misery with a bullet to the brain.

Hell has opened up, and the rapture has begun. Dan felt hot tears trickle down his cheeks as he holstered his pistol.

After his encounter with the undead mom and her infant, Dan was a changed man. He felt it was his duty, going forward, to put down as many of them as possible.

Dan arrived in Arco, Idaho before dawn. It looked like a slaughterhouse in the middle of town. Dead bodies littered the streets and many more walked them.

Dan had used all but one of his bullets mercifully killing the undead. The final round he was saving for his own exit plan. There was no way he was going to die at the hands of a demon and then return as one of them hungering for human flesh. Dan always told himself he was going out on his own terms, and he fully intended to honor that promise.

***

The back lot of the Food King grocery store was devoid of parked cars, and much to Dan's relief there were none of the moaning zombies roaming around. Two eighteen-wheelers were backed up to the loading dock; it looked like the warehouse crew didn't have time to unload the trailers before the shit hit the fan.

According to the article the illness had swept the nation with the infection rate surging exponentially day by day. Dan was hoping to avoid any more scenes like the two trapped in the car. If what he had seen so far was as widespread as the article suggested, he knew that wasn't going to be possible.

It was a tight fit, but Dan managed to back the four door Dodge between the two big rigs. He left himself enough room to partially open the driver's door so he could escape if he had to.

Dan found the cardboard dash protector that nearly every geriatric kept in their car; it was wedged under the front seat with a collapsible umbrella. It would keep out the light from the rising sun, but most importantly it would hide the inside of the car from the prying eyes of the dead. At last he felt safe enough to close his eyes. Ironically, the outside of the solar shield had the words, "HELP! CALL 911," printed in big bold red letters, and it was facing outward.

**

Dan awoke with a start to something beating on the windshield; he was disoriented and wondered where the hell he was. It felt like he had closed his eyes for only a heartbeat. Suddenly he realized the predicament that he was in, wedged between two tractor trailers with the monsters from hell wanting in. *"Dan. Dan. Dan,"* he admonished himself. "Smooth move Ex-Lax, now what are you going to do?" The .45 caliber pistol, with the last remaining round in the chamber, was on his lap where he had left it. Hefting the weight of the gun in his right hand he realized that his knuckles were whitening and the grip's checkerboard pattern was biting into his palm. He placed the barrel under his fully bearded chin. *You've got a decision to make*, he thought, *coward's way or...*

The thing pounded on the windshield again, more forcefully this time. It sounded like there was a rock in its fucking cadaver hands.

"911... do you need Police, Fire or Medical?" The male voice was followed by loud guffaws which puzzled him further, because in his mind he was convinced that at least

fifty of the flesh-eaters were waiting outside his General
Motors-made coffin.

More forcefully this time, and minus the laughter the same
voice shouted, "*Take down the sun shade and keep your hands where
we can see them.*"

Dan pulled the cardboard down and immediately noticed
the reason for the laughter. It was the writing on the other
side that they were getting a kick out of. He didn't possess the
energy to laugh even if he had wanted to. Relief washed over
the Vietnam veteran when he realized that at least a Company
of American soldiers were in the parking lot.

Dan placed his pistol on the roof of the car, squeezed his
frame from the vehicle and walked slowly, with his hands in
the air, out of the steel canyon.

"Do you have any wounds or bites?" a soldier asked
sternly.

"No sir," Dan replied, his hands still reaching for the sky.

"With all due respect sir, we need you to *completely*
disrobe." It was an order, not a request.

Dan complied without forming any resentment. Every
square inch of his body was thoroughly inspected by a latex
glove-wearing medic. Two soldiers kept their rifles pointed in
Dan's general direction during the entire exam.

"Good to go sir," the medic said to his superior. "Sorry,"
he said under his breath, loud enough for only Dan to hear,
"better safe than sorry."

"Hook up the rigs. *We're Oscar Mike in ten.*" The soldier in
charge strode away without saying another word.

Dan addressed the combat medic, "Where are you all
headed?"

"We've been shootin' and scootin' since Z day plus two.
We were based outside of Seattle. *Wow... I'm gonna miss Seattle...
shit hit the fan fast.* Anyway you'll be riding in the Bradley with
me."

"I don't have a choice?" Dan asked.

"No. And I'll tell you why when we get underway. Besides, if you would've seen Seattle, Portland, and Boise you would be begging us to take you." The soldier stared off into the distance and then reacquired eye contact with Dan. His eyes narrowed before he spoke, "You don't want to be out there alone. We've been ordered to muster all hands and make way for Colorado Springs, ASAP. It's the new Capital of the United States."

Dan was dying to unload the burden he was carrying and spew everything he had witnessed in his hometown of Stanley, all of the atrocities, as well as the details relating to Sheriff Blanda's horrific death. Bottom line, Ganz and his boys needed to pay. It was a long haul to Colorado. He was sure he would get his chance and hopefully all of his questions could be answered as well.

The two semi trucks joined the convoy of Humvees, Bradley fighting vehicles and eight wheeled Strykers from Fort Lewis. They had to push through Pocatello and continue to soldier onward to Colorado Springs.

Chapter 31
Outbreak - Day 6
Hanna, Utah

Daymon had been sitting on the hardwood floor for an
hour and a half. The fact that he could actually feel, through
the seat of his pants, the bumps and bangs of the zombies a
few feet away was supremely disconcerting, and to add to his
discomfort, Hosford wouldn't shut up.

"We're done for man. How in the hell are we going to get
out of this mess?"

Despite the plugs in his ears, Daymon could still hear the
moans coming from the restless pack of undead in the foyer.
He was feeling a little manic; all of his senses were under
assault.

"Robin Hood, you got any ideas?"

"Shhhh," Daymon put a finger to his lips.

"Fuck off! Don't you *dare* shush me."

Daymon glared at the shirtless lawyer, pushed the dreads
away from his ear and swiveled his head in the direction of
the open window.

"*Please*, be quiet... I hear an engine." His voice, dripping
with insincerity, sounded like it came from someone
reluctantly working in customer service. It worked; Hoss shut
his mouth and listened for the engine as well.

***

Cade was having a hard time shifting. He ground the gears, wincing after each violent clunk of metal on metal. Once on the straightaway he kept the RV in fourth gear and gained some speed.

How the old folks drove these things without killing everybody else on the road baffled him. The steering was sluggish and unresponsive and when he pressed on the brakes it felt like he was stepping on a pillow.

Yet another zombie wandered directly into the path of the motorhome. The impact knocked the shoes from its cold feet and sent it flying into a white picket fence. Now shoeless and punctured with multiple pieces of splintered wood, the ghoul stood and limped after the hit and run driver.

At the last moment Cade recognized the thicket of aspens in front of the two story house and wrenched the humongous steering wheel to the right. "Shit..." one word said it all. Screeching tires protested the sudden change of direction. The multi-ton RV was out of control and the brakes weren't responding. The bodies trapped under the vehicle were slowing it down slightly but not enough to prevent the impending collision. Cade was able to steer the thing a few feet to the left of the front porch. This wasn't turning out how he had planned.

With a sound like a bomb blast the Winnebago sheared off half of the stairs and dislodged a solid oak column. The RV finally came to rest wedged underneath part of the front porch.

Cade's eyes widened at the sheer number of approaching zombies. A pale face slammed into the glass on the driver's side, the jaundiced eyes hungrily following his every movement. Cade put the Winnebago in reverse and tried re-starting the engine.

***

Hosford crushed up against Daymon in front of the narrow window. They both had their faces pressed to the glass, trying in vain to catch a first glimpse of the approaching vehicle.

"He's coming in hot," Daymon said, watching the white behemoth barely negotiate the screeching right hand turn. Dangerously listing on two wheels, the RV plowed over two of the aspens before crunching like an aluminum can into the porch. A shudder resonated through the house as it was nudged off of its foundation.

"That had to be our guy... right?"

Daymon looked at Hosford, thinking, *this dolt's a lawyer?* It took every ounce of willpower to restrain himself from putting the Glock behind the fat man's ear and shutting his trap for good. Daymon was no murderer but the incessant yammering heaped upon the stresses of being trapped was getting to be too much. "Yes, master of the obvious, it did look like *our man.*"

***

After a few cranks the engine turned over and sputtered to life. Cade jammed the tree mounted shifter into reverse and gunned the engine. The wheels spun freely, gouging furrows into the brown grass. The full weight of the porch roof rested on the RV. It was going nowhere.

Resigned to the fact that he was back to square one... almost, Cade checked the driver's door, grabbed his rifle and moved into the passenger compartment.

Rotting faces were pressing against every window. After locking the side door he made the rounds and closed all of the curtains. Cade hoped it might buy him some time to plan his escape. He thought his options through: *Driver door - no luck, too many of them. Passenger door - hopelessly wedged shut from the impact with the porch, and lastly the back window was fixed in place and wasn't meant to open.* The zombies were now messing with the cabin door; the sliding latch jiggled but the door didn't open. *That had to be luck. These things can't really work a door knob,* Cade's inner voice told him.

Cade looked above his head. In the center of the low ceiling was a small pop-up air vent. He pushed it open, letting the noxious carrion odor permeate the inside of the Winnebago.

Cade thought someone as lean as Daymon might fit, but he knew that he had absolutely no chance of exiting through the small portal. Aside from the windows, which really weren't an option, the roof was the only way out.

Cade repeatedly bashed at the cheap tan plastic trim. The vent eventually lost out to the sharp blows from his rifle.

***

From their vantage point in the house, the men watched the vent pop out and skitter off of the vehicle's roof. A pair of gloved hands touched around the outside of the opening.

The zombies were reaching a fevered pitch.

"He's hosed... and so are we," Daymon whispered.

"*Noooo!*" Hoss screamed.

***

Cade fished the makeshift cloth earplugs from his pocket and reinserted them into both ears. With his back facing the house, lest he accidently shoot the men inside, he crouched down and began shooting holes in a rough circle through the thin aluminum roof. He used all thirty rounds, ejected the spent mag and inserted his last one.

Breaking glass littered the floor as the weight of the agitated zombies pushed the thin siding of the Winnebago inward and imploded the smaller wing windows. Cold gray hands thrust between the curtains, longing to get ahold of anything living.

A fit of dry heaves wracked Cade's body as the smell of the dead overwhelmed him in the hot cramped vehicle.

Momentarily ignoring the threat of being overrun, Cade used the butt stock of his carbine to pound on the weakened semi-circle over his head.

The combined weight of the zombies caused the RV to wobble on its springs. Cade was still trying to widen his

escape hatch when he noticed the side door beginning to
buckle inward. The interior of the RV began to heat up as the
first streamers of light from the rising sun found their way
inside.

It took a couple of minutes and a lot more rapid bashing
with his gun until the aluminum finally weakened enough so
that it could be bent outward.

Cade threw his carbine out onto the roof and pulled
himself up, mindful of the sharp edges. Everywhere he
looked the creatures were five deep. It was creepy being only
ten feet from a hundred walking dead. Cade shakily got to his
feet, ran the length of the RV and scrabbled up the porch
roof towards the open window.

Daymon's outstretched hand took the rifle and Hoss
pulled the winded man into the house.

"What happened?" Daymon inquired.

Peeling off the drenched tracksuit, Cade answered matter-
of-factly, "Operator failure." The icy tone in his voice
indicated that the topic wasn't up for discussion.

Cade thought it selfish on his part, but Brook and Raven
were the only two people in the world that he needed to be
responsible for, yet somehow he kept finding himself in the
company of others.

***

The first zombies to breach the RV were quickly crushed
to the floor. Like Black Friday at the Walmart, the second
wave of surging corpses crawled atop the pile, found the path
of least resistance, and began pouring through the hole in the
roof.

One of the zombies became lodged in the opening, his
lower extremities, still half inside the vehicle, were sheared off
by the crushing throng below. Now sans his lower half, the
little monster clawed his way forward. The slick blood trail
flowing from his shredded abdomen travelled down the
shingles and into the rain gutter.

"*Kill the thing already!*" Hoss screamed. The high pitched sound belied his large stature.

Cade leveled his carbine and shot the crawler in the eye.

"Oh my God, we're *fucked* now."

Cade didn't think it was possible, but the words spewing from the lawyer came out an octave or two higher than usual.

Daymon took his eyes off of the advancing ghouls. "Get ahold of yourself dude," he had had about enough. "All of your girlish crying is embarrassing."

More zombies poured from the hole and struggled up the blood slickened pitch.

Daymon took aim with the Glock and was firing rapidly into the crowd, he was scoring clean headshots but still the zombies kept up their forward progress.

Cade dropped a number of undead with his carbine; he had to make them all count because his last magazine was in the M4.

The dead were falling and sliding off of the roof, only to be quickly replaced by more of the flesh-eaters. Unexpectedly the Glock locked open, and before Daymon could reload the monsters were at the windowsill.

He dropped the pistol, slammed the window shut and quickly threw the lock. The ghouls were now hammering on the glass and trying their best to get inside.

"How are we going to get out of this one?" Daymon asked, looking at Cade for answers.

Cade knew that the only place they would be safe was the attic. Looking up he recognized the outline of the recessed, pull-down stairs. The trick was going to be actually getting ahold of the handle. He jumped trying to reach it, but came up a couple of inches shy.

Hoss finally got ahold of himself. "Get on my back."

Cade tried to ignore the lawyer's hairiness as he climbed onto his shoulders. Hoss nearly toppled over when he stood up but Cade quickly braced them by putting a hand on the wall. He stretched his arm as far as he could and grabbed the handle.

"I've got it... let me down."

Hoss took it literally and walked from under the operator's suspended body.

Cade's weight was more than enough to unfurl the folding steps, he fell faster than he anticipated and hit the floor with a bang, square on his tailbone. The ladder telescoped to its full extension leaving the last rung nearly touching the tip of his nose. Flat on his back, he stared up into the marginal safety of the attic, while dust and tufts of insulation rained down around him.

"That looked painful," Hoss said, shooing dust particles away from his face.

Cade ignored the smart ass comment. "Get up the stairs *now*."

Hoss reacted first. Like an elephant on a tight rope he slowly climbed up the creaking steps.

Cade grabbed his M4 from the floor and trained it at the window. "Hurry up... between us we have roughly thirty rounds left, and there are at least a hundred of them out there."

Hoss cleared the top of the stairs and Daymon began his ascent.

Cade covered the window until Daymon was in the attic and then started up himself. He was only three rungs up the ladder when the glass shattered and the zombies tumbled in. With deadly precision, the former Delta operator popped each one in the head. Their rotten bodies momentarily blocked the window, allowing Cade the time to turn and hurry the rest of the way up the flimsy steps.

Daymon was ready. As soon as Cade was in the attic he yanked on the ladder and it folded into the closed position with a loud thump. The only light in the cramped space filtered in through the small window in the decorative dormer.

"Where did you learn how to drive?" The question came from out of left field.

"Stow the insults Hoss. I had every intention of getting the RV here in one piece so we *all* could escape our uninvited houseguests downstairs." Cade let his gaze linger until Hoss curred out and looked away.

"I can't help it. The filter between my brain and mouth goes missing when I'm under great stress."

"If you don't have anything to say that's pertinent or useful then keep your mouth shut. *If you fail to do so I will feed you to those things outside.*" Cade's steely glare, even in the near dark, let Hoss know that he meant business.

Daymon went over to the other side of the attic and was inspecting the dormer window. "How are we going to get out of this one? We're trapped... we can only go as high as the rooftop."

"That's where I need to be, if this is going to work," he displayed the portable satellite phone.

"I haven't had cell service for five days... how is that going to help?"

"*Filter*," Daymon admonished Hoss before Cade had a chance to.

Hoss was very close to crossing the invisible line Cade had just warned him about. It was apparent the man didn't know how to observe *or* listen. How this man had passed the bar exam, let alone practiced law, mystified him.

Cade brushed the cobwebs from the window and wiped the husks of dead bugs from the sill. The dormer window was fixed in place and the only way it was going to open was by force. Once again the collapsed butt stock of the M4 came in handy. There was no more need for noise discipline. Cade relieved the window of glass, sending it showering down on the zombies below. Their raspy moans intensified as they became aware of Cade squeezing through the tiny window.

The angle was steeper than the front porch but he still
managed to scramble around to a safer perch.

Cade assembled the satellite phone and again tried to raise
Duncan. On the third ring someone answered; to Cade's
relief it was Duncan and his familiar southern drawl.

Chapter 32
Outbreak - Day 6
Camp Williams 19th Special Forces Garrison
Draper, Utah

Duncan Winters awoke from one of his famous nightmares. He hadn't had a Nam nightmare since the early eighties and this one didn't feature old Victor Charlie. The young men he had watched climb onto his Huey, full of so much bravado - with a healthy dose of fear thrown in - only to return in a muddy body bag, hadn't even made a cameo. These new nightmares featured walking corpses, dead kids that he hadn't gotten to know, and endless running. These new nightmares were still front and center the moment he awoke.

Duncan donned his fatigues and splashed his face with cold water. Shaving was out of the question. These days he loathed looking into the mirror. The man who peered back had suddenly aged ten years in only a week. He wore his boonie hat pulled down low over his forehead to avoid eye contact - he didn't want to get to know anyone, because lately, all of his new acquaintances were prone to dying.

Before he exited his sleeping quarters, he made it a point to take his weapon. The former Army aviator went nowhere without his stubby 12 gauge combat shotgun.

Only two steps out of the door he recognized the unmistakable report of a MK-19 grenade launcher. The rapid *thwomp-thwomp-thwomp* the 40 mm shells made as they left the barrel was unmistakable.

"What's happening?" Duncan asked a half dressed soldier, obviously on his way to the action.

"*The base is being overrun*," said the ashen-faced soldier, his voice trailing off as he continued running towards the action.

Duncan watched the man; one hand held up his unbuttoned pants and the other carried a rifle.

It was a miracle that Duncan had even heard the portable sat phone ringing. He instantly set his weapon aside and frantically felt himself up with both hands searching for the device. After the quick pat down he retrieved the phone from his thigh pocket.

"Duncan here." He strained to hear the voice on the other end.

"Prairie Fire, Prairie Fire, Duncan it's Cade, coordinates to follow."

Duncan knew the term *Prairie Fire* from his time serving in Vietnam. It meant one or more of three things: One, you are in contact with a much larger or superior force. Two, you are completely surrounded or will be. Three, death is imminent. He hoped for Cade's sake that it wasn't the latter.

"Copy that, standing by." Once again Duncan searched his pockets, looking for something to write with. A good aviator always carried a pen. He groped around and finally found a big hunk of white chalk and his well used Sharpie. Meanwhile, Cade had already begun reciting the GPS coordinates.

"Wait one, I wasn't prepared... can you please start over?"

"Copy that," Cade's voice sounded tinny and machinelike on the other end. "Coordinates are, 40 degrees, 28 minutes and 3 seconds north. 109 degrees, 55 minutes and 47 seconds west. I'm currently trapped on the roof of a two story house. How copy?"

Duncan scribbled the numbers on his fatigue pants and then repeated them to his friend. He could hear other voices in the background as well as the recognizable sounds of the dead. Cade confirmed the numbers repeated back to him were correct and added, "Look for purple smoke."

"Copy that amigo. I got *myself* a little Prairie Fire smoldering here." The aviator retrieved his weapon and headed for the parade ground where the lone Black Hawk sat.

Four successive concussions moved the earth underneath his boots. *Claymores,* the sound meant that things were bad, *very bad indeed.* In Vietnam if you had claymore mines going off on the perimeter of your firebase then it meant one of two things. One, the mines were being used offensively, detonated with a hand crank at the precise time the enemy were in the kill zone to maximize the casualties. Two, the mines had been set up with a tripwire to act as an early warning device and kill any unlucky sapper before he got near the wire.

Constant gunfire was the norm over the last few days. The soldiers had experimented with all of their weapons to thin out the moaning bodies. The Mark 19 grenade launcher was a failure, it only peppered their dead flesh with shrapnel. The grenadiers stared in amazement as scores of ghouls fell, only to pop back up and continue on, displaying the same unflappable zombie determination. It was a devastating weapon against living flesh but virtually useless against the dead. Claymore anti-personnel mines and hand grenades were equally ineffective. The supply of ammunition was at dangerously low levels, and aerial resupply wasn't coming.

Duncan contemplated asking permission from the major before taking the helicopter. The situation at the front gate was deteriorating at such a rapid pace, he feared he would never find Beeson and leave himself enough time to preflight and escape alive. To be fair he would take on as many people as he safely could. He thought back to the fall of Saigon in 1975 and remembered vividly the anguished faces of the South Vietnamese that didn't make his last flight. That Huey had been so loaded down that he thought he was going to be picking palm fronds out of his ass.

Duncan removed the tie downs from the rotor tips. There was no way that he was going to get atop the big bird to check the "Jesus bolt" if it even had one, so he made sure the tail rotor was sound and the other surfaces looked good. He strapped in and stretched his pant leg so he could clearly see the GPS coordinates. A few flicked switches later the engine whined and the sagging blades started their slow rotation.

Since he was not used to flying the Black Hawk he decided it would be smart to enter the destination into the computer now while on the ground. He didn't want his attention divided while he piloted the complex piece of machinery. The chicken scratch on his leg was hard to make out, but he felt confident that the GPS numbers were inputted correctly. Duncan took a moment to get familiar with the digital (AFCS) Automatic Flight Control System. He found that there were more buttons to push on the contraption than an ex-wife. When he was finally finished with the flight computer he looked up. Three hundred yards away, at his twelve o'clock, were half a dozen shambling ghouls.

Duncan felt his pulse quicken as his body flooded with adrenaline. Without glancing down he automatically found the collective and goosed the turbine. There was a flash of movement in his peripheral vision. A soldier streaked by followed by several trotting undead. The man abruptly turned and emptied a magazine on full auto into the collection of ghouls. Three fell at his feet. A look of recognition crossed his face and he changed direction, sprinting for the open fuselage of the medevac Black Hawk. Duncan pulled back on power to let the man close the gap.

The undead that escaped his *rock and roll* fusillade continued after him while two more crawled through the blood of their brethren.

Duncan watched until the desperate man was at the door, he launched his frame inside as the Black Hawk lifted from the ground. He could see one of the man's hands grasping at the canvas belt used to strap in the medical litter while the other flailed for another handhold. Duncan couldn't help him; he had to focus on flying the big beast of a chopper. Black Hawks were nothing like a Huey and he constantly had to remind himself of that.

A shriek rang out over the whine of the turbines and the noise of the rotor blades. Duncan glanced back to see one of the monsters receive a face full of combat boot from the screaming soldier. The female zombie's lower jaw tore free leaving her tongue to loll around in the open hole that used to be her mouth.

"*Persistent motherfuckers, they never give up.*" The man was shouting to be heard over the increasing rotor noise. He started to stomp on the ghoul's fingers. It felt absolutely no pain and maintained a vice-like grip on the bulkhead. Finally the man's combat boot won the battle. The monster tumbled thirty feet to the ground, the severed fingers raining down around her writhing body.

Duncan looked through the nose plexi and watched the zombie, dragging its shattered legs in search of fresh meat.

"Strap in, it's going to get bumpy." Duncan gave the soldier enough time to get seated and buckled before he banked the Black Hawk and began orbiting the battlefield.

A hundred feet below, the scene was chaotic. Fires raged, muzzle flashes winked, and sporadic explosions buffeted the chopper. The undead were surging around both the front and back of Camp Williams. The west side of the base suddenly brightened up. Row upon row of headlights cut through the haze and smoke of the constant ongoing battle with the undead. It gave Duncan hope for the people on the ground. The base housed more vehicles and weapons than able bodies. He had a tinge of regret for leaving with the only helo, but it couldn't be avoided. He kept circling looking for

survivors in need of help. It appeared that Major Beeson had
his troops executing a textbook strategic withdrawal.

Chapter 33
Outbreak - Day 6
Hanna, Utah

The humidity in the attic was stifling, and outside the day was beginning to heat up. Even the simple act of breathing was becoming a chore. A constant cacophony of sound from below added to their collective misery.

"When does the cavalry arrive?"

"Hoss, even if the cavalry does find us... how are you going to get your big ass through that small window?"

"I was trying to figure out a solution to that... if I stay in this sauna for a few more hours I should lose *some* weight. This is one big deja-vu after spending four days in the attic above my law office."

The banter continued. Considering their situation, Daymon could think of nothing better to do. "*Four days*... how much did you weigh before the freaks started walking?"

"*Too much*," Hoss answered dejectedly.

Daymon chuckled at his response.

Cade was probing the ceiling with his dagger and growing tired of the floor show. "I need you two to help look for weak spots, water damage or anywhere that these plywood sheets are compromised."

Hoss stood hunched over in the confined space and set about in search for a way out.

Daymon sat on his haunches trying to conserve energy. He hadn't had a drink of water for hours and was feeling it.

Hoss' voice carried from the other end of the attic, "Over here... someone give me a hand."

Cade tightroped along the rafters, watching his feet to make sure he didn't step where the insulation had settled. When he got closer, he could see the roof flexing above the big man's back. Hosford's stance made him look like a crouching Atlas, only not as svelte. Cade wasn't the same height as the lawyer so he had to push with his shoulder. The added force popped a row of the nails holding the plywood sheeting to the ceiling joists. Cade worked his knife between the cracks. The roofing paper cut easily but he had to saw the outer layer with the serrated edge of the Gerber. It was slow going; he was only through a few inches of the asphalt shingles. Sweat poured down his face, stinging his eyes.

"I'm gonna put my back into it again," Hoss said, getting himself situated. He grunted from the exertion and was rewarded with a few more inches of blue sky.

Daymon sidled up adding his back to the efforts. With a prolonged creak and the sound of popping nails the roof opened up some more, allowing them to hear the distant rotor blades beating the morning air.

Hoss rallied the troops; he didn't want to be the only one left in the attic, unable to fit his carcass through the window when help arrived. The fresh air pouring in the opening was welcome, and invigorated all three of them.

Cade pulled the canister of purple marking smoke from his side cargo pocket. It was the predetermined color he and Duncan had agreed upon. He pulled the pin and shoved the cylinder through the opening near his head; it rolled down the roof and plunked into the gutter. An angry, purple cloud spewed into the air. Anyone approaching by helicopter would have to be blind not to see it.

Cade put his back against the rooftop. "Big push... all at once."

With the three of them working together they peeled an entire sheet of roofing, shingles and all, free from the joists. The sudden weight leaving his shoulders caused Hoss to lose his balance. One wingtip shoe slipped from the rafter and his entire left leg followed, plunging through the lathe and plaster ceiling into the hallway below. A look of true horror flashed across the man's face as cold fingers locked onto his dangling extremity.

Cade instantly realized what was happening. Hoss started screaming and hyperventilating. *"My foot, they've got ahold of it. Help! Pull me up... don't let them have me!"*

Hosford's body was being pulled through the sixteen inch wide gap. Below, in the hall, the undead were jockeying for a piece of his pasty leg. They had already ripped off his leather wingtip and sheer black dress sock. Frigid fingers worked to pull the meat towards their open mouths, the multitude of gnashing teeth yearning for a taste.

Cade tried with all his might to save the man from a horrible death; it was a lopsided tug of war. He was fighting the undead as well as the pull of gravity. Hosford Preston's worst fear was becoming reality. He didn't want to be one of them. A piercing scream left his mouth when the jagged teeth clamped down on his bare toes. The three smallest ones on his left foot were amputated by the ghoul's grinding teeth. Blood sprayed onto the mob of flesh-eaters, exciting them all the more. Cade suddenly lost his grip on Hosford's meaty hand. The crush of dead accepted all three hundred pounds of him with clawing fingers and open jaws.

"Finish him!" Cade yelled loud enough to be heard over the bloodcurdling screams.

Daymon moved Cade aside and trained the Glock through the jagged man-sized hole. He aimed away from Hoss and fired three shots into the ghoul nearest the wailing man. If he had liked the lawyer even one iota, he would have emptied the

entire magazine into his glistening dome and spared him from
the fate much worse than death. Daymon's eyes narrowed to
slits as he watched the smug lawyer bleed out, bleating like a
lamb at slaughter. *It's a pity*, he thought, *that I won't be around to
see the fat fuck turn.*

Daymon quickly followed Cade out onto the steeply
pitched roof. He looked upward. The massive black
helicopter hovered, blotting out the bluebird sky. The white
aspens ringing the property danced and whipped about in the
downdraft, while tendrils of purple smoke wove through their
fluttering leaves.

Inside the house the dead were stripping the flesh from
Hosford's body and greedily consuming him. Daymon would
never know, but there wouldn't be enough of Hoss left to
reanimate.

Daymon watched the cable rescue ladder plummet from
the Black Hawk and strike Cade square in the face. Instantly a
fine red mist sprayed from the deep bloody gash across the
bridge of his nose. Without regard for himself, Cade grabbed
the ladder to stabilize it and motioned for Daymon to climb.
Neither man could hear himself think let alone communicate.
Cade waited until the other man was halfway inside the open
cabin before he started his ascent.

Even as he was bounced to and fro in the rotor wash he
thought, *Duncan's getting a hang of the Black Hawk. His hover isn't
as steady as one of the SOAR pilots, but not too bad for an old Huey
driver.*

As the helicopter gained altitude, Cade watched the
treetops disappear below his boots. When he reached the top
rung he was greeted by an extended hand. There was a trace
of a smile on Daymon's face, but Cade quickly dismissed it
and latched on. Once inside the vibrating Black Hawk he
noted the other passenger and then met eyes with the pilot.
Duncan was animatedly pointing at his helmeted head. Cade
understood what he wanted, located a flight helmet and

plugged the jack into the bulkhead, then crawled into the co-pilot seat.

With his familiar twang, Duncan welcomed Cade aboard. "How's it hanging Amigo?"

"Not as low as it was a minute ago. You got a bandage somewhere in this bird?"

Blood was still streaming freely from the gash. Cade tried to staunch the flow with his sleeve.

"Bandage... what you need my man is a *tourniquet*. I apologize for my boy Vincent. Chuckin' ladders out of helos isn't in his job description. From our brief conversation, turns out he was in culinary services at the base."

The young private's stammering voice cut in, "Yeah Sir... m-m-my bad. I was a cook... s-s-sorry."

"No worries soldier, it'll heal. Duncan, how is Major Beeson coping?"

Duncan put a finger up in the air, "Wait one." After he switched the intercom to ensure their conversation would be private, he answered Cade's question.

"It was inevitable with those bright lights inviting every dead Tom, Dick and Harry over for a bite. Camp Williams fell... it fell fast and hard. Like a big gal on roller-skates."

Cade ignored Duncan's gallows humor, it seemed to be his way of coping with the changed world - or not. "How many got out alive?"

"Put it this way. Beeson was prepared. The last thing that I saw was a long line of up-armored vehicles leaving the base. From the amount of muzzle flashes and explosions that I witnessed... they were givin' the dead hell."

"Sounds like textbook Beeson. As long as I've known the man he always has been prepared. He might have even been the very first Boy Scout and coined their motto."

Duncan snickered over the intercom, "Changing the subject on ya Cade." The tone in the old aviator's voice suddenly turned serious. "I've got bad news and I've got good news, which one do ya want to hear first?"

"Dealer's choice," Cade answered.

"I always liked to hear the bad news first... leaves a fella a
little somethin' to look forward to." Duncan took a second to
check the instrumentation before continuing, "The reason
that I bugged out of Portland when the crazies started biting
folks was to get to my baby brother's place."

Cade looked at Duncan from the co-pilot's seat, "So I
gather the bad news is we're going on a side trip." It was
more of an acknowledgement than a question. "Correct me if
I'm wrong, you said he lives near Salt Lake City... that's a *huge*
population center and I've made a point of avoiding those at
all costs."

"That's not lost on me. Did you already forget the shit that
we have been through together?"

"How can I forget the kids that went at the hands of the
Nazi bikers? I sure as hell won't forget how many undead
were streaming out of Boise. *That* was a close call... and Salt
Lake is several times more populated."

"Logan's place should be safe; it's about fifty miles north
of Salt Lake, up in the hill country. Also it's smack dab in the
middle of a lot of wooded acreage. From what he told me
last, it's made up of a series of semi-subterranean bunkers
with good fields of fire, water, the works. The place wasn't
very elaborate the first time he gave me a tour."

Cade broke in, "When was that?"

"The late nineties, he was getting ready for the Y2K bug
before anyone in the lamestream media ever got wind of it.
You and I both know how that one panned out."

"Nothing but a whimper, *but... a lot of people got rich off of the
panic*," Cade said while he scanned the airspace on his side of
the helicopter. He had stopped looking groundward early into
the flight. All of the dead bodies and walking dead made him
fear for Brook and Raven. Lately a palpable sense of
impending doom settled in his gut every time he thought

about their wellbeing and whereabouts. "When were you there last, and can you find it from the air?"

"Late last year, and it's much improved. Can I find it from the air? No telling. But rest assured I won't burn all of our remaining fuel searching. I guarantee we'll have enough fuel to get to Colorado Springs."

"I'm curious... after Y2K fizzled what prompted Logan to keep prepping?"

"Lately, my little brother feared that a looming financial crash was imminent. Not only is Logan a 'prepper' but he's a Mormon also... so as you can imagine, he's more than ready for any and all hardships. I'm sure he's still in denial his favorite type of horror movie has become reality. No better reason than that for me to ride this thing out at his place."

"What do you mean by *his favorite type of horror movie?*"

"You wouldn't believe me if I told you." Duncan waved his hand in a dismissive gesture.

"Try me..." Cade hated not knowing all of the details going into a situation.

"Not only is my baby bro Logan a fan of the movies and such..." Duncan looked at Cade, and acting against everything his inner voice was telling him, continued his confession, "he was into the zombie walks or whatever they *were* called, and he also belonged to a zombie apocalypse preparedness group."

"You have got to be shitting me."

"I wouldn't shit my favorite turd." Duncan cackled. "And it's a good thing our friends in the back aren't listening in. I'm afraid we would have a mutiny on our hands if they were privy to all of this. As far as Logan is concerned, he didn't believe this zombie apocalypse was going to happen, it was all just for fun, role playing type stuff... but I hope that he was taking notes."

"Can't wait to meet him." Cade was envisioning a thirty-something, Dungeons and Dragon playing, comic book reading nerd.

"Grab my go-bag, it's next to the bulkhead there. Look in the top pouch, there's a small notebook, on the first page are the GPS coordinates to my bro's place. Punch in the lats and longs and we'll see if we can surprise him."

The Black Hawk hit another patch of turbulent air; everyone was jostled in their seats.

While he keyed in the coordinates Cade continued the interrogation. "I hope this prepper sibling of yours doesn't put a Stinger man portable up our tailpipe."

Duncan's southern inflection made the words sound all the more ominous. "That thought has already crossed my mind, lad, and I've taken the time to acquaint myself with the countermeasures on this bird." A shit eating grin spread across the aviator's face. Cade pretended not to notice.

"How old is this baby brother of yours?"

Duncan let out a cackle. "His nickname is *Oops*. He's your age. I think you two will hit it off famously."

"Duncan, I'm very grateful that you lived up to your word. You fly. I'll navigate."

"That reminds me. Do you still want to hear the good news?"

"Hell yes, seeing as how I've yet to hear even a shred of good news since day one of this monster march."

"Brace yourself. The last news that Beeson heard out of Colorado Springs was that quite a few civilians - including *women* and *children* - had escaped from Fort Bragg and relocated there."

Before Duncan was halfway through telling Cade the news he could see the former Delta Operator's face soften, his usual steely determined look replaced by what appeared to be a newfound hope. Cade let out a whoop and pumped his fist, "*Yee-Haw!*"

It was the most emotion Duncan had seen from the stoic fella since they met, days ago, back in Oregon.

"I suspected you had a little cowboy in you," Duncan said, as he switched the intercom to include the other passengers in case they wanted to communicate anything.

"Someone win the lottery up there?" Daymon asked.

"You could say that." Cade pumped his fist again and gave Duncan a spirited high five. Cade felt it in his stomach first, the helicopter was slowly descending. Duncan was bringing them down, closer to the thick canopy of trees.

Changing the subject, Duncan asked, "Who's the fella with the spider on his head?" He was obviously talking about Daymon and his full mane of tightly woven dreadlocks, and apparently didn't care that the man was listening in on the comms.

"Says his name is Daymon, he's proven himself capable against the walkers... the guy's deadly with his crossbow, the best I've ever seen."

Duncan welcomed the young man aboard. "Good to make your acquaintance, son. My name's Duncan Winters, glad to meet ya."

"Likewise dude." Daymon nodded and smiled, although inwardly he still seethed at the disrespectful comment. "You need to know... where you're headed... that place is crawling with those things. I've seen them with my own eyes. My mom lived there. There ain't nothing living there now. I couldn't get closer than Provo. The fuckers were rushing my Suburban so I turned around and was headed home to Jackson Hole before I met Mister Glock in my face."

"You did the right thing son," Duncan said. "But don't worry, we're going northeast of the city... way up in the hills."

Daymon hated people who told him not to worry. *I've been worrying since that bitch of a mom threw her baby boy in the dumpster,* he thought, *don't worry my ass.* "I know, I know, but it still doesn't feel good. It's like there will be no closure for me. I already miss her." Daymon's voice trailed off. He was certainly not finished mourning the loss of the lady he considered his mom, the one who adopted him thirty-two years ago. Suddenly he exploded, *"The right thing to do is nuke the fuckers responsible for this nightmare that I can't seem to wake up from."*

"Someday, someone will put the pieces of the puzzle together and pinpoint where it all started. I'm sure the CDC is working hard to find an antidote," Cade said. He shivered thinking about the ramifications if he were wrong.

"I've been thinking that this thing... It's got to be manmade. Mother Nature can be cold and cruel but she ain't evil. You know what I'm saying." Daymon's eyes were welling up with tears which he made sure to conceal from the others.

Duncan kept scanning the Black Hawk's gauges while he listened in on the conversation.

Cade looked Daymon straight in the eyes. "I concur, but *anger* won't serve you well now. Keep a level head and stay frosty."

Wiping the tears with his sleeve, Daymon uttered a simple, "Thanks."

"Believe you me Daymon… there will be a judgment day," Cade intoned without removing his eyes from the gray ribbon of highway clogged with cars and death. Without realizing it, even after subtly admonishing the younger man, somehow a trace of anger had crept into his voice.

Off to the port side of the ship, thunderclouds were beginning to form in advance of the usual afternoon sky show. The Black Hawk dipped and then immediately regained the lost altitude. Cade normally liked roller coasters but the constant turbulence near the mountain range was doing a number on his empty stomach.

"So this crossbow master is the only tagalong you picked up this go around?" Duncan instantly wished he could take the words back. He knew the hurt that his friend harbored after their harrowing journey from Oregon to Utah. Five fine people died too soon and he feared the man sitting to his right still shouldered the blame.

After a barely perceptible sigh, Cade responded. "There was another guy - a small town lawyer - he didn't make it out of the farmhouse." After a moment of thought, Cade added coldly, "He would've been nothing but a dragging anchor anyway."

In the back of the Black Hawk, Daymon pursed his lips, fighting to suppress a knowing grin.

***

Eden, Utah.

As Duncan skimmed the tree tops, he knew his brother's property was nearby. It had been a number of years since he had even set eyes on the property, and that had been from the ground.

Vincent broke in. "I think I see something on the left side. Looks like a bunch of airplanes in a clearing."

Duncan slewed the Black Hawk to the left for a better view.

An unimproved dirt runway bisected the expansive green meadow; the open ground was entirely surrounded by thick forest. Civilian airplanes were parked on both sides of the airstrip. Several different models of Cessna, a couple of Piper Cubs, a Beechcraft Bonanza and a Bell Jet Ranger helicopter were scattered about the grounds. The closer they got, the more confident Duncan was that his brother Logan was somehow responsible for the rural airstrip.

"Starboard side, one body," Cade said, informing Duncan of the contact.

A man emerged from the trees shouldering a long black rifle. Sunlight glinted off of the high powered scope attached over the barrel, and a big muzzle brake capped off the business end.

"I was only kidding earlier about the shoulder fired missile, but that guy's got a cannon pointed at us," Cade stated dryly.

"I'm no expert, and furthermore my eyesight isn't what it used to be, but that looks like one of those Barrett fifty-cals. I've seen what a fifty caliber round can do to a fuselage... that

thing might as *well* be a missile." Duncan put the Black Hawk
into a hover.

"Slowly rotate the bird and show them she's unarmed."

"Good idea Cade," Duncan said, a huge grin spread across
his face.

"There's no chance we're going to get shot out of the
sky... *is there?* Vincent asked nervously.

"Not another Hoss..." Daymon hissed, prompting Duncan
to once again block the passengers from talking on the
comms.

The man aiming the sniper rifle abruptly tilted it
downward and waved the chopper in.

Duncan picked a spot away from the dirt airstrip, well
clear of the other aircraft. The Black Hawk flared and settled
into the spongy grass.

Cade noted the soft landing but detected an abnormal
shudder when Duncan powered down the rotors. Duncan
noticed the anomaly as well and looked over to see Cade
nodding his helmet.

Cade made sure the M4 was nearby and ready while he
watched the seemingly unarmed man approach.

Duncan flicked the comms back on and looked behind
him at the two passengers. "I'm getting out for just a second,
can you guys stay put?"

"I've got nowhere else to be," Daymon muttered.

"Me neither," Vincent said shrugging.

Duncan left the rotors spinning, disembarked the medevac
Black Hawk and strode towards the man.

Cade exited the helo, M4 at the ready and scanned the
woods and static aircraft for any threats. He turned to check
on Duncan in time to see him warmly embrace the other
man; they hugged for some time. Cade's attention was drawn
to the nose of the helicopter; Duncan had drawn wicked
shark's teeth around the chin. *I'll be damned, that wily bastard.*

He had also scrawled the word "Oops!" underneath the white teeth.

A clue that only his brother could decipher, Cade thought. *Brilliant.*

Duncan waved Cade over. He yelled to be heard over the turbine noise from the helicopter, "Cade, this is my younger brother Logan."

Logan was about even in height with Duncan; Cade had a couple of inches on both of them. When Logan smiled, his eyes scrunched up. The goatee and handlebar mustache made him look like he belonged behind the bar in an old west saloon.

Cade extended his hand in greeting. "Good to meet you. This old man has had nothing but good things to say about you."

The same southern inflection that Duncan spoke with was evident when the younger man opened his mouth. "I wish I could reciprocate but he always gave me hell..." Feeling a little sheepish, Logan added, "not really, he taught me everything I know."

"And everyone tells me that I don't know shit... now I feel sorry for you bro." Duncan's infectious laugh filled the air.

Logan's voice lowered, he seemed more serious. "How did you get the Black Hawk?" he asked Duncan as he worried his black goatee.

"That's a long story, I'll tell it in its entirety when I return. I'm gonna take Cade and the two fellas we picked up to Colorado Springs."

"Yeah, yeah... I heard from a Ham radio operator in Denver that the government is relocating there," Logan added.

"Where did you get the .50 cal?"

Logan belly laughed. "It's a Barrett M82A1. I got it at the big gun show in South Jordan last summer. Pretty good deterrent... huh?"

"Not out in the open like that. Pretty good way to get yourself killed little brother, especially if you were to point that rifle at the wrong military chopper."

"I saw "Oops" on the nose. I knew it was you. I usually reserve this thing for the stray Cessna that sees the strip. Let's go to the compound... you guys can stay as long as you want."

"No. I gave my word. We've got to go ASAP."

"Before you boogie, do you need anything big brother?"

Duncan swiveled his head indicating no. "Cade, how are you set on ammo?"

"I could use a couple of mags full of 5.56 and some loose 9 mm for the Glock."

Logan motioned to the trees. A figure in a ghillie suit peeled from the background and advanced towards them. "Jamie, can you spare a few AR mags full of .223 or 5.56?"

The boonie hat came off and with it the foliage obscuring the sniper's face. There was an attractive brunette woman under the ghillie suit.

"I can give you all three of mine. There's plenty more where they came from in the facility."

Cade took the magazines and thanked the woman warrior. It was then he noticed the other figures, at least a dozen, scattered in the shadows along the forest's edge.

Duncan cleared his throat and reached out for his kin. He gave his brother his satellite phone and another bear hug. In his best Schwarzenegger accent he said, *"I'll be baack."*

Cade gave Logan a nod of his head, turned and walked back to the helo.

Duncan stayed behind for a few minutes and held a private conversation with his baby brother and then forced himself to walk back to the Black Hawk. Before he had covered half the distance, he looked back at Logan and mouthed the words, *I love you brother.*

Parting was always difficult for Duncan. He had made a vow to his brother that he would come back as soon as possible.

As soon as they left the ground Cade punched in the coordinates that would direct them to Colorado Springs.

***

"Looks like downtown Baghdad the morning after "Shock and Awe," Cade said as he surveyed the Salt Lake metro area from the co-pilot seat in the Black Hawk. The only movement below was the walking dead. Smoke and pieces of newspaper and trash carried on the wind. Fires still smoldered from the widespread looting that had taken place between the initial outbreak and the formal declaration of martial law.

Cade had watched the footage of looting and zombie attacks alike live on satellite television the first day and night after the outbreak. He wondered how the people partaking came to the conclusion that a new fifty-inch flat screen and a case of vodka were going to help them in times like these.

"Look at that mess. You all see, I wasn't talkin' out of the side of my neck," Daymon looked to Vincent for validation.

"Sure is a shit show down there," Vincent said without making eye contact.

"Anyway, can we go and check on my Mom?" Daymon asked, his voice conveying his desperation.

Duncan's southern drawl entered the conversation. "Daymon, I fully intend on coming back this way in a day or two. While I'd like to help you find your Mom and Pop right now, I can't, and there isn't sufficient fuel to loiter anywhere. I'm sorry, son."

"Just drop me off then."

"That would be suicide. You told us you couldn't get close in that big green Suburban of yours," Cade said. "On foot... you wouldn't last a second."

Daymon knew it would be futile to argue, it was three to one. Lost in his own thoughts, he turned towards the window and watched a dying United States flash by.

***

"Ding. Your seatbelt light is now extinguished; feel free to move around the cabin."

Daymon rolled his eyes. He was still getting over the fact that he was out of options and being *shanghaied* to Colorado Springs. He really didn't appreciate the standup comedian show.

"We are now leaving the city limits of Boulder, Colorado. Our airspeed is a comfortable one hundred knots and thanks to a slight tailwind we should be arriving at our destination before O'dark thirty." Duncan's strange brand of humor earned snickers from Vincent and Cade both.

With a not so gentle tug, Daymon disconnected his helmet from the onboard communications system and closed his eyes.

***

Denver had been more of the same: death, destruction and multitudes of walking dead. Everyone aboard the Black Hawk had long since grown accustomed to the sights, smells and sounds now dominating the landscape.

Duncan had done some calculations or made a semi-educated guess - he wasn't certain which. He deduced that they would be on fumes or forced to find a landing spot on the outskirts of Colorado Springs. Duncan hoped he was wrong, and they would have enough to get them all the way to Schriever AFB, but he had a gut feeling they would be doing some walking before the day was done. He switched the comms and let Cade in on the bad news.

***

They were twenty miles south of Denver when Duncan noticed a slight shimmy transmitted through his stick. When he was piloting a UH-1 Huey, he knew what every little shake, tremor or abnormal sound meant. The Uh-60 on the other hand was like a new girlfriend - unfortunately he didn't know how to read her. The one thing that Duncan was certain of, whatever his new girlfriend was trying to tell him, it was anything but good. The vibrations continued and started to become more pronounced.

Cade sensed that something was wrong, Duncan was scrutinizing the instruments more closely and his body language seemed different.

"What's up Duncan?" Cade probed.

Before he could answer, a shrill alarm sounded, reverberating throughout the ship.

The moment the instrument panel lit up like a Christmas tree Cade knew that they were in for trouble.

"*Everyone brace for impact!*" The collective felt like it was stuck in quicksand, the rest of the controls were also responding sluggishly. Duncan cursed his decision to follow the I-25 freeway. Although he knew the black strip of asphalt led south, directly into downtown Colorado Springs, he failed to take into account the fact that the roadway was scattered with motionless vehicles and the undead associated with them.

Veering sideways with gut churning g-forces, the helicopter started to spin.

In the back jump seat, Vincent tightened his seatbelt and silently waited for the impact, fully expecting to die.

For Daymon, opening his eyes to the harsh sunlight was less painful than leaving the young lady he had been frolicking with in his dream. "*Ain't that just my luck!*" he exclaimed. "*About to get lucky and then I wake up feeling very unlucky.*"

"*We're going down...*" Vincent looked out his window wide eyed, "*and those things are everywhere.*"

"Take this... it's loaded." Daymon gave the Glock to Vincent and produced an extra magazine. "There are a few rounds in this too."

"What are you going to use?"

Daymon patted the neon green handle of his machete and braced for the crash landing.

Duncan wrestled with the controls; he managed to regain a somewhat straight heading, but it was a herculean effort. *She's got the altitude*, he thought, *the airspeed should be enough if I point the nose down a little.* The Black Hawk quickly fell through three-hundred feet AGL while keeping sixty knots of forward momentum. A successful autorotation required altitude and airspeed, but most importantly a clear LZ.

The freeway was a straight stretch dotted with vehicles and walking corpses. The airspace was devoid of trees and power lines but a toll station still loomed ahead. The metal framework rose at least forty feet into the air and spanned all eight lanes of the freeway.

Duncan and Cade waited for the impending collision in silence. The rotor was not receiving power from either engine; fortunately it was still spinning and providing lift. While no expert on the UH-60, Duncan had a hunch the transmission was shot. It was a fleeting thought of no importance - nothing was going to stop their free fall.

Bracing for impact, both men peered between their feet through the plexi-glass chin bubble. Someone was looking out for them; they watched the metal framework flash below the helicopter without making contact.

"That was close," Cade said.

"We're not down yet."

A multitude of cars and trucks rushed by, it was like looking through a kaleidoscope filled with shiny colors. Zombies reached skyward, futilely grabbing for the falling helicopter.

Duncan became aware of the safety barrier at the last second. The taut cable separated the northbound and southbound lanes, running parallel down the freeway's grass median. A UH-60 wasn't meant to land moving as fast as it was, but he had no alternative. Duncan thought back to his training so many years ago. The final, but very important, component to landing a helo without power is to pull as much cyclic as possible at the very last second. In theory the ship would settle, without pranging, and roll on its wheels, bleeding off any excess airspeed.

The median blazed at them, a sharp jolt reverberated upon impact through the rigid airframe and directly up everyone's spine.

So much for theory, the experienced aviator thought.

The Black Hawk bounced twice before its left wheel caught on the cable. Newton's law reared its ugly head, for every action, it states, there is an equal and opposite reaction. The opposite reaction *was not* pretty. The massive Black Hawk did a one-eighty, the starboard side slamming against the cable barrier. The violence from the sudden neck-breaking halt sent every loose piece of equipment flying around the crew compartment; dangerous missiles seeking flesh and bone.

Daymon caught a face full of Duncan's canvas go-bag. A medical kit popped open resulting in a white explosion that filled the air with bandages and gauze.

Vincent's head crashed into the bulkhead, the blow temporarily knocking him out.

After all of the kinetic energy had bled off the Black Hawk ground to a halt and made one last death rattle. Duncan was awestruck that the rotor blades hadn't disintegrated into a million tiny pieces and some stroke of luck had kept the helicopter from rolling. White acrid smoke drifted up inside the cabin of the broken bird but thankfully no flames materialized.

The voice of *Duncan Airways* invaded all but Daymon's helmet. "Head count. Who's still among the living?"

"Barely," said Vincent, his voice sounding weak.

Daymon remained silent and tossed the old man's go-bag up front to him.

It was a miracle, Duncan thought, *the shotgun strapped to it didn't knock him out or claim a few of his teeth.* Luck, it seemed, was always on Daymon's side.

Cade could see that the door next him was jammed shut; the helicopter had absorbed a lot of energy and settled up against the divider on his side. He unbuckled his seatbelt and armed himself with the Colt M4 before he entered the passenger compartment. He found his tactical helmet. It had been thrown around in the crash and was partially buried under bandages, gauze and medicine bottles. He put it on in place of the bulky flight helmet. Cade noticed that Vincent, now fully alert, had somehow gotten ahold of the Glock 17. Knowing full well the soldier was only a cook back at Camp Williams, Cade had to ask him some embarrassing questions. "Have you qualified with a pistol lately?"

"It's been a while, but the last time at the range I scored pretty well."

Now the hard one, Cade thought. "Have you killed a man in combat?"

Before Vincent had a chance to answer, something fleshy impacted the starboard side. Slimy palm prints appeared, followed by the sneering face of a female zombie smacking its yellowed teeth on the glass.

Cade singled out the former camp cook, looking him square in the face. "Don't hesitate. Aim for the head. Most importantly, they aren't human anymore, *shoot to kill.*"

Cade recognized the unmistakable sound of a shotgun round being chambered. Without needing to look, he instinctively knew Duncan was in the fight and good to go. "*Out, everyone out now.*" They were in store for some running and gunning and if they didn't find transportation quickly their day was going to end very badly.

***

I-25 Twenty miles south of Denver

Daymon was the first to open the door and set foot on the brown grass outside of the helicopter. "*We've got company. Bring your A-game!*" he bellowed, brandishing the machete in his right hand.

Cade watched the man work, his dreadlocks whipped behind him as the deadly blade cut the air in front. In a matter of seconds four zombies lay decapitated, in a semi-circle, near Daymon's feet.

Cade spotted a legion of undead pressed around a livestock transporter a few hundred yards to the north; they were obviously attracted to the animals trapped inside. He could hear the sound of the hungry zombies clearly from his position. Some of them were starting to amble in their direction, drawn by the commotion of the downed Black Hawk. There were far less of the creatures to the south but Cade sensed that the noose of undead was tightening around the small group. They were caught in a catch twenty-two; for every zombie they killed, many more would be attracted by the resulting gunfire.

Duncan discharged the twelve gauge point blank into the walker nearest him. The moaning ghoul's face disappeared in a viscous spray of decomposed dermis and muscle. For good measure he introduced the thing's skull to the butt of his combat shotgun.

"This way!" Duncan made the decision for all of them. They would be going south, and so was the situation they found themselves facing. Although he couldn't see well enough to make out the writing on the side of the squat vehicle, he did recognize the unmistakable yellow horse-drawn stagecoach above the words. It was a Wells Fargo armored truck wedged in a sea of stalled cars.

Vincent's pistol bucked four times. Two 9 mm bullets found their mark, and two sailed high. The scrawny zombie fell to the roadway. Many more were closing in from the left.

Cade emptied an entire magazine into the throng of undead, squeezing off well aimed single shots. The act saved Vincent's life. Cade rammed a new mag home and exhorted Vincent to keep up. Both men followed the trail of dead zombies left by Duncan and his deadly accurate shotgun.

211

They were getting into a rhythm and fighting as a team; whenever one of them had to reload the others would pick up the slack. Cade couldn't help but admire the poise and grace the lanky black man exhibited as he struck down the walking dead. The fluid cuts of the razor sharp machete reminded him of the swordsmen from the late night Kung Fu movies he used to watch as a kid. Hard as it was for Cade to believe, Daymon was better with the steel blade than the crossbow.

Zombies were falling fast. Cade was still worried that if they didn't move it soon they would find themselves surrounded and out of ammunition.

They covered the open ground rapidly, with Daymon in the lead. Duncan trotted in the middle of the group and Cade took the rear, keeping the walkers on their six, at arm's length. Vincent was of little use, but he did show courage; a lot could be said about that.

Daymon kicked one walker away from the back of the armored truck and lopped the top third of another's head clean off. The skullcap twirled through the air like a flipped coin. It landed on heads presumably, the remaining slab of frontal lobe cartwheeled through the brown grass. Daymon paused momentarily to smile at his handiwork.

Duncan walked the perimeter of the truck, shotgun at the ready. Both the driver and passenger door were closed and locked. A dead guard in full Wells Fargo regalia sat slumped in the driver's seat, maggots squirmed under his exposed skin. *It's going to reek in there*, Duncan thought, as a shiver of revulsion wracked his body.

Daymon waited by the rear doors while Vincent and Duncan crawled in.

"There's no money in here..." Vincent said, sounding truly disappointed.

"What were you gonna spend it on... hookers and blow?" Duncan queried half-way seriously.

Duncan checked the ignition, there were no keys dangling from it. He turned his head away from the decomposing driver and drew in another lung full of semi-fresh air. The security guard had died doing his job; there was a puckered entry wound in his neck right above his Kevlar vest. The ensuing blood loss killed him and left his uniform saturated. Fully repulsed, Duncan reached into the dead driver's pants looking for their ticket out. He found two things in the corpse's pockets: lint and squirming fly larvae. "*We have no keys goddammit.*" Duncan's pissed off drawl echoed from the armored truck's interior.

Cade's attention was drawn by Duncan's verbal outburst. As he watched, the driver's door opened and out tumbled a bloated corpse.

"*Daymon... check the ground on that side for the keys. There is no way they up and walked off on their own.*" Cade immediately regretted his last statement. He envisioned an undead Wells Fargo guard lurching around the countryside, the keys to the truck jangling away, still hooked on his belt. That was the last thing they needed.

"*Got 'em!*" Daymon held the keys in the air and jingled them for effect. "Fuckers left 'em in the back door."

"Quit yer yappin and give them here." Duncan was getting nervous. The mass of undead had given up on the meat in the trailer and were shuffling towards the source of the gunfire.

Cade was putting lead downrange at the walkers. He ejected the thirty round magazine and rammed the last one in the well.

A puff of diesel exhaust enveloped Cade. "Daymon, you ride shotgun..." Cade fired ten more rounds, only four zombies fell. "I'll watch our six." Cade vaulted in and sealed everyone inside.

Daymon pinched his nose shut and climbed into the passenger seat, one long leg at a time. "Man, it stinks to high heaven up in here," his voice had taken on a Duncan-esque nasally twang. "Step on it boss."

Duncan reversed into a compact Hyundai, pushing it back several feet to free the armored truck. Slamming into first gear, he powered the large truck around the pickup blocking them in. A sickening crunch emanated from the undercarriage. Duncan grimaced, because he knew he had rolled over the guard's body. "Sorry buddy..." Duncan truly felt bad for the man and had to vent. "For Christ's sake, he was merely trying to do his job, in the middle of all this pandemonium; the fleeing people, zombie attacks." Duncan pounded the steering wheel. The same steering wheel the guard had clutched in his death grip. "Look at what he gets for staying the course. I can't believe that anyone would feel the need to pop an armored car in the middle of the end times."

"Finished?"

"Yes dear." Duncan made it sound like he was answering to his angry wife.

"Daymon... Vincent, are either one of you injured... bitten?" Cade asked.

"Good to go," Vincent replied.

"I got a few scratches from the bitches... no bites though," Daymon replied, before stating the obvious, "that's an instant effing death warrant."

Duncan wove around the wrecks, hitting and pushing more out of the way than he was able to avoid. He wasn't being shy about running over the dead. The twenty-five ton rig rolled on six wheels wrapped with bulletproof run flat tires. Duncan was confident; as long as he looked ahead and chose the right route they had a good chance of making it out alive.

The sun dipped behind the Rocky Mountains. The complete absence of light was significant, and the high desert between Denver and Colorado Springs might as well have been the dark side of the moon.

Duncan had been dreading this moment since the crash landing. He flipped the headlights on providing the dead a beacon to hone in on visually. As if on cue a zombie high fived the window inches from his face; the hand shaped stain came along for the ride. Creeping down the freeway at ten to fifteen miles an hour with the headlights summoning the undead was extremely nerve-wracking. Like he learned to do in Nam, Duncan was starting to compartmentalize his feelings and thoughts - tucking them away in the far reaches of his mind to be dealt with later. He focused on their destination at the end of I-25.

***

The armored car crept along a scant fifteen miles an hour. The sprawling campus of the darkened Air Force Academy stretched to the base of the Rockies. *No incoming officer material this year*, Duncan thought as the Cadet Chapel materialized from the dark, the spires standing out like obsidian skeletal fingers reaching to the heavens.

Duncan kept up a steady pace weaving in and out of tight spots. *Thank God*, he thought, *this isn't a rental*, as the screeching of metal on metal sounded inside the truck. It reminded him of fingernails on a chalkboard. Duncan despised the sound; the only thing worse was the fingernails of the dead scrabbling on the outside of the armored truck.

Cade was resting his eyes and on the periphery of sleep when Vincent's voice pulled him back.

"Check out these things. They're peepholes or something." Vincent unlatched the two inch square portal nearest him and moved his face closer to peek outside.

"Not a good idea, soldier." Cade snatched the young private by the elbow and pulled him away. One second later and he would have gotten the Three Stooges treatment.

A single grimy finger poked through the hole and blindly rooted around.

"Almost lost an eye there, *Curly*, that's a firing port," Cade said as he snapped the hatch shut, forcing the pasty digit to retreat.

"Th..th..thanks... I shoulda known. C..c..can I shoot that nosy f..f..f..fucker?" Vincent stuttered.

Daymon sat reclined in the passenger seat with his head tilted back. His eyes were shut in an attempt to keep the monsters on the other side of the glass from becoming fodder for future nightmares. "Save the bullets Vinnie... if this truck goes tits up, we'll need all four of them, one for each of us."

Chapter 34
Outbreak - Day 7
I-25

"Sir, we have a contact. Slow mover... looks to be paralleling I-25."

Staff Sergeant Brody Johnson had only been back in the states for two days; already he had seen more combat in Colorado Springs than he had in two tours in Iraq. Although he hadn't been shot at yet, he had seen more Zs amassed in one place than he could fathom, and unlike the insurgent's shoot and scoot mentality, once they saw you, the dead were like the Eveready Bunny, they just kept coming. It was a difficult transition for the hard charging young commander, but he sensed he was turning the corner.

When they landed at Schriever there was no down time at all - he and his crew had been thrust back into action the moment their boots hit the ground. The Bradley fighting vehicle he commanded still had Middle Eastern sand stuck in every nook and cranny, the engine was running poorly and required maintenance.

The Bradley was perched atop an elevated dirt berm inside the fencing on the northwest corner of Schriever AFB. The lone vehicle was responsible for guarding a big swath of the base. A quick reaction force standing by was ready and could assist anywhere on the perimeter they were needed.

The staff sergeant hailed "Springs," the new Capital of the
United States. "Golem Actual, Golem Six-One here, how
copy?"

"Go ahead, Six-One."

"Golem Actual - be advised we have an inbound vehicle,
two klicks outside of grid November-Whisky-One-Two.
Vehicle appears to be a two axle delivery truck. I see three,
possibly four thermal hits inside. How copy?"

"Copy that, observe and report, Golem Actual out."

Golem Six-One's gunner tracked the vehicle until it
disappeared behind an obstruction. "I lost him in the clutter,"
Wilkes responded, sounding irritated.

Fifty feet from the dirt berm, right outside the wire, a
handful of zombies quietly milled about. The moment they
noticed the vehicle commander move atop the Bradley, they
started moaning.

"When you get a clean line of sight, flash them," the track
commander ordered his gunner.

"Copy that Sir."

Sergeant Wilkes kept his face pressed to the optics mast.
"Sir, the vehicle didn't reappear."

"If memory serves - isn't there an eighteen wheeler
blocking that underpass?" Commander Brody asked.

"The engineers were worried that the supports were going
to fail so they left it for the time being," Wilkes answered.

***

The survivors surged to the base on Z-day plus one; many
had already been bitten and had to be quarantined. Within
twelve hours every one of them turned. B.J. heard
secondhand how hard it was on the soldiers to put thousands
of them down. Many of the men recognized loved ones or
members of their community, making the job all the more
difficult. Over the last two days survivors had stopped
showing up altogether.

Staff Sergeant Brody Johnson felt a strong urge to go help the travelers. *The human race*, he thought, *was quickly becoming an endangered species.*

***

"This is Golem Actual, Golem Six-One requesting permission to assist civilian survivors, how copy?"

"Roger that. How many Zs are at your AO?"

"Only fifteen, Golem Six-One out."

"Golem Actual, notify Golem Six-Two that you are going off base. Sit-rep every five mikes. How copy?"

"Roger that, Golem Six-One out.

"Wilkes, hand me up the quiet carbine."

The black SCAR rifle emerged butt stock first. B.J. charged the weapon and sighted on the nearest Z. He flicked off the safety and said, "Night, night," with as much compassion as he could muster. His finger tightened on the trigger. *Breathe, squeeze easy.... pop.* The suppressed rifle was extremely quiet; the first zombie hitting the ground drew more attention than the actual sound the kill shot made leaving the rifle.

The staff sergeant had an excellent firing position from the Bradley cupola; one by one he sent the rest of the monsters to a final dirt nap.

***

The Bradley vibrated violently one time, like a dog shaking water from its coat. The exhaust pipe belched black smoke and the engine finally turned over. A clunk from the transfer case indicated that Specialist Cooley was about to back them off of the earthen berm.

Commander Johnson sprang from the top of the Bradley to let them through the secondary fence, the track easily negotiating the tight turn. Johnson scanned the area outside of the primary fence for ghouls. Satisfied all was still clear, he opened up and followed the tracked vehicle outside of the wire. As quick as humanly possible, with imaginary zombies nipping at his heels, Johnson locked the fence up and vaulted atop his Bradley.

Specialist Cooley steered the armored vehicle along a maintenance road intersecting the freeway. In a few short minutes they were moving south and dodging stalled cars on I-25.

"I have the vehicle in sight. It isn't moving sir and... there are Zs all over."

"Light 'em up Wilkes," ordered SSGT Johnson.

Electric motors whined as the turret rotated on target.

***

Duncan slowed the heavy vehicle down. When the headlights illuminated the mangled semi, he stepped on the brakes and brought them to a complete stop. The tractor was wedged against the overpass supports; the double trailer connected to it was jackknifed, blocking all four lanes.

"Dagnabbit," drawled Duncan as he searched for reverse.

Daymon opened one eye and peered at Duncan. "Is that the best one you've got? I've heard nuns pop off better."

"Mind your business and spot for me."

Bang. Something heavy slammed onto the roof. The two men in the front seat flinched and looked up as if they could see through quarter inch plate. A zombie tumbled down onto the engine cowl and crushed its face onto the windshield.

Zombies were mindlessly pushing each other off of the roadway above. The armored truck's idling engine and intense headlights were an irresistible lure. Every time one of the creatures swan dived atop the armored car the resulting impact was amplified tenfold inside.

"*Get us out of here... now!*" Cade yelled. They were on the verge of being trapped; killing himself with his own Glock was not an option.

"*I'm trying.*" The vehicle finally started creeping backwards.

Daymon feigned a look at each mirror. "OK, spotting for the driver. On the left... we have *zombies*. On the right... we have *zombies*. Can one of you guys look out the back... I'm sure there are *zombies* back there also."

"I don't need smartass remarks. I can't see a fucking thing. What's blocking us in?" Duncan was losing his cool.

"Like I said... *zom*..."

Staccato bursts of heavy machinegun fire bounced off of the cement walls and roof of the underpass. The fireworks show lit up the night on both sides of the truck. Daymon's face appeared demonic, bathed in red from the flashes of light. He had been in mid-sentence about to push Duncan's buttons some more, when the flesh-eaters surrounding them started disintegrating before his eyes. Bits and pieces of zombie bounced off of the walls. The tractor trailer rig was being splattered with flying chunks of decaying flesh and fractured bone. Toxic bodily fluids painted the sides of the double trailer and ran off in yellow and red rivulets.

"Wh..who's sh..shooting at us?" Vincent's disembodied voice asked from somewhere in the dark.

"Those are tracers from a large machine gun... someone's saving our asses," Cade answered, while he twisted his head struggling to see where the fire was coming from.

As quickly as it started it was over and once again quiet and dark below the underpass.

Duncan revved the engine and felt the truck start crawling in reverse up the slight incline. It was a bumpy ride; the fallen zombies were bursting under the weight of the Wells Fargo truck. Duncan successfully choreographed a three point turn before the armored truck grudgingly delivered them the final thirty yards uphill. Duncan had no idea what to expect or who their saviors were. A pinpoint of light flashed off to the right shoulder of the Interstate.

"What do you make of that?" Daymon asked.

Duncan nervously checked the mirrors while dabbing beads of sweat from his forehead. "My Morse code is rusty... I think the first letters were F-O..."

"*Follow them*," Cade ordered.

"To the point my brother," Daymon let his gaze lock with Cade's.

Cade processed the silent interaction. He wasn't able to decipher whether it was a silent challenge or if he was just Daymon being Daymon. After all, the man was good at acting abrasive.

"Can't be any worse than staying put and letting ourselves get surrounded again," Duncan added as he engaged the transmission. The armored truck lurched forward and they blindly followed the tracked vehicle.

From the brief glance of the silhouette Cade surmised it was a Bradley fighting vehicle, and since it was rolling solo they had to be close to their base. He had a feeling that he was going to get some sort of closure, one way or the other, in the coming hours.

***

The Bradley sped east on the gravel two lane road. Duncan had his hands full trying to keep up. They were running with the lights on, but the dust being kicked up by the tracked vehicle made their headlights virtually ineffective.

"Where do you think they're taking us?" Cade noticed that Vincent had somehow shed the stutter, but decided not to mention it to him.

"We're on a United States military reservation. I noticed surveillance domes spaced a few hundred yards apart on the perimeter fencing, standard United States base security. The same stuff went up everywhere after the 9/11 attacks."

A building loomed. It looked like a very large bomber hanger. Cade had been on airbases like this all over the world. The pieces were falling in place... they had finally arrived at Schriever AFB in Colorado Springs.

The hangar doors parted only wide enough to allow the two vehicles entry; brilliant fluorescent lights illuminated the interior of the expansive hangar. The building was designed to be large enough to service two C-5 Galaxys at the same time.

Cade noted that several prefab buildings were erected inside of the hangar. Multiple rows of empty hospital beds also drew his attention. They stretched the length of the hangar, spaced uniformly like the grave markers at Arlington. Cade estimated they numbered in the hundreds. "If this is a quarantine building gentlemen... clearly someone was anticipating a lot more survivors."

Two men in full level four bio hazard suits motioned for Duncan to stop the truck.

"Looks like we're going to get the once over," drawled Duncan as he shut off the engine.

"It's in our best interest to cooperate. Be ready to relinquish any weapons. It's most likely their SOP to disarm, disrobe and disinfect us," Cade said, just trying to be realistic.

"Wow boss. You make it sound like a fuckin spa treatment," Daymon retorted.

Cade took note as three soldiers dismounted their M2 Bradley and joined the welcoming party. Two of the three were armed with SCAR carbines held at the low-ready position. Cade figured they were being cautious in case anyone in his group suddenly died and reanimated.

"Gentlemen, are any of you armed?" The soldier speaking to them was a staff sergeant; he was obviously the commander and the highest ranking of the three. Cade couldn't see his uniform well enough to discern his unit, but he was Army.

Duncan took the lead. "Yes Sir, but we're low on ammunition. Thanks for saving my ass... our asses back there. It was looking a little hopeless for us."

"To be honest, I had a hard time believing what I was seeing when you entered our assigned sector. Denver is hot with the infected and we haven't seen anyone arriving from the north in a couple of days. The good thing is that the dead aren't here in large numbers *yet*."

"Well, I still owe you one staff sergeant."

"Now... the weapons please."

223

Daymon relinquished his machete - rather reluctantly.

Cade dropped the mag and cleared his M4 before handing it to the SSGT.

Duncan racked all of the shells from his shotgun and handed it over butt first.

"I left the Glock in the truck," Vincent said clearly without stammering or stuttering.

"*Follow me*," said one of the men in the rubber suit. His voice came through the speaker sounding thin and unnatural. The four survivors complied. Each were led to a separate exam area and ordered to disrobe.

Vincent received a thorough once over. The doctors, or whoever they were, appeared to be looking for obvious bite wounds. He also had to stand in front of a thermal body scanner, he had no idea what for. After the battery of tests he was pointed in the direction of the showers.

Duncan got the same treatment and retired to the showers after a few extra debriefing questions.

Daymon didn't go so easy. He had a hard time with the authority being heaped upon him. The soldiers handcuffed him and let the doctors check him out under their watchful eyes.

Cade received the most scrutiny. The gash on his nose was cleaned and sutured while the attendee grilled him about the injury. The man in the suit also asked him about the scarred over gunshot wounds on his shoulder and neck.

"Hunting accident," Cade replied.

"So you hunt two legged prey?"

"No comment. *Are we finished here?*" Cade was growing tired of the inquisition and found it hard to follow the advice he gave the others.

"For now, but my superior is going to want to talk to you about the conditions outside."

Cade locked eyes with the doctor. "I need to know if there are any survivors from Fort Bragg on this base. My wife

Brooklyn and my eleven-year-old daughter Raven may have been refugees from there. *Do you know anything?*"

"I'm sorry to hear about your situation. I know that a few helicopters arrived here from back East a few days after the outbreak. I wasn't on base yet when they arrived so I can't be certain exactly where they came from. The base is getting more crowded day by day. Our guys are coming back from deployment in waves; I suggest that you find Major Freda Nash. If anyone knows who, what or where... it's her."

Cade knew the major but didn't let on. "Thanks. It's the little bit of hope that I needed. Where can I get some chow?" *There's no way*, Cade thought, *that I'll be able to sleep.*

***

Cade took a very long hot shower, totally oblivious to the other three survivors.

Daymon stared at Cade's tattoo; the word "INFIDEL" arced from one shoulder blade to the other, rendered in black Old English lettering. It reminded Daymon of the "THUG LIFE" tat that Tupac Shakur had on his stomach and took with him to the grave. "Looks like my man likes his bacon," Daymon paused for comedic effect but not one person laughed at his joke. Not wanting to lose the center stage he tried another one liner. "Or his wife caught him doing someone he wasn't s'posed to be doin'." *Crickets*. Daymon was nonplussed, "I'm getting some sleep. It's been real fellas." The track commander directed Daymon to the round the clock cafeteria and also where he could find a place to sleep.

The Bradley commander singled out Vincent. "Private, get dressed and come with us. Someone will give you the standard orientation in the morning. The enlisted sleeping quarters are down by the flight line, we'll take you over there. Should be plenty quiet going forward, most of the C-130s and C-5s have already landed. Springs is only about fifty percent cleared and that means we've got plenty of doors to kick and lots of Zs to deal with."

225

Vincent looked at Duncan and Daymon, snapped them a
quick salute and followed his newfound superiors.

Duncan put on a clean pair of ACUs, said "Adios" to
Cade and Daymon and set off in search of a rack with clean
sheets. The man was bone tired from all the running. *Hell,* he
thought, *even a hot rack with week old bedbug infested sheets would do.*

Only Cade and Daymon remained. Cade spoke first, "You
might want to stick around. I have a feeling someone with
your skill is going to be in demand around here."

"I think I have to sleep on that. I do have a strong feeling
that my mom is dead... it's a gut feeling and I always trust my
gut." Daymon put up a closed fist, waiting for a bump.

Cade reciprocated, "In that respect, you and I are alike,
and my gut tells me I'll be seeing more of you."

"So far this parting of the ways has a kinder, gentler feel to
it... unlike our *gun in my face* first meeting."

"I'm sorry... it was necessary considering the
circumstances," Cade replied casually.

With a *think nothing of it* flick of his wrist, Daymon walked
out of the exam cubicle.

Cade had come so far and overcame so many obstacles to
find his family. The feeling resonating in his bones tried to tell
him that everything would be all right. The former Delta
Force operator was left sitting half naked and alone, while his
hopes and doubts battled for supremacy in his head.

Chapter 35
Outbreak - Day 7
Schriever AFB
Colorado Springs, Colorado

She had been running nonstop for what seemed like an eternity. Every time she reached a seemingly safe refuge, a pack of the fast moving zombies would cut her off.

A crumpled galvanized steel garbage can lay between her and a darkened alleyway. Brook vaulted the obstacle with ease and set her sights on a low-hanging fire escape.

The undead had tapped into a new wellspring of energy and were now sprinting after her, moving more fluidly than before and faster than she had ever seen. The ghouls snarled and moaned, clicking their teeth - anticipating her meat.

Brook leapt for the bottom rung and snared it with both hands. The ladder was supposed to slide down but it didn't budge.

"Get away from me," Brook screamed. With all of her might she pulled herself up the ladder one rung at a time. She felt a tug as one of the creatures caught ahold of her boot. Their combined weight pulled the ladder down and dropped her into the crowd of hungry zombies.

Brook awoke thinking that she was dead, but quickly realized someone was banging on the screen door.

"Auntie Brook... Auntie Brook. Get up, our brother is coming."

Her next waking thought was one of gratitude - she was thankful that she was alive and more importantly that the superfast and agile zombies weren't real.

"OK... I'm getting dressed. Come in for a moment girls."

Raven stirred on the top bunk bed. "Mom, what's wrong?"

"Get up sweetie. Aunt Annie is going to have her baby."

Raven stretched and yawned and then greeted the twins.

Sierra and Serena calmed down and waited on the bottom bunk for Brook to get dressed.

"Is your mom in any pain?" Brook didn't expect accurate information from the young twins.

Sierra answered, "Not really... but she says she's really hungry."

"She *is* eating for two... Why don't you three go and get some food and then hurry right back."

"Ewww, the food is awful here," Raven stated.

"The food's not for you... it's for Annie."

The twins retreated further into the bottom bunk to escape Raven's dangling legs.

Brook bolted from the room on her way to the infirmary.

"What wrong?" Dmitri asked in broken English. The orphaned boy had adopted Brook and Raven. He was still half asleep on the top bunk adjacent to Raven's.

"Everything is OK Dmitri. It's real early. Go back to sleep," Raven said.

The three girls were off on their mission to get Annie something to eat. Before the screen door slammed shut Dmitri had already resumed snoring.

Chapter 36
Outbreak - Day 7
Over Kansas

Ari decreased throttle. A slight clunk sounded indicating the aircraft's separation. The refueling boom sticking out of the Pave Hawk's nose retracted to a more aerodynamic position. The KC-135 pilot pushed the throttles to gain altitude while he initiated a hard bank to starboard. The first two pit stops were done in the dark and had required the tanker to fly ahead and loiter in a racetrack pattern, waiting for the slower Pave Hawk to rendezvous. The KC-135 out of MacDill AFB in Tampa, Florida and the black helicopter had already performed the delicate dance three times during the thousand mile flight. It was obvious to Ari that the tanker pilot and crew wanted to return home and he couldn't blame them.

Ari Silver had been pushing the Pave Hawk hard on their return flight. The earth flashed by underneath the HH-60G at one hundred and seventy knots; Kansas was but a gold and brown blur basking in the glow of the rising sun.

"Three down, none to go," Ari updated anyone that cared to listen. It had been a long grueling stretch of flying, Ari was fatigued, but at least the hardest part, aerial refueling, was over. He shifted in his seat, his butt happy that the finish line was getting closer.

General Desantos adjusted his boom microphone before responding, "Where are we right now?"

"Sir, we're passing over Garden City, Kansas."

Ever since Ari had relayed the message from the SATCOM that Annie Desantos had gone into labor, Mike Desantos had started acting fidgety and impatient, a far cry from his normal stoic and reserved demeanor. "That should put us close to the Colorado border... right?"

"Sir, yes Sir. You are going to be meeting your son before twelve hundred hours."

A huge grin sprouted on the Delta Force commander's craggy face. Even though it smelled like road kill inside of the helicopter and the undead Chinese national was still kicking and squirming in the bag at his feet, today was the best day of Mike's life.

Chapter 37
Outbreak - Day 7
Schriever AFB
Colorado Springs, Colorado

Cade picked at his powdered scrambled eggs. No matter how much Tabasco he put on base chow it always tasted the same. He should be grateful, he thought, it was the first hot food that he had eaten in days, and the first meal he had had the pleasure of attempting to consume without having to be hypervigilant of his surroundings. He chose a seat in the far corner of the building where he could watch the comings and goings. The only other people occupying the cafeteria appeared to be an aircrew. The three men and a woman attired in blue flight suits talked animatedly amongst themselves.

Cade looked at his Suunto. It was 0330 and soon more soldiers would be filing in for morning chow, he was sure of that.

A man approached with a plate of the same runny eggs and a cup full of something hot, tendrils of steam wafting up. The older man sat down gingerly, thrust his meaty hand across the table and introduced himself. "Hi, name's Dan."

"Cade... good to meet you," he said pumping Dan's hand.

"What brings you here at zero-three-thirty?" Dan queried, while he stirred the soupy eggs with his fork.

"Just got in from the outside." Cade finished the last of his
meal and changed the subject. He pointed with his chin. "Is
that coffee?"

"Big urn of it over that way," the bearded man pointed at
the end of the steam tables with his fork and started talking.
"I had one of the worst nightmares of my adult life..." Cade
asked Dan to wait one; he had already extricated one of his
legs from under the table and was intent on getting some
coffee.

Cade returned with the steaming mug and sat down ready
to listen. Guessing that he had at least three hours to kill
before the civilians would be out and about, he decided he'd
let this gentleman waste a couple for him.

"As I was saying, I've had claustrophobic nightmares - I
was a tunnel rat in Nam and I don't want to go there. I have
had people shooting at me in my nightmares... always lived."
Dan took a long pull of his coffee, dried his mustache and
then resumed. "This one... was too real. It was a zombie
nightmare. Slow movers... hungry as hell. Well, when they
finally got me I was taken to their leader, the biggest zombie
of the bunch... red hair flowing everywhere..."

This got Cade's attention. He leaned in.

"...the bastard hooked me up to his motorcycle and
dragged me down the main street of the town where I grew
up. In my nightmare, I noticed a sign on that main drive,
"Welcome to Stanley, Idaho, Population 100." The sign still
stands there today... let me remind you. I escaped from there
twenty-four hours ago." Dan intentionally left out the
incidental details, *sleeping with thoughts of suicide fresh in his mind
and being caught off guard by the U.S. Army*, it was a little bit
embarrassing. "I've got a black hole in my heart... I had to say
goodbye to some good friends two days ago. I've lost friends
to old age, illness, war, accidents... when you get to my age
that's gonna happen. My friends were murdered... *that's
personal.*"

Cade cataloged all of this in his mind while the orator paused for effect.

"But I digress. Anyway, take a guess what the sign read right before I woke up?"

Cade longed for some more coffee but he was enjoying the story. "I have no idea."

Dan cleared his throat. "The numbers on that sign, which hadn't been changed since the last census in 2000, had been crossed out and changed to zero. I presume to reflect all of the people killed by Ganz and his gang."

"You mean the man in your nightmare, the large redheaded biker is real, and not your personal bogey man?" Right then Cade knew the murderous biker that had tried to kill him was still alive.

"That man is responsible for killing my good friend, Stanley's only Sheriff, Bob Blanda, his teenaged daughter Irene and countless others. Almost forgot old Bo, another good man gone." Dan swiped a napkin from the table, dried his eyes and blew his nose. "I thought all of that shit was behind me. Now I don't even want to sleep... couldn't, even if I wanted to. What's an old man to do?"

"Talking it out is a great start."

"I've been a loner for so many years... all the talking goes on internally. I've been stuffing *everything* since Nam."

"Thanks for your service." Cade said with a nod of his head. "Marines I presume."

"Oorah," Dan smiled but didn't offer the other details. During *his* war, there were very few Marine Force Recon members in the MACV-SOG groups that actually were part of the hunter killer teams. Nearly half of the men over fifty-five he had ever met in a bar claimed Vietnam service, and quite a few declared elite unit membership. In Dan's opinion, if you talked about it, you were full of it.

"Army," Cade stated, waiting for the cross branch ribbing that was sure to come.

"Son, *thank you for your service* and for lettin' me bend your ear. I'm gonna go see if I can hold a wrench for someone at the motor pool - gotta feel useful somehow."

Cade watched the honored veteran return his tray and head for the door. He truly admired men like Dan, they had paved the way for him and he was grateful for that.

Cade looked at his watch, *0430*. Only an hour had passed, the coffee wasn't doing its thing and he wanted to rest his eyes. Instead of succumbing to the overwhelming draw of sleep he opted to give caffeine another try.

Two steps removed from the coffee urn, Cade was tackled, and two thin arms encircled his waist. Off balance, he did the cup of full Joe dance, barely spilling a drop of his coffee.

"Daddy, Daddy..." Raven screamed Daddy for several moments; she was clearly going into shock.

Cade wrapped her up in a big bear hug. "Raven... Raven, take a deep breath – relax - it's for real, it's me."

The two twin sisters stood rooted, mouths agape. "Where is *our* Daddy?" Sierra asked.

"That I don't know, girls," he softened his tone. "Was he supposed to be back tonight?"

"I don't know, but we miss him." Serena spoke for the two of them and then broke down, quickly followed by her sister.

Now all three girls were bawling and Cade was at a loss.

"Raven, pull it together, I have an important question that I need you to answer."

Her chest heaved a few more times and she gazed at her Dad through swollen red eyes. The bewildered look was replaced by one of pure relief. "OK... I'm pulled together." A slight curl of her lip told Cade she hadn't lost her smart-aleck streak.

"Listen closely. Where is your mom?"

"She's in the infirmary," Raven said between sniffles.

Cade's heart skipped a beat; his stomach felt like it always does at the two minute warning, about to step out of a perfectly good aircraft at thirty thousand feet on a HALO insertion. He swallowed once and told himself to follow his own advice and *pull it together*. "What happened to Brook? Please tell me she didn't get bit by one of those things."

"Dad... pull yourself together, Aunt Annie is in labor. We were getting her some food because Mom says that she's eating for two."

Going from one emotional extreme to the next was almost too much for Cade, grateful as he was that the latest swing of the pendulum hit on the desired outcome. "Get the food. I haven't seen your mom in more than a week."

The sisters picked out Jell-O and a tapioca pudding. Apparently this looked like pregnant person food to the eight-year-olds.

Cade discarded his coffee cup and helped carry the *food*. "Sweetie, how are you doing? Is everything OK?" he asked Raven.

He was greeted by silence. It was his daughter's default when something traumatic had happened in her life. She had acted this way when her parakeet Samson died when she was five years old, and Cade suspected this would be her default as an adult.

Brook, on the other hand, always confronted her problems head on, wrestled them to the ground and beat them into her way of thinking. Cade had barely enough time to process the fact that his daughter was alive and well and within arm's reach. He was trembling with the knowledge that his wife Brooklyn was alive and well somewhere on the base.

Chapter 38
Outbreak - Day 7
Schriever AFB
Colorado Springs, Colorado

The double doors to the small medical center swung open. Raven led followed by the maternal twin sisters. Cade walked a few steps behind the group. The euphoria that he still felt from holding his little girl put him in a semi-transcendental state, and the swinging doors almost got him in the face on the return trip. The last thing he needed was a broken nose to go along with the deep horizontal gash that was already there.

Annie was in the hospital bed, her legs being held prisoner by a pair of stainless steel stirrups. It looked like the deck of the Starship Enterprise. She was surrounded by all manner of monitors and diagnostic equipment. Brook seemed swallowed up by the electronic machines; her small stature added to the effect.

"Push... breathe deep." Brook was at home in this setting. *What a nurturer she is*, Cade thought as he watched things unfold. "Push... breathe deep." She had no idea that she was being watched.

"Girls," Cade said in a near whisper, "your Mommy doesn't need the food now... it looks like you two are about to have a new brother or sister."

"A brother," the two twins answered in unison.

Cade smiled, happy for them and Mike.

Brook caught some movement in her peripheral vision and turned her head a few degrees. "Push... push... breathe deep. *Cade!*" she yelled his name. It caught her totally by surprise and Brook's exclamation caught Annie by surprise, causing her to push again. "Here he comes...." Brook had lost the professional nurse voice that she used at work. Her words wavered; Cade could tell that she was on the verge of tears.

Cade watched the doctor hand the baby off to Brook, the cries that could only come from a newborn filling the air. It was at once the most beautiful sound and the most angst inducing. Brook swaddled the little baby and handed him to Annie. "It's a boy. Mike is going to be very proud."

Annie clutched her baby boy closely as her daughters circled in to meet their new brother.

Brook snapped the latex gloves from her hands and closed the distance to her family.

Cade already had Raven in his arms and received Brook fully. She looked him in the eyes, reached up and gently probed his injured nose. Her loving touch silently conveyed every emotion she was experiencing. No words were spoken, their little family was back together and that was all that mattered.

A short while later, Brook watched Annie and her daughters fawn over Mike Junior. She was grateful that the birth had none of the complications she had prepared for. Cade rubbed off on her more than she would admit. "An ounce of prevention is worth a pound of cure." He was fond of that phrase.

The medical carts that Brook liberated proved worth their weight in gold. The multiple infections that had Carl near death were responding to the antibiotics. He was slowly surfacing from the depths of his coma and had even given Brook's hand a gentle squeeze.

Suddenly the door opened behind Brook. The twins
started shrieking and rushed past, totally ignoring her, focused
on whoever had just entered the infirmary.

By the time Brook recovered from the shock of the
screams, Mike Desantos had both girls in his arms. He looked
beaten up and dirty. It was bittersweet. He missed the birth
but he was still among the living. Now he would get to meet
his namesake.

Mike spotted Brook and Raven and gave Cade thumbs up.

Without saying a word Brook slipped from the room with
her loved ones in tow.

***

Cade was fast asleep between Brook and Raven. They
were on the bottom of two bunk beds that were pushed
together. It was still a little uncomfortable, but after being
apart from them he wouldn't have it any other way.

"Cade," Brook whispered in his ear, the subtle vibrations
of her voice tickling a bit, "I have something to tell you..."

"After all we've been through... I'm sure we each could
write a book about our time apart," Cade whispered back
groggily.

Raven stirred, said something unintelligible and then went
quiet.

"I... am... pregnant," Brook spaced the words out to soften
the blow.

"*How?*"

"The usual way and you were involved. *What*... did you
miss that day in health class?"

"Honey... I am going to need some time to process this."
Cade cloaked his face with his open palms, then rubbed his
eyes in case he had drifted back to sleep and was dreaming.
He found that he was in fact wide awake and was going to be
a dad again.

"I gave myself two tests - both positive. I was late by a
couple weeks before Raven and I left Portland. I thought it

238

might be from stress, what with you looking for work and us going to see Mom and Pops." As soon as she uttered the words, Mom and Pops, the events of the past few days came crashing back. Like the brisk gust of wind preceding a downpour, the loss of her parents hit her square on.

Cade embraced his wife and let her grieve. They fell asleep in each other's arms.

***

Cade popped up in bed with a feeling of impending doom firmly rooted in his gut. The details of the nightmare teased on the periphery of his memory, his accelerated heart beat and the sheen of perspiration still clinging to his body evidence enough that it had been a very bad one.

Sleep was out of the question, the adrenaline coursing through his body made the decision for him. Cade's black Suunto indicated he had only been down for a little less than two hours. It was 0900 and time for some coffee.

The room was empty. Cade had a feeling that Brook and Raven were probably fighting over who got to hold little Mike Junior.

***

Cade was lacing up his boots when someone rapped sharply on the door.

"Who is it?"

"Airman Davis and I'm looking for Cade Grayson."

"Come in Airman Davis..."

Cade wondered who sent *Doogie Howser* to fetch him. The incredibly young looking, baby faced E-2 stood at attention. After a moment of awkward silence Cade broke the ice. "Stand down, I'm retired."

"I'm sorry, Sir. The person who sent me here holds you in such high regard - I thought you were a Medal of Honor winner... or a General or something."

"I'm flattered, but let's get to the point. Who sent you?"

"I'm not at liberty to say. Will you come with me?"

Cade continued cinching up his boots, rubbed his scruffy beard, and nodded an affirmative.

Chapter 39
Outbreak - Day 7
Grand Teton Pass
Jackson Hole, Wyoming

The steady thrumming of the tracks slapping the pavement produced a mesmerizing cadence. The vehicle's power plants strained to propel the tonnage up the granite mountain. Three things worked against them: heat, altitude, and grade. The trailing Bradley struggled to keep the pace, so the commander in the lead vehicle had his driver halt, and ordered the rest of the procession to do the same.

Staff Sergeant Sean O'Malley adjusted his stance in the commander's seat; the top half of his body benefitted from the cool mountain winds. On the other hand his lower extremities still suffered, cooking in the cramped, kiln-like interior of the Bradley fighting vehicle. Why the Army hadn't upgraded *all* of their vehicles with the new climate control systems crossed his mind as he longed for a dash of Gold Bond powder down below. He knew that bitching about it would be asinine because compared to the blast furnace heat of Afghanistan, Wyoming felt like Antarctica.

O'Malley was still in a state of disbelief he was home. He still had a hundred and thirty-nine days and a wake up before he was *supposed* to rotate home. If someone in the Stan would have told him seven days ago he would be in Wyoming on this date, the bearer of the good news would've received a great big sloppy kiss. If that same person would've leveled with him and told him the truth, that he would be back in the United States shooting fellow Americans, he would have called said person a fucking lunatic. The once jovial redhead, of Irish descent, just wished everything would get back to normal; this surreal nightmare was taking him to places he never wished to visit.

Two Bradleys, two Humvees and a fuel truck made up the small convoy. Staff Sergeant O'Malley, call sign Tempest Seven, was in the lead Bradley. In addition to his driver and gunner, six soldiers of the 4th Infantry Division out of Fort Carson rode in the troop compartment. All of the soldiers were combat veterans and had recently returned from the big sandbox; to a man they were ready and itching for any reason to dismount the rolling sauna.

The Humvees held four soldiers each, also from the 4th ID. Bringing up the rear was another Bradley fighting vehicle. It held three living crew members and eighteen corpses, stiff with rigor mortis, stacked like cordwood in the troop compartment.

O'Malley adjusted the binocular's focus, and the undead woman's features sharpened up. She tottered stiffly towards his column. An adventurous black mountain bird swooped down to feed on a charred corpse. The walking sun-baked cadaver paid the raven no attention. The zombie was focused only on the soldiers in the noisy machines and the meat on their bones.

O'Malley still couldn't believe what he was looking at. She wasn't the first zombie he had come across; in fact he had lost count of how many of these things he had put down since he returned from the other war. A Muslim extremist wearing a suicide vest - that he could believe - he had seen the aftermath with his own eyes and had picked up the body parts of friendly Afghan troops; their only mistake: waiting in line for a hot meal. That had been real... too real.

At some point he hoped that someone would explain, why? Why did they come back in the first place? Why did they keep hungering for human flesh after they died? Why didn't they feel pain? O'Malley had a million questions, but only his orders to follow, recon Montana, Eastern Idaho and Wyoming before returning to Colorado Springs via Jackson Hole, Wyoming.

The driver's voice crackled in O'Malley's earpiece. "Some pileup we've got here Sir. Does it appear navigable?"

O'Malley, busy glassing the apex of the Teton pass, answered without removing the binoculars from his face. "We're going to have to move some of the wrecks, at least the ones that aren't fused to the asphalt, and it should be no problem if *our* vehicles don't give up the ghost first."

***

Staff Sergeant O'Malley and the thirty-two men under his command had left Colorado Springs three days before. The patrol consisted of one M978 fuel truck, five Humvees, two Deuce and a Half transports and two Bradley fighting vehicles - including the one he was perched atop. They were patrolling northeast of Boise, Idaho, when they rolled into an ambush. The pitched battle proved to be deadly for both sides. IEDs planted by the roadside immediately destroyed three Humvees and disabled both Deuce and a Halfs. Heavy machine gun and small arms fire tore into the disabled vehicles killing the remaining survivors.

O'Malley's gunner returned fire. The 25 mm cannon chewed up several SUVs and half a dozen bikers including their Harleys. One of the tracer rounds found a Humvee fuel tank resulting in a massive explosion. The greasy black fireball roiled into the sky.

O'Malley called in the ambush requesting a dust-off and air to ground support. His call for air was immediately denied. Aviation fuel had been getting scarcer by the day, and even

calls for medical evacuation were being turned down.
O'Malley made a difficult decision and broke contact. The
commander was feeling a little like George Custer, all alone,
surrounded by the enemy, desperately wanting to get back
inside the wire in one piece.

After pulling back and regrouping they returned to recover
the bodies of his soldiers. He would never be able to purge
the images from his memory, nor did he wish to forget the
atrocities committed by the evil deviants. All of the dead had
been stripped of their uniforms and left naked and defiled for
the crows to feed on. Some had swastikas gouged into their
dead flesh, the rest were desecrated with the interlocking
letters N and J.

O'Malley was livid and wanted retribution. His hopes were
dashed by the response that he received from the brass. His
commander at Fort Carson acknowledged his dire situation
but he indicated their air resources were "Stretched thin" -
whatever that meant. The man did say they would be
diverting RPAs from Salt Lake City to gather after-action
intelligence. *Predator drones*, he thought, *were great for Intel during
an engagement, but no help getting the wounded the attention they needed
afterward.* Staff Sergeant O'Malley was disheartened after the
exchange and came to the bitter conclusion that, ultimately,
he was on his own.

The sergeant had another tough choice to make. Should
he push on or turn the train around and limp home? *This
mission was a clusterfuck from the get-go*, he thought, *a long circuitous
route through Indian country - only something a desk jockey could dream
up. Screw them; they can finish this circle jerk with their UAVs.*
O'Malley put his index finger in the air and twisted his hand
around.

The other soldiers knew it meant they were going home...
or what was left of it.

***

Teton Pass
Jackson Hole
There were at least twenty vehicles of all makes and
models twisted together into one big clusterfuck of a road
block. Some of the cars had caught fire and were nothing but
scorched bare metal. Charcoal blackened corpses remained
seated in many of them. The inferno had been so hot the
metal sign announcing the 8,431 foot elevation of the Teton
pass had wilted and now rested on its side with the base still
cemented into the roadbed.

Of the many zombies milling around the blocked road, the
female was the closest. She would be the first one of the day.
The walker's flesh was pale, her eyes were jaundiced and her
gait resembled that of a drunk's. Black blood had dried on her
tank top days ago. Even though she had been petite by most
people's standards, her midsection had bloated up horribly.
To O'Malley she looked like a pear with legs, albeit shriveled,
scabbed up cadaver legs. He took the binoculars from his eyes
for a moment and then replaced them, hoping the scene
would change. He really didn't want to continue putting down
infected Americans; it was deeply troubling to him, and deep
down, against everything he stood for. The young
commander was aware of the dark cloud of depression
hanging over his head. The only solace from the guilt he was
feeling was in the mantra he kept repeating in his head, *orders
are meant to be followed.*

O'Malley's head reflexively turned toward the sound he
knew all too well. It usually preceded the annihilation of an
enemy stronghold or the demise of a stubborn insurgent
sniper. The cough-pop, followed by the whoosh of the solid
propellant igniting, meant one of the four vehicles and the
crew inside were certainly doomed. From the left of the
column, partway up the canyon, a Javelin anti-tank missile
arced up out of the pines.

Tempest Seven gaped as the tail of white smoke traced a
path directly for his convoy. Training kicked in and he started

barking orders into his throat mike. *"Tempest One-Six we are
taking fire, reverse course, reverse now."*

Before they could follow orders, the driver and the
security man in the tanker truck were killed, only seconds
apart. The sniper watched as the dying driver popped the
clutch, the semi truck lurched and stalled at the rear of the
convoy, effectively sealing off any means of retreat.

The reassuring sound of the .50 cals gave O'Malley reason
for hope as the Humvee gunners started returning fire, uphill,
at their unseen enemies. The ground troops banged on the
inside of the track, clamoring to get out.

Staff Sergeant O'Malley tracked the streaking projectile
with his eyes; it only took the Javelin two seconds to cover
the short distance before striking the trailing Bradley,
Tempest One-Six, directly on its top where the armor was
thinnest.

The first mini detonation sounded as the penetrator charge
popped the hull, allowing the eighteen pound HEAT warhead
access to the innards of the armored fighting vehicle.
Explosion number two sounded like a thunderclap, sending a
shockwave of pressure and intense heat rolling over the entire
line of vehicles.

The driver and gunner died instantly when molten
aluminum from the skin of the track entered the crew
compartment. Secondary explosions from the onboard
ammunition cooking off masked the report of the high
powered sniper rifle being fired at them.

The gunner atop the third vehicle was instantaneously cut
in half by flying fragments of razor sharp aluminum and steel.
His dead fingers locked on the trigger, emptying the .50
caliber machine gun into the dirt berm on the roadside. The
gear strapped to the rear of the Humvee quickly caught fire,
black oily smoke obscuring Tempest One-Six from the
commander's view.

Small arms fire started impacting the skin of O'Malley's
M2. "*Lower the ramp!*" he screamed to his driver over the din
of battle. It was the last order he would ever give. An enemy
sniper scored a direct hit, the .50 caliber round caving in
O'Malley's face. The only thing distinguishable from his neck
up was the Kevlar helmet firmly strapped to the remaining
chunks of his skull.

At the rear of the M2, the thick blast door covering the
troop area slowly descended. Before the ramp hit the ground
the 4th ID soldiers charged out.

The sound of the ammo cooking, along with the booming
25 mm cannon atop the intact Bradley, was deafening.

Sergeant Jeffries, acting on muscle memory and instinct
launched out of the track, his M4 rifle at the ready. The
sensation of the cool mountain breeze was a welcome feeling
after being cooped up inside the armored fighting vehicle.
Jeffries moved to the right side of the Bradley hoping to seek
cover from the withering fire from the concealed snipers. *They
must be well trained soldiers*, he thought, because their firing
positions were well planned out, scattered amongst the
boulders and trees. The other five soldiers formed up next to
him, awaiting his orders.

Suddenly the wind changed direction, carrying with it thick
acrid smoke and the smell of rotting flesh. Jeffries covered his
face and struggled to draw in a breath of fresh air. The
chemical laden smoke seared his eyes; he found opening them
was almost impossible, it felt like he had been pepper sprayed.

Jeffries felt a body bump into him. "Staff Sergeant, is that
you? I can't see a damn thing... I got smoke in my eyes." A
stiff gust of wind redirected the smoke, revealing the open
maw of the undead female he was conducting a one sided
conversation with. Cold pustule covered arms wrapped
around his shoulders. "*Get off me!*" The sergeant tussled with
the rank smelling walker, lost his footing and fell in a heap.
The zombie fell on top of him, clamped her yellowed teeth

on his ear, and shook. Jeffries' screams, shrill and animal like,
drew the attention of his squad.

Corporal Byrd turned toward the sound; it reminded him
of the insurgent video Al-Jazeera reveled in showing over and
over again, the U.S. soldier being decapitated by Iraqi
insurgents had made the exact same sounds as Jeffries.
Shaken by the events unfolding before his eyes, the corporal
leveled his rifle at the scrawny form, but held his fire because
he didn't want to risk fratricide.

Jeffries pushed the monster away and was frantically
calling for a medic when he collapsed unmoving. It was too
late, the Omega virus was already surging through his
bloodstream and it would only be a matter of minutes before
he reanimated.

Corporal Byrd had the feeding zombie in his sights when
the world around him erupted in fire and pain, followed by a
never ending darkness. The second Javelin had plunged into
the remaining Bradley and detonated. The earthshaking blast
killed the dismounted soldiers instantly.

Bookended by the burning hulks of armor, the two
Humvees couldn't move. The drivers maneuvered the
vehicles to and fro trying desperately to escape the kill zone.

Large caliber rifle fire continued booming from the high
ground. One by one, starting with the drivers, all of the
remaining 4th ID soldiers fell dead or dying.

The one sided massacre was finished in less than five
minutes. America's new Civil War had just begun.

Totally oblivious of the ammunition cooking off,
unphased by the flesh melting heat, the undead moved in to
feed on the wounded soldiers.

Chapter 40
Outbreak - Day 7
Guild Headquarters
Jackson Hole, Wyoming

Ian Bishop retrieved the Cobra two-way radio from his back pocket. "Yes, what is it?"

"Sir, we initiated contact with a five vehicle convoy. Two Bradleys down, there are still two Humvees and a fully loaded tanker truck intact. What are your orders?"

"All of this is important, so listen very carefully. Destroy the radios *right now* and then make the vehicles vanish except for the tanker. Bring it to town, we can unload the fuel."

"Copy that," Joshua answered.

"How many soldiers were there and what branch and unit were they from?"

Joshua knew what to look for, he had seen combat in Iraq early on and had even been there when Baghdad fell. For the last six years he had worked as a Spartan mercenary earning the trust of their founder Ian Bishop. "There are thirty-two enemies KIA. They're all Army, 4th Infantry Division, if my memory serves, that unit calls Fort Carson home. What do you want done with the bodies?"

Fort Carson was in Colorado Springs, a little too close for comfort, Ian thought, as he ran his hands through his short cropped hair and pondered what to do about the mess. It took but a second. Being a Navy SEAL had taught Ian to think quickly and decisively. Failure to do so in combat was a good way to make the Grim Reaper's acquaintance. "Collect the weapons and ammo and throw the corpses in the ditch and burn them. Sterilize the area. I don't want any evidence left behind, not so much as a charred dog tag. Make sure you don't leave any undead soldiers either. Good work Joshua, if they had been able to get down into the city center our jig would have been up."

Ian hoped the patrol didn't have time to radio wherever they called home to report the ambush. He didn't want the remnants of the U.S. military to have any reason to send aerial reconnaissance or more boots on the ground out looking for them.

With a concerned look on his face Bishop switched the frequency on his radio and called his number two man.

Carson answered immediately. "Yes."

"Are our air defenses in place yet?"

"They're in transit, overland, and less than a day out."

Ian Bishop shook his head in disgust and continued pacing the room. "And the Minot mission?"

"We have secured the packages and they are in transit as well."

"Excellent, Carson, things are falling into place. In a few short days we will be a formidable adversary... that is, if anyone has the nerve to challenge our authority."

Bishop ended his conversation with Carson. He then took a walk to find Robert Christian and deliver the positive news.

Chapter 41
Outbreak - Day 7
Schriever AFB
Colorado Springs, Colorado

"Carl. Squeeze my hand. I know you're there."

The heart rate monitor blipped along the same as it had since Carl succumbed to the infections wrought on him by his undead assailant.

"Cade is coming to see you soon, don't you want to say hi to him? You two got along so good. Remember his bachelor party." Brook had no idea what went on that night but at this point she was grasping at straws and wanted another sign - any sign - that he was coming out of the coma.

Brook was out of ideas. Time was going to have to heal Carl's wounds. She swabbed some water on his tongue and lips. *Come on brother, keep fighting,* she thought, *it's only you and I, Mom and Pop are gone.* "Don't go anywhere. I'll be back big brother."

She had a good feeling that Carl would be OK. The way he tackled his alcoholism and got sober proved he was a survivor. Brook left her brother and headed for the door. She wanted to go and check on Annie and the little pink Mike Junior.

Carl opened his eyes; the light attacked his optic nerves like microscopic razor blades. He didn't know where he was

251

or how he came to be in the hospital bed, but he had
recognized his sister's voice urging him to join her. His nerves
were waking up along with his brain. It felt like a million red
ants had taken up residence under his skin, their gnashing
pincers rending scraps of his flesh to take to their queen.
Supernovas of white hot pain erupted all over his body. The
sound that he forced from his throat was but a rattle of
suffering and misery. "Help me... sis."

Chapter 42
Outbreak - Day 7
Schriever AFB
Colorado Springs, Colorado

"Freda Crash, you're a sight for sore eyes."

The petite major visibly blanched. "Wyatt, who the eff told you my new nickname?"

Cade grinned at the no nonsense woman. They went way back. If there was an important op running anywhere in the world, it definitely had Freda's fingerprints all over it. "What happens in Bagram, *does not stay in Bagram.*"

"I've never driven a Hummer before."

Cade took the opening, "From what I've heard, *nobody* else will be able to drive that Hummer... at least you didn't take out any aircraft."

Blatantly changing the subject, Freda said, "I met Brook, lovely lady. You wouldn't believe what she did for Desantos' wife."

"And I presume I don't want to know." Cade arched his eyebrows, his body language contradicting his words.

"Do you want to know why I need your ear?" Freda asked, throwing her hands up in a display of mock disgust.

"I need a favor from you... then, I might take listening to what you have to say into consideration. In the past, every

time you needed to tell me something I usually ended up
tangling with an HVT."

"Wyatt, there aren't any more high value targets. There are
only the undead and opportunist breathers."

"I came here from Portland. Getting here was like that
movie Planes, Trains and Automobiles, only throw in an ass
load of walking dead. I almost bought it more times than I
can count. A few days back I had a run in with a large gang of
outlaw bikers, and their leader, a big redhead bastard. Richard
Ganz fancies himself as the new owner of Idaho. The waste
of skin has had a hand in a number of murders."

"Why didn't you put a bullet in his brain? You're good at
that... I've seen the after-action reports."

"OK. Here is my after-action report: We drove. We killed
zombies. The bikers killed lawmen and National Guardsmen.
Ganz and his boys killed my friends and tried to kill me.
Lastly, I sent a few of them to hell... but Ganz, he slipped the
noose. I had him in my sights outside of Boise but he was out
of range. *The bottom line is... this mutt needs to die.*"

Cade broke it down to all of the specifics that he knew
first and then added the second hand information that Dan
had provided.

"I'll see if I can help you with your problem. Sounds like a
worthy endeavor. But... you need to hear me out. OK?"

"I owe you that much." Cade instantly regretted leaving
the door cracked open.

Freda Nash's face regained its normal hue. "Mr. Grayson,
can you be back here at thirteen hundred hours?"

"I'll clear my schedule."

"One more thing soldier."

"Yes Ms. Cra..." Cade almost uttered her nickname but
thought better of it. Retired or not, he was still addressing a
major.

"Forget what you may have heard about how I procured
my nickname."

"What do you speak of...?" Cade said, feigning ignorance.

"Thirteen hundred, I'm going to find an eye in the sky. *Do not be late.*"

Cade left the meeting with a sense of urgency. He needed to find the old Vietnam Vet named Dan, and he had a little less than three hours to make it happen.

***

The Airman that fetched him minutes ago was still standing outside the major's door. *"E-2 Davis. Come with me!"* Cade barked.

"Sir?"

"Officers rarely joke and this is no exception." Without a backward glance, Cade walked briskly, off to find someplace he could stop and continue the charade in a more private setting.

He must be with the Joint Chiefs, Airman Davis thought, *or military intelligence.* His monkey mind ran through the possibilities as he followed close on the heels of mister whoever the hell he is.

A machine gun rattled off a sustained burst somewhere near the perimeter.

"Those things aren't taking a day off, are they sir?" Davis stammered nervously trying to make small talk.

Sir, Cade thought, *the ruse must be working.* He was pleased with his human hijacking so far.

Cade stopped so fast that E-2 Davis practically marched up his back. "I need you to find two civilians for me. An older gentleman named Dan; he's a retired Vietnam vet." Cade pantomimed, "Bushy gray beard, ball cap," and holding his hand at the gash on his nose, "he's about this tall."

"The other man's name is Duncan Winters. Ex-Army aviator and also a Vietnam vet. Ruddy complexion, narrow squinty eyes and he talks like a cowboy with a healthy twang in his voice. Got all of that?"

"I think so. I mean, *yes sir.*" The E-2 remembered who he was addressing and saluted.

Cade returned the salute. "Bring them to the Space
Command complex by thirteen hundred hours. Don't let me
down."

Still holding the salute but looking a little shaky Airman
Davis repeated himself exhibiting more enthusiasm, "*Sir. Yes
sir.*"

Chapter 43
Outbreak - Day 7
Schriever AFB
1300 Space Command Operations
Colorado Springs, Colorado

Cade rapped on the solid door. Major Freda Nash let him inside the secure operations room. The first thing he noticed was the abundance of flat panel monitors. The only place that Cade had seen more screens was the rear wall in a *Best Buy* store. Cade was in man cave heaven gazing at all of the shiny TVs.

Major Nash cleared her throat.

Cade recognized the other petite woman; Valerie Clay was the Speaker of the House. It dawned on him then that she was next in succession and therefore, since Odero was dead, she was now the President. The lady wore an olive drab long-sleeved shirt, khaki pants and a pair of sturdy hiking boots. To Cade it looked like she was a Sierra Club member and not the Commander-in-Chief. A colonel stood in the wings, obviously letting the major run the show. Seeing as how Major Nash was the satellite wizard it made perfect sense. Behind the colonel, President Clay's stone-faced Secret Service agents stood at attention trying to remain inconspicuous.

"Madame President, you already know General Mike
Desantos, let me introduce you to Sergeant First Class,
retired, Cade Grayson."

"Good to finally meet you Mr. Grayson. I have heard
nothing but good things about you. I want to personally
thank you for bagging Uday and Qusay."

The news stunned Duncan. He knew Cade was special,
but he had no idea he was Tier-One. Dan also was taken
aback. He beamed at the revelation and couldn't wait to thank
the hero.

"It was my pleasure Madam President."

"Sorry, I didn't mean to snub you two gentlemen. Major
Nash briefed me. Your service in Southeast Asia will never be
forgotten. If you would consider passing on your war fighting
knowledge to our young men and women here in Colorado
Springs I would be extremely grateful. With so few of us left,
everyone is going to have to cross train and learn how to
combat this new enemy. I believe the window is about to
open... Major Nash will take it from here."

Cade knew instantly what he was looking at, and judging
by the constantly changing numbers in the lower left corner
of the display, the image was coming from somewhere in real-
time. It was the two tone gray gun camera feed from a Reaper
or Predator UAV.

"President Clay, the Colonel and I wanted you men to see
this with your own eyes. Cade has vouched for the two
civilians and I concur they can remain. Let me stress - what
you see here *does not* leave this room."

The image on the largest screen continued to slowly rotate
as the UAV circled the target.

"The video on screen number one is streaming real-time
from an HQ-9 Reaper." Nash inserted a Bluetooth enabled
Plantronics ear bud. *"Zoom one stop."* She was giving orders to
some PS3 veteran sitting in an air-conditioned trailer at
Creech AFB in Nevada.

The magnification increased; the forest that dominated the screen disappeared. A wide open courtyard surrounded by multiple buildings that varied in size took its place. A long access road snaked from the compound, and at least thirty pickup trucks and SUVs were parked haphazardly on both sides.

Dan squinted his eyes. Although the compound looked tiny from the drone's altitude, he instantly recognized it.

Major Nash continued, "Colonel Shrill authorized me to redirect these assets from other areas. Cade Grayson appealed to me to surveil a group that is taking advantage of the citizenry and also responsible for a number of murders. Based on the images captured during the first Keyhole Sat pass, we have decided to retaliate decisively and with impunity."

"Oorah," Dan added, he was in total agreement.

Screen number two lit up. The satellite imagery was less grainy than the Reaper's feed. The compound remained in the center of the screen, but from a different angle. It looked to Cade like U.S. military vehicles were parked on the premises. Two Humvees and a lone M1A1 Abrams stood out in stark relief. People were evident, moving about, inside and around the target area.

The more the merrier, Dan thought. *They didn't spare any Stanley citizens.*

Once again the image changed, the same vehicles reappeared only magnified much larger, and it was evident that all three of the military vehicles were adorned with Nazi flags.

"That's Ganz and his boys," Dan muttered.

The magnification increased again.

Duncan noticed he could actually read some of the license plates on the parked vehicles.

Dan gritted his teeth as Richard Ganz's likeness came into view. It was surreal seeing the dirtbag again; his red mane appeared close enough to touch.

"Can anyone positively identify the individual on the screen?" Nash asked.

Dan answered forcefully. "That's Richard Ganz. *Tell your pilot to send a missile up his ass.*"

"In due time," Nash replied. "Let the record indicate we have positive target identification."

Cade couldn't believe with all that was going on in the world anyone would find it necessary to document for the record all the minute details to justify killing this scum. *If he had his way,* Cade thought, *he would snatch the fucker, bring him back and get medieval on his ass.*

President Valerie Clay stood, arms crossed, wearing a serious look on her face.

Major Nash ordered the attack to proceed. "*High Roller, you are guns free.*"

The gray image being transmitted from the Reaper changed attitude as the UAV banked to get the proper firing angle.

"*Go to color and zoom two steps,*" Nash ordered the sensor operator.

The camera zoomed in and the gray image disappeared for a millisecond. The flat panel now reproduced every color in vivid HD.

"*Missile away,*" the Reaper driver stated without a hint of emotion.

Ganz was still in the reclining chair reading an *Easy Rider* magazine.

Hot exhaust from the disgorged Hellfire blurred the Reaper's sensors for a fraction of a second. It reminded Cade of a heat mirage on a desert road.

The missile's journey from the aircraft to the targeting pip was brief. One moment Ganz was enjoying the afternoon sun, fidgeting with his rock star hair, oblivious to his fate, and the next he disintegrated into hundreds of meaty pieces. It was a direct hit. The twenty pound warhead annihilated Ganz, the two Pit Bulls and eight other people in the immediate vicinity. Body parts rained down around the smoking crater.

Duncan looked on with morbid fascination as the little people scurried away from the carnage, sprinting to take refuge inside.

"*Missile away*," sounded again from the pilot.

The largest building in the Aryan compound imploded from the second Hellfire strike.

A man's form stumbled from an out building, fully engulfed in flames. It looked like a movie special effect, but no one yelled cut, or rushed in to douse the flames when he finally crumpled to the ground face first.

Everyone in the room stood at rapt attention watching the display of firepower. The Humvees were aflame, white sparks and flashes meant the ammo onboard was catching fire. In all, six missiles rained down. In a matter of minutes the whole compound was burning out of control.

The Reaper continued to orbit, airing the funeral pyre to the remote viewers at Schriever AFB.

Dan watched with grim satisfaction as the buildings crumbled one by one, mesmerized by the dancing orange flames. *Rest in peace Bob and Irene.*

Duncan was pleased that he was witness to the biker's demise. He looked at Cade, "That's payback for Rawley and the kids."

Sharing the sentiment wholeheartedly, Cade nodded in agreement, wishing only that he could've dispatched the psychopath himself.

The image from the circling Reaper disappeared, leaving the rest to their imagination.

Major Nash turned the lights on. "Is there anyone in attendance not satisfied with the outcome?"

No one spoke up.

"Outstanding. Dan and Duncan, I have to respectfully ask you two to leave the room now."

***

Colonel Shrill was still the base commander, President
Clay made that very clear. Shrill saluted the newly minted
General and then introduced himself to Cade. "We've
received some disturbing intel. A cabal of very wealthy men
has their sights set on taking control of the country. They
have been waiting patiently for an event such as Omega to
happen."

The large monitor came to life. An image started the slow
rotation much like the Reaper feed. Cade could tell that this
UAV was flying much higher. The target looked like a ski
town. *Banff, Whistler, Sun Valley?* The mountains ringing the
valley floor looked very familiar but Cade couldn't pinpoint
the locale.

"They've taken over Jackson Hole, Wyoming. The fact
that the ski town was full of tourists and summer workers
complicates things and limits our type of response. The group
covertly call themselves the Guild. Before Omega the media
referred to them as the Marzenberg Group - named after
Kaiser Von Marzenberg. The real goal of the Guild is to
maintain all of their members in the ruling class and establish
a permanent lower class. I'm sure that you all have heard of
them, they have had their hand in every Presidential election
since the late forties. Some would argue that they have
actually chosen every President since then and have enough
politicians in their pocket to manipulate the electoral system
to make it happen. The man currently steering the group is
none other than one of the biggest land owners in the
country, Robert Christian. It is also a longstanding rumor that
more than one former President is a Guild member. To put it
succinctly; they have lofty goals and will stop at nothing to
achieve them."

President Clay cleared her throat and interjected, "I was
contacted more than once by their lobbyists. They wanted to
build some political capital with me so they could manipulate
my future voting. I'm one million percent sure that the people

funneling opinions into Odero's ear were hand-picked by the Marzenbergs. They might have gotten him elected and then became his puppet masters. We will never know... unless..." The President smoothed the pleats in her khakis and looked intently at the two Delta operators.

Not much could cause Cade to squirm - the look Valerie Clay gave him almost did.

Shrill continued the briefing, "There's more information in the dossier Nash has prepared."

"Mr. Grayson, I would normally ask something of this importance in a private setting, but time is running out. I urge you to please consider throwing your hat back in the ring." Finishing up, the President made it very clear that China was down and out with 1.4 billion problems of her own, but still the winds of war were blowing.

***

Duncan and Dan waited outside of the secure room. They swapped recollections of their tours in Nam and shared their post apocalypse experiences. Each man had his own reason to talk to Cade and they didn't have to wait long.

***

General Desantos exited first and switched a bulging manila envelope stamped "TOP SECRET" to his left hand, saluted the two veterans and then continued on his way.

After a short wait Cade emerged, appearing exhausted and beaten down - like the weight of the world was resting squarely on his shoulders.

Duncan deferred to Dan and waited for him to have a word with Cade.

"You made an old leatherneck's day. Thank you." Dan was overcome with emotion.

"I simply repeated your story Dan... *you* made your own day." Dan saluted his brothers in arms and left them alone in the hallway.

"Cade my man, can you help an old boy rustle up some transportation?" Duncan inquired.

"After you saved my ass, how could I not? I'll make sure
the General goes to bat for you."

"I don't want to be a pain in the ass... but a Huey would
be preferable. After the Black Hawk decided to fall out from
under us, I want to stick with what I know."

"Where are you going to go?" Cade's voice softened. He
knew Duncan was close to his baby brother. He also knew he
was going to miss the old warhorse.

"Do you really need to ask? I know you're brighter than
that."

A guilty grin crossed Cade's face. "No I didn't. You and
Oops need each other. Blood is thicker than water - as the
saying goes."

"You read my mind, *Delta boy*."

No thanks to Nash, Cade's secret background was out. He
was a little pissed because he really didn't want his past
involvement in Special Operations revealed. It was too late
now. *At least only Dan and Duncan harbor the knowledge*, Cade
thought.

"I need to run something by Daymon. Have you seen
him?" Cade asked.

"No, not since we had the medical inspections. I'm going
to get some chow; do you want to join me?"

Remembering the egg smoothie from earlier, Cade shook
his head side to side. "I have some catching up to do. Family
waits."

"Take it easy... *Wyatt*. I'll keep my eyes peeled for Daymon
and tell him you want to talk."

Before leaving Cade gave Duncan a slap on the shoulder,
"'Til we meet again Amigo."

Cade looked at the bulging envelope in his hands. He
turned it over, hefted its weight, and wondered what
information it contained that warranted the words "TOP
SECRET."

Epilogue

Cade found Brook by her brother's bedside. "Is he back among the living?"

"I was getting ready to leave and see the baby when I heard him utter something. He's been in and out. I gave him something for his pain and now he's asleep." Brook's lip started to quiver. Cade knew it meant she was headed for a good cry. All he could do is hold her close while the sobs rocked her small frame.

"I didn't want to sedate him but he was begging me. Carl is a recovering alcoholic and any drugs are a no-no."

Cade saw that his wife - the nurse - was conflicted. He stroked her hair while he watched his brother-in-law's chest rise and fall under the thin sheet. Carl looked at peace. "Sounds like you did the right thing. He wouldn't have asked if he really didn't need it," Cade said, trying to assuage her guilt.

Brook wiped her tears and blew her nose. "It'll be getting dark soon. I *really* need some alone time with my family."

"Is he going to be alright by himself?"

Brook nodded; she bit her lower lip trying to prevent another volley of emotion. "Let's go," she said in a wavering voice.

They walked back to their quarters hand in hand.

***

Cade sat on the edge of the bed. Raven lay curled up in a ball spooning with her mom. She was fighting the good fight willing her eyes to stay open. "Daddy?"

"Yes sweetie." Cade stroked his daughter's temple.

"When are we going home?"

Cade looked to Brook for help. At a loss for words she silently shrugged and closed her eyes. Cade waited for a moment to put some thought into his answer. "This is going to have to be our home for a while." Cade never lied to his little girl, but intuitively he knew that she needed something to hope for. "If I can make it happen... we will go home some day."

"Will my Lady Gaga poster still be on the wall in my room?" Raven was losing her battle with Mister Sandman.

Cade smiled, "Yes sweetie."

"Daddy?"

"Yes sweetie."

"Did you think you would ever see Mommy and me again?"

"I was certain that I would."

"Why?" Raven yawned, her small form shifting under the thin sheet.

"Because when I asked you to take care of Mom, you told me, and I quote, "*Nothing shall befall Mom when I am on the job.* Isn't that right?"

He didn't receive an answer. Raven was fast asleep, wrapped in her mother's arms.

###

Thank you so much for reading Soldier On! I hope you had as much fun reading as I had putting the "movie in my mind" in print. Look for Book Three - In Harm's Way: Surviving the Zombie Apocalypse - available Spring 2012. Shawn Chesser

Feel free to find me on Facebook.

ABOUT THE AUTHOR

Shawn Chesser, a practicing father, has been a zombie fanatic for decades. He likes his creatures shambling, trudging and moaning. As for fast, agile, screaming specimens... not so much. He lives in Portland, Oregon, with his wife, two kids and three fish. This is his second novel.

9 780988 257603